THE
LAZARUS
TRAP

DAVIS BUNN

WestBow
PRESS

A Division of Thomas Nelson Publishers
Since 1798

visit us at www.westbowpress.com

For Isabella

With all my love

*"A wife of noble character,
who can find?"*

Published in Nashville, Tennessee, by WestBow Press, a division of Thomas Nelson, Inc.

WestBow Press books may be purchased in bulk for educational, business, fund-raising, or sales promotional use. For information, please e-mail SpecialMarkets@ThomasNelson.com.

ISBN 0-8499-4485-6 (trade pbk.)
ISBN 1-5955-4184-5 (mass market)

Printed in the United States of America

06 07 08 09 10 QWB 9 8 7 6 5 4 3 2 1

HE DID NOT KNOW WHERE HE WAS, ONLY THAT HE WAS returning from a far, dark place. The smell was the only thing he was sure of. He used it like a rope, pulling himself hand over mental hand back from the pit. There was a sharp familiarity to the smell. He knew he had been in a place before that had worn this appalling odor like a badge. In this addled moment, that knowledge was all he had.

He arrived back to a point where he could open his eyes.

He lay on a concrete floor under a cold fluorescent sun. Pain attacked with the return of sight. His head thundered. Every inch of his body cried out. His mouth felt gummed shut.

A bellowing thirst drove him to move. Testing each motion before committing, he managed to roll over. Next to him sprawled a snoring mountain of beard and leather and stink. He crawled around the other man and searched for water.

"Well, lookee here. The dead is commencing to rise."

The words were meaningless. But he knew the tone. It fitted into the blank puzzle of his brain. It connected to the smell. He spotted a sink in the corner. He used a bench that was bolted to the floor to push himself to his feet. Only when he started shuffling across the yawning distance did he realize he had no shoes.

Bending over the sink almost dislodged his skull. The faucet creaked open. He stuffed his mouth under the flow and groaned as he drank. He doused his head, then used his one remaining jacket sleeve to dry his face. The other sleeve appeared to have been torn off. Colored threads dangled over his shirt like military braid. If only he could remember the battle!

He blinked through the sheen of moisture. Two sides of the chamber were the same grey-painted concrete as the floor. The other two were floor-to-ceiling metal bars. He shared the lockup with perhaps a dozen other men. More than half were still sleeping. Two youths in shiny athletic gear argued in words that he could not piece together. Only one man, perhaps the largest in the cage, met his eye. His weather-beaten features and flat, dark gaze had once probably sparked with intelligence, but now were merely aware.

The stranger waved him over. "You come on over here and sit yourself down."

He hesitated.

"You heard me. Get yourself on over here."

He shuffled over. The stranger waited until he was seated, then turned to the youths and said, "Give the man back his shoes."

One youth responded with a curse.

"You want to get on the wrong side of me? That really what you want?"

"What are you, his mama?"

The other youth said, "No, man, it's just fresh meat. The dude's looking after his own self. Wants to get the meat all close and cozy. Ain't that right, meat?"

The man said, "I'm not asking you again."

The youth took off the soft black loafers and threw them. Hard. "Wait till your honey drifts off, meat. I'll be watching."

"Don't you listen to him. Put your shoes on."

"I'll be watching," the youth repeated. "Got me a blade with your name on it."

The man eased forward a trifle. The youth was suddenly blocked from view. "The difference between y'all and me is, I know what I'm in for. I made a mistake. Again." The giant spoke with a steady monotone. As if he'd been over this terrain a billion times. "I fell. Again."

"Like I care."

"When I fall, these days what I do is I drink. After that, I got a problem with my anger management. So you two best hush up while you still can. Otherwise I'll have to spend time on my knees for smashing you like a couple of shiny bugs."

The mountain let the silence hold a moment before turning around. "Do you know your head is bleeding?"

He reached up and touched the spot that thundered the loudest. His fingers came back red. But when he spoke, it was about what worried him the most. "I don't know who I am."

"Me, I go by Reuben." Nothing seemed to surprise this man. "I heard the cops talking about you. You were at a bar they had under surveillance. The bartender and his ladies, they had a scam going. They was slipping something in the johns' drinks and rolling them. What you want to be going in a place like that for?"

"I don't remember a thing."

"They brought you in on account of you duking it out

with one of their own. Sounds like you might need some of that same anger management yourself."

"I hit a cop?"

"You tried. That's what counts. Looks like they're the ones that connected. Turn around and let me have a look at your head."

When he did not move fast enough, the man swiveled him easy as a doll. Fingers probed the wound. "They gave you a couple of good licks, that's for sure." Reuben held up fingers. "How many you see?"

"Three."

"Follow my hand. No, don't move your head. Just your eyes." The fingers went back and forth, then up and down. "I used to be an ER nurse. Which is where I got hooked the first time. That place is full of the most awesome drugs. Okay, cross your legs."

Reuben poked beneath the kneecap, making his leg bounce. Then Reuben gripped his chin and the base of his neck and swiveled the skull, still probing. "You getting dizzy?"

"No. But everything hurts."

"It ought to, after what you put your body through." Reuben dropped his hands. "Probably shoulda had a couple of stitches. But you don't seem concussed."

"But I can't remember."

"Weren't you listening? You got drugged, you took a couple of hits with the stick. You're gonna need a while to wake up."

A steel door clapped open as a guard stepped from the bullet-proof viewing station across the hall. "Adams!"

"That you?"

"I told you, I don't know—"

The cop pointed straight at him. "Jeffrey Adams! Front and center!"

The black man helped him rise to his feet. "Ain't everybody gets called back from the pit, man. Question is, what are you gonna do when you find out who you are?"

WHEN THE OFFICE STAFF STARTED HUSTLING IN AT A
few minutes after eight, Terrance d'Arcy was at his desk
as usual. Just another Tuesday morning in downtown
Orlando. Except, of course, for the seeds of mayhem he
expected to watch sprout. Any minute now.

When his secretary knocked on his door and asked if
he wanted anything, Terrance did not acknowledge her.
She gave him ten seconds of her patented mask, then
left. Terrance remained as he was, his wireless keyboard
in his lap and his back to his office. The credenza behind
his immaculate rosewood desk held three flat screens.
One showed quotes from the European markets and
early currency dealings. The second was tuned to
Bloomberg News with the sound cut off. The third
scrolled through his daily cascade of e-mails. Terrance
saw none of it. His fingers remained locked in stillness.
Waiting.

Then the middle monitor burst into sound. An hour
earlier he had keyed in several words to unlock the volume. Though he had been hoping for it, still the voice
hit his shock button.

"—explosion," the newscaster intoned. "Reports are
sketchy at this point. But it appears that several floors of

the Rockefeller Center have been destroyed. Police are refusing to rule out terrorist—"

Terrance slapped the keys to kill all three screens and bolted from his chair. He did not run down the hall. That would appear unseemly. He walked at a pace just slightly slower than a trot. He skipped the elevators and took the stairs. Only when the steel door slammed shut behind him did he bound up the three floors to the penthouse.

When Terrance entered the chairman's office, he was greeted with Jack Budrow's customary glare. The CEO detested Terrance d'Arcy. When time had come for the board to approve Terrance for the senior vice-presidency he now held, Jack had voted against him and for Terrance's corporate enemy, Val Haines. Jack suspected that Terrance had counterfeited documents and effectively stolen the promotion, as Val maintained. Terrance's admittance to Jack's inner sanctum was a constant irritant. There had been times when Terrance wished he could wind back the clock and dislodge himself from the whole affair. But today, this minute, he was delighted to be here. Positively thrilled.

Terrance d'Arcy considered himself to carry a true Englishman's heart. This despite the fact that he was only half British by blood, had lived most of his life in the U.S., and could not disengage his American twang no matter how many elocution coaches he hired. But one did what one could. Terrance's suits were staid Saville Row. His shirts were Turnbull and Asser and starched to perfection. His cufflinks were twenty-two-carat-gold Dunhills. His only other splashes of color were his reddish-gold locks, a sprinkling of freckles that women considered boyishly attractive, and a four-

hundred dollar I Zingari tie. Terrance had a polite word
for everyone. Combined with his freckles and his crystal
blue eyes, this was enough to charm those who did not
know him well.

Jack Budrow's office encompassed almost a third of
the former Dupont Building's top floor. Dupont had
erected the structure in the early eighties as an investment property, back during the first faint glimmerings
that Orlando might become a regional powerhouse.
Dupont had been right, but too early. The rents were
too high for back then, the lobby too ornate, the building too New York flash for the gentrified South. But
times changed. In the ensuing quarter century,
Orlando's dismal downtown had experienced an
extreme makeover. Money and power and strict zoning
enforcement had removed most of the dives, spruced
up the remaining smaller structures, bricked the streets,
and added art deco streetlamps with hanging floral
arrangements. Newer high-rise centers shouted big
money. Now the Dupont's atrium was too squat, the
marble too dull, the chandeliers not flashy enough. The
metallic pinnacles fronting the building's stepping-
stone roofline were now faded by the fierce Florida sun.
Insignia, Jack Budrow's company, had obtained the
long-term lease for a song.

The wall opposite Jack's desk held a shoji screen of
antique hand-painted silk. Behind this resided an eighty-
two-inch plasma screen, the largest made. Jack used it for
teleconferences and showing guests what was supposed
to be an introduction to Insignia International. Terrance
thought of it as a five-minute stroll down Jack Budrow's
personal hall of fame. Today, however, the screen showed
three talking heads on *Good Morning Orlando*. Which,

for Jack Budrow, was about par for the course. *Good Morning Orlando* newsbreaks ran an ice age behind the national wire services.

Terrance walked to the desk, picked up the television's controls, and switched to Bloomberg News.

The CEO barked, "Do you mind?"

"Ease up, Jack." This from the third man in the room, Don Winslow.

"Last I checked, this was still my office. Change back the channel!"

"Ease up, I said." Don came out of his customary slouch. "You got something?"

"Listen."

"—We can now confirm that the top two floors of the Rockefeller Center building fronting Forty-Eighth Street were completely destroyed early this morning by what appears to have been a massive explosion. No report of casualties has yet come through. According to preliminary police reports, the early hour spared New York from what otherwise would have been a massive death toll, as debris rained down on sidewalks that two hours later would be jammed.

"The floors were home to Syntec Bank, an international merchant bank based on the island of Jersey. Police refuse to comment on the possibility of a terrorist attack. Adjacent buildings have been evacuated while a full search is underway . . ." The announcer touched his earpiece, then added, "We now take you live to our reporter at Rockefeller Plaza."

The rap on the door startled them all. Terrance killed the television. Budrow's secretary, a stone-faced woman of indeterminate years, opened the door. "There's a caller on line one."

Jack's voice sounded raspy from the sudden strain. "I said no interruptions."

"This one is for Mr. Winslow. The caller knew he would be in this office and insists it is urgent."

Don asked, "He give a name?"

"It is a woman, sir. All she would tell me is that you are expecting the call." The secretary was clearly displeased with having her authority breached. "She was most adamant."

Don said to Jack, "I guess I better take it."

"Put it through, Consuela. And no more interruptions."

When the door shut, Don said, "This must be Wally."

Her name was Suzanne Walton, and she was a former cop. She had been working narcotics in Baltimore and got greedy. Don had insisted they hire her as their outside security consultant. When Terrance had asked what for, Don had merely replied, *In case we ever need ourselves a hammer.*

The phone rang, and Don hit the speaker button. "Winslow."

"I been trying to reach you for an hour."

"My cell phone's doing a fritz."

The woman asked, "You heard?"

"We were just listening to Bloomberg. They're talking terrorists."

"They do that with everything these days." The woman's voice rattled like a deluge of glass shards. "It'll pass."

Terrance watched Don smile approval of her attitude. "So what now?"

"You get confirmation. I get payment."

"We'll be waiting." Don glanced at Terrance, then added, "You need anything more, you go through Terrance d'Arcy."

"Who?"

"The man who signs your paycheck." Don gave her Terrance's cell phone number. "My dance card's about to get extremely full. When you talk to Terrance, you talk to me."

"I don't like change."

Don's tone hardened. "Deal with it."

They waited through a long moment, then the line went dead. Click and gone. Terrance shivered once more. He really had to meet that woman. See if reality lived up to the mental image and the one photo he had obtained through his sources. Wally was a tall brunette who would have been truly striking, had it not been for the scar running from her hairline to her left eyebrow. That and her dead-eyed cop's gaze. Well, former cop, actually.

Don stretched his arms over his head until his joints popped. Don Winslow was executive vice president of Insignia, a company whose revenue topped two billion dollars a year. He was a graduate of Columbia Law School and earned a high six-figure income. But the man looked like a tramp. He could take a top-line suit straight off the rack, wear it five minutes, and look like he had fed it to his three Dobermans. The only hairbrush Don owned was the fingers of his right hand. He was a tennis fanatic, a long-distance runner, a fitness freak. He possessed no waistline to speak of, boundless energy, and a total absence of moral convictions. Terrance admired him immensely.

Don asked no one in particular, "Can you *believe* this?"

Jack responded as only Jack could. "With our luck, they'd already finished their appointment and left the bank."

"No, Terrance checked that out carefully." Don wagged his fingers. "Remind the man."

"I downloaded their latest schedules at midnight. They both showed at the Syntec meeting beginning at six-thirty this morning."

"Which is a little odd, if you think about it," Don said. "Our Val does love the New York nightlife."

"They obviously wanted to get in and get out before the bank woke up."

"Astonishing," Jack Budrow mused, perhaps for the thousandth time. "I still can't believe that Val Haines was a thief."

Don gave Terrance a sideways look. "Right, Jack."

"Well, really. The man's been a trusted employee for almost seven years. Of anyone on my payroll, Val would be the last person I would ever imagine to do such a thing. It's positively astonishing."

"Astonishing," Don repeated, still watching Terrance. "Absolutely."

"And he was at it for almost three months," Terrance added. The pleasure of watching his corporate nemesis crash and burn was exquisite.

Jack Budrow shook his head. "Being so wrong about someone is unsettling."

"Tell you what I think, Jack." Don pointed with his chin at the television screen. The top of the New York building was a smoldering ruin. "Looks to me like you won't need to worry about him anymore."

A TRIO APPROACHED WITH FLAT COP EXPRESSIONS.
One wore a rumpled suit. The other two, a man and a
woman, had gold detective badges clipped to their belts.
"Jeffrey Adams, that right?" The male detective slid into
the seat behind the desk. He was burly and pockmarked
with eyes the color of congealed molasses. "You recognize me?"

His cop escort had led him into a bull pen of an office
and manacled his wrist to a metal plate clamped to a
desk's corner. His wooden chair struck his bruised body
like a paddle. Across the room a phone rang and rang.
"No, sorry."

"Wish I could say the same." The detective swiveled
far enough around to ask the woman, "You got a Kleenex
or something? The guy is leaking."

"Thank you." He accepted the tissue and applied it to
his oozing temple. Mentally, he repeated his own name.
Jeffrey Adams. The words meant nothing.

His one free hand lay limp in his lap. His suit pants
were filthy and one knee was torn. The ringing phone
sounded like a panic alarm. The absence of any knowledge was like a vacuum inside his brain. The mental void
threatened to collapse his head like an empty paper bag.

"I'm Lieutenant Dangelo. This is Detective Suarez. The suit over there is Peters from the DA's office. You got any recollection of taking a swing at me? I'm asking on account of the state you were in at the time. When I restrained you, you tried to lay me out with a round-house. Which is why you got clipped."

"No," his partner corrected. "First you tore his jacket trying to restrain him. When he wouldn't calm down, then you clipped him."

"Mind telling me why you were in the Barron's Club last night, Mr. Adams?"

"I have no idea."

"Do you realize you could be facing felony charges for striking an officer?"

He made a procedure of inspecting the stained tissue. "It looks like I'm the one who's bleeding."

The prosecutor leaned on a desk across the narrow aisle. He wore a heavy brown suit and an expression to match the cops'. "How long have you lived in Des Moines, Mr. Adams?"

Des Moines. The name echoed through his pounding skull. "I don't remember."

"You don't know how long you have resided in your own hometown?"

"I told you. Everything is very muddled. Was I drugged?"

The prosecutor exchanged glances with the cops. "Have you been through this booking process before, Mr. Adams?"

"I assume you've pulled up my records."

"There are no outstanding charges or convictions," the woman detective said.

"Barron's is an odd place for a tourist to visit, Mr.

Adams. Where did you learn about the place?" When he did not respond fast enough, the prosecutor barked, "What exactly do you recall about last night?"

Their gazes formed a pressure that shoved him with rude force. He deflected it as best he could by turning away. Midway across the bull pen, a woman wept and wrenched a handkerchief as an officer filled in a form. At another desk, a narrow-faced black man responded to a cop's questions with the flat drone of someone already claimed by a fate he loathed.

He was surrounded by other people's tragedies. The air was tainted by jaded indifference and a trace of the chemical odor from upstairs. But he was terrified of examining the space where his memory should have resided. The internal nothingness bore the metallic taste of death.

"I asked you a question, Mr. Adams."

"Look. I honestly don't remember anything about last night." He looked from one face to the other. "Or anything else."

The two detectives looked at the suit. The prosecutor shrugged. "What have we got?"

"He solicited an undercover cop," the male detective said.

"In other words, we got nothing. You know the drill. What exactly did he say? Was money mentioned?"

"He flashed a roll."

"I take that as a negative." The suit shook his head. "Unless I'm mistaken, stupidity is not a crime in this city."

"How do we know that's all it was?" The male cop upended a manila envelope on the desk. A driver's license and a gold watch tumbled out. These were followed by two bundles of cash. One was rolled up tightly and held by a rubber band. The other was in a gold money clip. "Mr. Adams, were you in Barron's to buy drugs?"

He reached over and picked up his driver's license. He had not seen a mirror. He could not even identify the photograph as belonging to his own face.

"Are you a user, Mr. Adams? Like a little snort from time to time? Somebody told you Barron's was the place to score a few rocks?"

"If I am not going to be charged, could you please release the handcuffs?"

The trio exchanged a glance. The woman leaned over and opened the manacle. An odor rose from her, a smoky, metallic scent that hinted at the night where she operated. She set the manacles on the desk and moved back. He could see it in her flat, hard gaze, the nearness of something more awful than losing his memory.

He rubbed his wrist. "Can you tell me what drug they used on me?"

"Tit for tat, Mr. Adams. Would you be willing to testify in court that you were drugged and rolled while visiting the Barron's Club on West Hundred and Eleventh?"

"If I can remember any of it."

"You don't recall being dragged outside?" The woman sounded doubtful. "I heard you protesting. You want us to believe it's all gone blank?"

Their hostile disbelief and his own empty panic were a terrible mix. His words sounded a lie in his own ears. "I don't remember a thing."

The woman snorted. "You believe this guy?"

"This is going nowhere," the suit agreed.

The male detective said, "Mr. Adams, we probably saved your life last night. All we're asking in return is help in prosecuting your attackers." The detective's chair creaked as he turned to the prosecutor. "I still say we should press charges."

The suit replied, "You got none to press. One look at that guy's head, and his attorney would be screaming foul all the way to settlement."

The male detective said, "I didn't see any wrongdoing on the part of any police officer. Did you?"

The female detective smirked. "I don't remember."

The prosecutor asked, "Mr. Adams, how much longer do you plan to remain in New York?"

"I'm not sure. A few days." Until he remembered where he lived. And what he would be going back to.

"Where are you staying? Or do you not remember that either?"

When he did not reply, the suit rose from the desk. "I'm out of here."

The woman leaned forward and said, "Mr. Adams, a word to the wise. If you want company, have your concierge arrange it. The Barron's neighborhood might like to claim it's stylin' these days. But the area between Morningside Heights and Harlem is still high risk." She pointed at the two wads of cash. "We have a name for people who carry this much money and a Cartier tank watch into the Upper West Side at one in the morning. We call them dead."

"Would you tell me what drug they used—"

"You come back when you feel like providing information we can use to prosecute your attackers, Mr. Adams, and we'll be happy to help."

"But I'm telling—"

"The door's behind you, Mr. Adams. Have a nice day."

THEY REMAINED LOCKED INSIDE THE CHAIRMAN'S OFFICE.
Terrance stationed himself on the suede sofa with the
silver-plated arms, using the remote to switch back and
forth among the wire channels' televised broadcasts. He
kept the sound turned down to a low murmur. There was
no need for outsiders to know what occupied every shred
of their concentration. Jack Budrow made no further
objection to Terrance's holding on to the control. The
CEO slipped into a glowering silence so complete he did
not seem to notice Terrance at all. Which was not altogether a bad thing. Don remained where he was, pret-
zeled into a visitor's swivel chair.

Waiting.

The morning stretched out over several eons. None of
them made any move to return to their offices. They had
no interest in showing themselves and being drawn into
the normal office routine. The chance of getting real
work done was nil.

Waiting.

If Terrance had scripted the moment in advance, he
would have seen himself pacing. All his computers
would be busy with search missions. Don would have
gone out for a ten-mile run. Jack would be wounding

some hapless office prey with his acidic bluster. But none of that happened. They hunkered down. They did not speak. They scarcely acknowledged one another's presence. The deal had already been talked to death. They were tied together now. The implications of what they had set in motion buffeted them every time the television showed another glimpse of the blackened bank.

Waiting.

They were lunching on salads and sandwiches when notice finally arrived.

Terrance fumbled with the remote and scarcely managed to cut off the television before Consuela opened the door. "I'm very sorry, Mr. Budrow." The secretary's concrete facade was fully shattered now. "I know you said you weren't to be disturbed again. But there is something, well . . ."

"It's all right, Consuela. Come in." Jack did his part well, Terrance had to hand it to the man. He showed the proper distracted concern watching the office's stone lady come totally undone. "What on earth is the matter?"

"I'm really not . . ." Consuela gave a frantic little hand-wave. The young woman behind Consuela took that as her cue. Terrance recognized the newcomer as Val Haines's PA. She looked even more distraught than Consuela.

"Tell me what it is," Jack ordered.

"Sir, there's been an explosion," the young woman said.

Jack was instantly on his feet. As was Don. "In which factory?"

"No, sir. It's not . . ." The woman began leaking tears.

"My dear young lady." Jack moved around his desk, all fatherly concern now. "What on earth has happened? Is it your family?"

"It's Val."

"Who?"

Consuela took over. "Val Haines, sir."

"What about him?"

"He and Marjorie Copeland. They're in New York."

"I know that." He helped Val's secretary into the suede chair across from where Terrance still sat. His sandwich dangled from his right hand, napkin tucked into his shirt collar. Just another busy exec watching his world shift out of normal rotation. Jack said, "Consuela, get this young lady a glass of water."

"I'll do it." Don moved for the executive bathroom.

Jack waited until the woman had taken a sip and almost choked in the process. "Now try and give it to me straight."

"Val and Marjorie had an early morning meeting at Syntec," she said.

Terrance made his first contribution. "Our bank for international funds transfers."

"Yes, sir." Normally Val's PA did her best to pretend Terrance was invisible. An ethereal vampire who did not register on her screen. Today she was too distraught to notice who spoke. "Syntec's been hit by terrorists."

"What?"

"I saw it on the news," Consuela confirmed. "There's been some huge explosion. Two floors of the Rockefeller Center were totally demolished early this morning."

Now both women were crying. "I checked his calendar. Val had a meeting set up for six-thirty. Right before the bomb went off."

"That isn't possible." Jack pointed a shaky finger at his desk and ordered nobody in particular, "Get on the phone. Call their hotel—"

"I've already done that," Consuela replied. "Nobody answered. His cell either. Or Marjorie's."

Don now. "This can't be happening."

"It's almost one. Val hasn't shown up for any of his other morning appointments. The lunch they had scheduled has called twice." She cast frantic glances at them all, pleading with them to tell her it was a dreadful mistake. "I don't know what else to do."

Terrance had a sudden chilling sensation of standing just beyond the gathering's visual range. A conductor's white baton was in his hand. He counted off the beats. One, two, three silent seconds. Okay, now. On the downbeat. Hit it.

As though on cue, Jack turned to Don Winslow and said, "What would you suggest?"

Terrance's baton continued to count off the cadence of shock and sorrow. Don followed the silent script to perfection. His hand even shook as he raised the telephone receiver and dialed information. "I need a number for New York police. What? Oh. Right. Manhattan."

He hesitated then, staring at Terrance as though making sure he held to the proper beat. "Missing persons, I guess . . . No." Another hesitation. Then he dropped his voice a full octave. "No. Scratch that. I think I might need to speak with Homicide."

Both women began weeping full out.

"MR. ADAMS? I'M DR. MARTINEZ. WHAT SEEMS TO BE THE problem?" The doctor was a slight lady with tired eyes, a soft voice, and a fleeting smile. "Other than the fact that your temple is bleeding."

He had spotted the walk-in clinic's address on a street sign just down from the police station entrance. The clinic was connected to an inner-city church housed in a renovated warehouse. The exteriors of both the church and the clinic were painted an orange that hurt his eyes. The clinic's waiting room held a dozen plastic chairs, a cross on one wall, and health posters on the others. The waiting room was crowded with faces that gave his wounds only a cursory inspection. He had discarded his jacket outside the police station. Other than the tear on his left knee, his remaining clothes were stained but intact. He had dozed through a two-hour wait, then awakened to the sound of someone calling a name he was still having trouble claiming as his own.

He told the doctor, "I can't remember anything."

"A lot of people would pay money to trade places with you." The examination rooms were curtained alcoves in a long, open chamber. The floor was faded linoleum. The air was stained with the odor of a strong disinfectant.

From behind other curtains came soft voices. Somewhere a woman moaned.

"Have a seat on the chair there." The doctor swept the curtain around the ceiling corner and enclosed them in an off-white realm. "I don't suppose it would be proper to ask if this has happened before."

He liked that enough to smile, the first in a very bleak day. "Cute."

"I was always a sucker for puns." She slipped on gloves. "Can I have a look at your head?" Her touch was as soft as her voice.

"I wish I knew what happened," he said.

"I imagine you do." She unscrewed a bottle and dabbed a cloth. "This may sting a little."

In the distance a baby wailed. The doctor paid it no mind. She had an unshakable calm similar to the cops', but with a compassion that showed in her eyes as he related what the cops had told him. He asked, "Does that sound like any drug you know?"

"What I know, Mr. Adams, is that you have suffered multiple traumas to your system. Just a cursory examination of your head shows another spot where you have been struck hard. How old are you?"

"I have no idea."

"I'd put your age at thirty, maybe thirty-one. Young enough to heal fast." She taped a bandage over his temple, then touched a place at the back of his skull. "Does this hurt?"

"Ow. Yes."

"It's going to hurt even more, because I want to clean off this clotted blood. No, don't touch. Hold still, please." She had to tug to dislodge the blood from his hair. "You really should have a scan. But we don't have the equipment here." She probed the base of his skull, then began the same twisting, turning routine Reuben had. "Do you feel disoriented? Dizzy? Nauseous?"

"No. I was put through the same routine earlier."

"The cops let you see a doctor? Why didn't they clean you up?"

"An ER nurse was in the lockup with me. He did the finger thing and the head twist and said I didn't appear concussed."

She came around to reveal another quick smile. "Did he charge?"

"He should have." He looked down at his feet. "He saved my shoes. And maybe my life."

"What was he in for?"

"He says he got drunk."

"If we canned everybody in this place who fell off the wagon, you'd see tumbleweeds blowing down the center aisle. Have him stop by when he gets out. We're always on the lookout for good nurses." She shone a light into his eyes. "Follow the light. Good. Okay, how many fingers?"

"Three."

"Close your eyes and bring your left forefinger up and touch your nose. Now do the same with your other hand. Good. Well, I agree with your nurse's opinion. But I'd still like you to stop by the hospital and have a scan. As for the drug they slipped you, there are several options." She began making notes on a metal-backed clipboard. "My guess is GBH. That's the street name, which stands for Grievous Bodily Harm. It's a tablet derived from an anesthetic known as GHB. The user remains vaguely conscious, but loses muscle control. Behavior can often become extremely erratic, sometimes illogically violent. Which mirrors what the cops said."

"But I don't—"

"Remember. Right. Not a total surprise. I assume you were drinking alcohol?"

"The cops said I was tanked."

"Had you done any other drugs?"

"I don't . . ."

"The bar where you say this all took place has quite a reputation. You went there for some reason. There are a lot of other bars you could have gone to for a drink, Mr. Adams. Safer places closer to your hotel. I assume you're staying somewhere midtown?"

"I wish I knew."

"So what we have is a night of heavy drinking, with possibly some recreational drug use added for good measure. Then you were slipped something that brought you to the verge of unconsciousness. After which you were struck repeatedly on the head." Another swift smile. "I'm surprised you made it this far on your own steam, Mr. Adams."

"Everything hurts."

"You'll get over it. I don't want to give you anything for the pain unless you're in desperate agony. It might only slow the process of your brain ridding itself of whatever toxic mix it's struggling through already. Can you manage?"

"Maybe."

"Come back if you can't. I'll leave a note in your file saying whoever is on duty should give you a prescription for Percodan."

"Can you suggest someplace for me to stay?"

The doctor halted in the process of reopening the curtains. "Excuse me?"

"I don't know where I was booked. I need someplace to sleep."

"Wouldn't you prefer someplace south of the park?"

He found himself unable to confess just how desperate he was not to lose connection to the one face that seemed concerned about him. "I'd rather stay around here."

She drew the curtains aside in a slow sweep. "The Everest is around the corner on Lenox. It's clean and safe. Or as safe as you can get in this area."

"Thanks."

"Trauma such as you've experienced can result in a sense of severe disorientation. More than likely your memory will begin to return in a series of flashes. It could be very disconcerting. Remember what I'm saying, Mr. Adams. This is a normal part of the process. But if you have not seen any improvement within the next forty-eight hours, I want you to stop by and see me again." A final smile. "Now go get some rest."

———

He stopped at a men's store midway down the same block as the Everest Hotel, desperate to get out of clothes that felt glued to his frame. He dared not move enough to try anything on. He pulled items from the shelves and carried them to a Hispanic shopkeeper who watched impassively as he peeled the cash off his roll.

The shopping bag formed his only luggage as he entered the hotel. The Everest was a postwar brownstone conversion with an ancient mosaic on the lobby floor and an authentic brass railing around the check-in counter.

The desk manager was a light heavyweight who showed no curiosity whatsoever over his battered state. "How do you want to pay for this?"

"Is cash okay?"

"Cash is always okay by me. Long as you don't mind leaving me a two-night deposit. You got some kind of ID?"

"Yes."

"The authorities, they're very big on us keeping records. Me, I'm not so worried." The clerk could have easily tossed his new guest across the room. His neck was too thick for the shirt collar to be buttoned. His shoulders formed lumpy ridges beneath his jacket collar. "Long as my guests are willing to pay for the service."

"How much extra?"

"Call it another twenty a night."

Remaining anonymous until his head straightened out sounded like a very good idea. He set another forty dollars on the counter.

The desk clerk made the bills disappear. "Enjoy your stay, Mr. Smith."

Soon as he entered the room, the bedside clock caught his eye. He stood on the frayed carpet and stared at the red numbers counting out time that was not his to claim. Somewhere there was a life ticking away without him.

He picked up the phone. The receiver felt sticky with old sweat. He pulled out his shirttail and wiped it down. He dialed the operator.

"Desk."

"How do I get an outside line?"

There was a click and a dial tone. Val dialed information, then pulled out his driver's license. He gave the state and city and name in response to the automatic prompts, wishing he did not feel like he lied with every word.

An operator came on the line. "That listing is for Des Moines?"

"Yes."

"I have several J. Adamses but no Jeffrey. Do you have a street address?"

He read off his license, "One eighteen Hawthorne Boulevard."

"One moment. I'm sorry. We have no listing for that address."

"What about under a different first name for Adams?"

"Sorry. No Adams on Hawthorne."

"There has to be. Could you please check again?"

The operator muted the line. Then, "No Adams on Hawthorne, no Jeffrey Adams at any Des Moines address."

He stared at the face on the license.

"Can I help you with another listing? Sir?"

When he remained silent, the operator hung up.

Slowly he set down the phone and slipped the license back into his pocket. His head throbbed with the compounded pressure of needing desperately to know, yet being increasingly afraid of the answers.

He took a blisteringly hot shower, then opened the door, rubbed down the glass, and spent half an hour in front of the bathroom mirror. There was a larger mirror on the wall opposite the bed. But the lightbulb in the hotel room's only lamp was yellow and weak. When he had been with Dr. Martinez in the clinic, he had absorbed a trace of her weary confidence. Now the tight coil of unease twisted and writhed in his gut.

Even with the bruises and the smudge stains beneath his eyes, he studied a strikingly handsome face. The lines were strong and clearly drawn, which made the swelling around the cut on his temple even more noticeable. His hair was a dark blond with a hint of a wave. His chin had a slight cleft and his lips were a trace overfull. His irises started as dark green around the outer edges and lightened toward the pupils. But their color was not so important. Nor did his looks hold his attention for long. The hollow void at the center of his gaze dominated everything.

This stranger's face stared back at him, blank and wounded. He put a dry bandage over his right temple. Over and over he watched his mouth form the words "Jeffrey Adams." Try as he might, he could not force himself to claim his own name.

The bed was soft as a sponge. He lay down and was instantly enveloped in cheap sheets and the odor of someone else's ashes. He rolled back and forth, trying to find a position where he was not being poked by the springs. Finally he rose and stripped the bed. He folded the bedcover and stretched it out on the floor. On that went the mattress cover, then a sheet. He lay down and covered himself with the second sheet and the blanket. An instant later he rose again, crossed the room, and turned on the bathroom light. He lay back down on his pallet. He fell asleep to the sound of television gunfire from the next room.

The dream came in stages. Before he saw anything, he smelled the odors. The air was rich with the fragrance of burgers on the grill and overripe oranges. Gradually the world came into focus. He stared up into a deep blue sky. Dappled fruit pulled ancient tree limbs down to where they almost touched a manicured lawn. To his right the sun descended behind the roof of a sprawling ranch-style house. *His* house. The dusk was intensely vivid, as though each image he examined was cut with crystal blades and set upon a backdrop of endless blue. Even the laughter he heard behind him was etched in perfect clarity. He knew he should have been able to name the people laughing and talking. Especially the woman who was laughing loudest of all.

The woman stepped into view. She was slender and taut. She wore shorts almost hidden by one of his old short-sleeve shirts starched until it hung on her like pin-striped armor. She had hair that he knew smelled of honeysuckle. And a smile that caught every fragment of the day's remaining light.

She called out. One word. She said, "Valentine!"

The next thing he knew, he was standing in the center of the drab hotel room. His chest was heaving. His legs trembled so hard he had to lean against the wall to make it to the bathroom. He washed his face, taking care to avoid the fresh bandage on his temple. Then he leaned on the bathroom sink and waited for his heart to calm down.

It had been such a happy scene. He could still hear the laughter. The woman with her lovely brown legs stood before him still, smiling at him with a special sense of ownership.

So why was his chest crimped by a tight and ancient sorrow?

He left the bathroom light on and the door fully open. He returned to bed, chased by the worst question of all.

———

This time, sleep was not swift in coming. The pallet was so thin he could feel the frayed carpet threads beneath his shoulder blades. The room smelled of age and dust and a multitude of worn-down visitors. His gaze measured the hard-edged shadows formed by the bathroom light. How many other hotels had he stayed in? How many other places had he thought he would never forget? What multitude of memories had he possessed, events he was certain would remain branded upon the fabric of his life?

Yet now the hunger to remember was tainted by the dream. Fading sorrow flavored his night like the prison's lingering scent. He rolled over. With his ear pressed against the pillow, he could hear a couple shouting from the floor below.

Exhaustion and pain finally carried him into a half-sleep where he argued with himself. He stood before another mirror and shouted at an indistinct face.

His sleep deepened; the dream sharpened. He looked into a mirror cracked with age, as though scarred by all the faces that had studied its depths. His awareness expanded until he saw an antechamber with a floor of broad Mexican tiles. The ceiling was ribbed with hand-painted beams. To his right, a trio of peaked wooden doors were open to a lazy summer breeze. In the mirror he saw rows of tall candles, rising like flaming steps. He knew then where he was, and what it meant.

He was in a church. He was instantly certain church had once been important. Back then, he had searched out structures like this one, where the faith of cultures and centuries was on display. He had liked the sense of standing united against the rush of uncaring time.

He knew he was dreaming, yet knew as well that this visit had actually taken place. He had come with another person. A woman. He dreaded seeing her again, even in an image he knew was just a dream. She had brought him here. She had found this church, one of the oldest in Florida, dating back to the earliest Spanish conquistadors. They had come because she had insisted on it.

The candles were placed in three metal stands that formed a U. Seven pews rested in the center space shaped by the flickering barriers. He watched as the image in the mirror deepened and extended until the woman came into view. It was a different woman from the first dream. The sight of her crystallized the moment with the intensity of an animal's howl.

He had a sudden ability to touch every memory connected to this moment. Audrey. That was her name. Audrey d'Arcy. She had loved him with depth and passion. She had brought him to this church because she yearned to see him reconnected to a life he had given up as utterly and hopelessly lost.

Audrey sat alone in the middle pew. She was an intensely striking woman, with determined features and an intelligent strength. He knew she was also tall, such that if she rose to her feet she would stand only a few inches shorter than him. And she loved him. So much it tore her face into fragments. She had suspected from the beginning that he would refuse her love. And yet she had loved him still.

The candles burnished her copper hair, forming a halo or a crown—he could not tell which. He watched helplessly as, in the dream, he turned away, following the same course he had taken in real life. His heart keened a dirge of loss and yearning, for that had been the last time he had ever seen her.

In his dream she called to him, a one-word litany that mirrored his own remorse. She cried, "Valentine."

The shock woke him up a second time. His heart thundered and his chest heaved. The veil had been pierced with the precise agony of regret.

He rose from the pallet and stalked about the room.

He pumped the stale air in and out of his chest. He strove as best he could to halt the sudden torrent of images. He was no longer asleep. But the nightmare stalked him. The memories clamored like wolves.

He beat at his temples, and one fist came away red. Still the memories tore at him. His name was not Jeffrey Adams. He felt assaulted by a storm of mystery. Why he carried an ID with someone else's name, he could not say.

He clenched his eyes shut. But the image only intensified. He stopped pacing. He no longer leaned against the wall of a dismal hotel room. Instead, he stood in an office corridor. He looked at the closed door to a corner office, and knew it should have been his. He also knew he hated the man inside so fiercely that just seeing the closed door filled him with acidic rage. He turned away, consumed by a desire for vengeance and destruction.

He opened his eyes, but the image did not go away. He saw himself moving farther down the corridor. He entered another office and stared down at the desk. He looked at the name on the document awaiting his signature.

The image vanished. He stood once more in the threadbare hotel room and stared at his reflection. He could finally put a name to this face. He also knew that he wanted to know nothing more. But he was certain he had no choice.

He spoke to his reflection, greeting himself and all the mysteries yet to be revealed.

"My name is Val Haines."

BY THAT AFTERNOON, WORD HAD SPREAD ABOUT THE explosion and the missing personnel. Solemn workers clustered about the office's open-planned center. Terrance knew they were talking about Val and Marjorie. Mostly Val. Marjorie Copeland was a colorless woman with a severely disabled child. She did her work, served her time, and left. She was in it for the medical and the security. Val was something else entirely. Terrance had once heard a trio of secretaries refer to Val as Häagen-Dazs in a suit. When Val's wife had left him two years earlier, the office women had declared her legally insane. When Val's ex revealed in court that she had been having an affair with Terrance and was carrying his child, Terrance had become the office leper. The fact that Val had never fully recovered from the loss had only added to his mystery and appeal.

Terrance's secretary knocked on the door and announced, "Don Winslow called to say the guests have arrived and you should stop by his office."

"Tell him I'm on my way up." Through the interior glass wall he spied Val's secretary weeping on a young man's shoulder. Val had a lot of friends. The young guy, a newcomer doing his stint in petty accounts, looked close to tears himself.

He opened his briefcase and extracted the folders from his office safe. They felt radioactive in his hands. He took a deep breath. He had slept only three and a half hours last night, but he felt as energized as if he had just returned from a month's holiday.

"I'll be in the boardroom if anyone needs me." Terrance noticed his secretary's red eyes. "Any word about Val?"

"Nothing."

"This really is terrible. Be sure and interrupt us the instant anything further is discovered."

Terrance headed for the elevator. When the doors closed around him, he sighed with genuine pleasure, loving the tight adrenaline gleam in his eyes.

Terrance said, "Let the show begin."

———

Four days earlier, Terrance's entire world had been permanently canted within the space of a few minutes.

Two, to be precise.

Friday evening, he and Don Winslow had been seated in Terrance's office. Terrance had the inside drapes open, a rarity. The floor's central arena was quiet. A couple of gofers hustled through last-minute duties. Otherwise the weekend wind-down was complete. He and Don were running through a possible timeline. As in, when they might head out into the sunset, and how. There was a nice low-key tone to their discussion. They had been through this several times before, basically just kicking ideas around. Terrance didn't mind the repetition. Talking about this stage of the game made his blood fizz.

Then Terrance's private line rang. The one that

didn't go through either the main switchboard or his secretary's desk.

As soon as the voice came on the line, their evening grew far less frivolous. He knew instantly that this caller was not the sort who would take time out for idle chatter. Whatever this man had to say, it would be bad.

The caller confirmed it with his first words. "I've got some serious juice."

"Hold on." Terrance hit the mute button and looked over at Don shuffling paper like a coach going over his early-season playbook. "You know about the chap who is counsel for the SEC?"

Don glanced up. "I know we're paying a retainer to some joker who hasn't done diddly for us."

"He's about to earn his keep," Terrance said, and hit the speaker button. "Go ahead."

"What, we're into public performances here? I don't think so."

"Nonsense. I'm totally alone." Terrance hushed Don's paper rattling with a look. "I merely want to jot down some notes as we talk."

"Long as you don't jot down my name."

"Certainly not. You mentioned something about bad news?"

"Bad as it gets. Unless, of course, you're squeaky clean."

Terrance watched Don as he spoke. "Well, of course we are."

His contact announced, "The Securities and Exchange Commission is growing concerned about possible irregularities in your company's books."

Since Insignia was traded on the New York Stock Exchange, any possible illegality that implicated the sen-

ior management required a direct intervention and public inspection of their accounts.

Don huffed like a guy taking a blow to the solar plexus.
This shook Terrance harder than any news the Wall Street
guy might deliver.

"You say something?"

"Just clearing my throat." Terrance couldn't quite
erase the tremor from his voice. "Can you perhaps give
me further details?"

"What, you're saying this isn't enough? Give me a
break here."

"We are indeed grateful. But details might prove
crucial."

"All I know is, they're planning to make a public
announcement before they pounce."

Terrance watched Don grow paler still. Making a statement at the outset of an investigation, rather than once the
teams arrived and began digging, meant they were confi-
dent of finding something. "You're certain of this?"

"The confab ended an hour ago. They brought in
Legal. Meaning me. From what I heard, they've got
everything but the smoking gun."

Don grabbed his notebook and wrote out a single
word. His papers spilled unnoticed to the floor as he
jammed the page in front of Terrance's face. *When?*

Terrance struggled to keep his tone light. "I'd certainly
appreciate hearing your best guesstimate as to when
they'll arrive."

"Sooner rather than later. I'd say you've got until the
end of this week. Four days max."

Terrance and Don silently tried to come to terms with
the news. The caller finished, "You don't call, I don't
answer."

"Understood," Terrance said.

But the line was already dead.

Terrance punched the button and said to his superior, "This is not good."

"Tell me about it." Don tried to rub the blood back into his features. "But at least we know more than we did five minutes ago."

Terrance pointed at Don's papers sprawled all over the carpet. "We need a minimum of four more weeks to put these plans into motion."

"There's no time for that. We've got to act now. Tonight."

"But the timing is not up to us."

"Isn't it?" Don stared at him. "You heard what your contact just said. Our train's about to hit the wall."

"We still haven't answered the most crucial question. Unless the pair we want to pin this on chooses to disappear now, they can always deny involvement."

Don Winslow had a wolf's face. Everything drew back from a fleshy predator's nose. Big bony growths encircled eyes that glowed almost golden, holding a fierce life and no compunctions whatsoever. Don Winslow was as close to a true psychopath as Terrance had ever known. Terrance envied Don's utter lack of remorse and coolness under the strain of wrongdoing. Like now.

Don replied, "That's the first dumb comment I've ever heard you make."

"But—"

"Pay attention, hoss. Either we clean up our tracks and get ready to show the world three pairs of lily-white hands, or we're toast."

Terrance knew Don wanted him to say the words for them both. The chasm yawned there before him. He remained mute.

Finally Don said it. "They've had their chance to disappear. Now we'll just have to make it happen."

Terrance found it odd, how it seemed as though they had always been headed in this direction. From the very beginning. "How?"

"You find out their movements for the next few days. We need them together and away from here." Don stooped and gathered his papers. "Don't we have the auditors and outside counsel coming in?"

"In four days. It's their periodic review."

"Well, at least that's in our favor."

"What do you have in mind?"

"You just be ready. We're going to war. That's all you need to know."

Upstairs, Don appeared his normal rumpled self. It was hard to tell whether the man's frenetic force was new and genuine, or just an uncovering of his constant interior state. Don said, "Quarter past three, and this day already feels two years old." He pointed at the ceiling. "Our man Jack has needed some major help staying sold on the idea."

"Tad late to be altering course."

"He knows that. Which only makes his grousing worse."

The phone buzzed. Don hit the speaker. His secretary announced, "Your guests are in the boardroom."

"Tell Jack five minutes." Don cut the connection and went on, "Been on the horn twice more with New York's finest."

"What did they want?"

"About what you'd expect. Have we heard from either of

the missing employees, what were they doing so early at the bank." Don held out his hand. "One of those files for me?"

"Yes."

He leafed through the pages. "We have any unfinished business?"

"No. None."

"Ready to face the hired guns?"

"Anytime."

He smiled at Terrance with all but his eyes. "As of this morning, how much do we look to clear on this?"

Terrance held the door for his boss. "Why don't we go upstairs and share that bit of news with our guests?"

———

The boardroom had the powder-keg scent of coming tempests. Whatever lighthearted chatter the five men and two women might have brought in with them, Jack Budrow had successfully choked off. His pallid features and clenched jaw shrieked calamity. The company chairman gripped the arms of his chair so hard that his knuckles looked carved from chalk. "You're late."

"Sorry, Jack." Don nodded his greeting to the room and slid into his customary slouch in the nearest open chair. He waved his hand at Terrance. "You know our in-house numbers whizzo."

Terrance grimaced with all the skill of an actor entering the role of a lifetime. "Good afternoon, all."

The two external board members watched Terrance with worried gazes. Insignia's outside counsel and external auditors greeted him with subdued murmurs. Terrance could almost see the antennas searching the air for danger. And who they were going to blame.

Jack said, "You know I detest being kept waiting."

"Just going through the wreckage one last time," Don replied.

The senior attorney cleared his throat. "That, ah, does not sound good, Don."

"It isn't. Believe me. I assume you all have heard about our missing employees."

"I was just filling them in," Jack said.

"Right. We would have preferred to postpone this meeting until we know more. The day has already held enough trauma. But this can't wait." Don waved at Terrance. "Might as well go ahead and destroy their day."

"Enough histrionics. Just get on with it," Jack groused.

Terrance remained where he was, staring down the table's length to the company's chairman. Jack Budrow's grandfather had started the family business from the front porch of the family home. Back then it had been known simply as Budrow's Dairy. Jack's father had made the name change, realizing that Budrow's was too cracker to fit a company he intended to grow into an empire.

The dairies had been expanded to include beef cattle ranches. A total of fifty thousand Florida acres. Then came the orange groves and fruit-packing plants. Another twenty-seven thousand acres total. All bought at near Depression prices.

Nineteen years later, the builders started stopping by the farm.

Palm Beach was expanding west. Lake Worth was about to move from sleepy cow town into the big league. Budrow owned or controlled under long-term lease almost every available acre. Jack's dad led the builders through a merry waltz around his cow stalls. He pretended to have no interest whatsoever in selling. Finally one came up with the idea of not buying the property outright, but rather taking Budrow on as minority partner. Which was what Budrow had been after all along.

One development led to another. On and on, each one richer than the next. The state tried to condemn other parcels for building the Florida Turnpike and the Bee-Line Expressway. Budrow hired an army of lawyers and held out for a minor fortune.

Then the mouse kingdom came calling. Overnight, Budrow's fortune was multiplied tenfold.

The old man remained in feisty control right into his nineties. Finally a massive heart attack felled Jack's father one midsummer dawn as he stooped over his cane, supervising the milking operations on his family homestead. A man with a personal fortune of almost half a billion dollars, coming to rest in a pile of dirty hay. The local press had a field day.

At the age of sixty-three, a bitter and impatient Jack Budrow had finally inherited full control. Despite Jack's best efforts, however, he could not fill his old man's shoes. He tried. Time and again he tried. But the massive South American ranches he invested in never panned out. The Patagonians might herd good beef, but they proved even better at milking empty promises. Whenever Jack or one of his minions flew down, they were handled like royalty, flown about on a company chopper while the locals painted visions of vast holdings and untold wealth. Just a little more time and money, they repeatedly promised, and the half-million acre spread would finally start turning a profit. But Insignia's gold just kept sliding into a bottomless pit. When the board finally revolted and forced a sale of the interlinked ranches, Insignia retrieved one and two-thirds cents on the dollar.

In concept, Jack Budrow's other business projects made sense. But his move from minority investor into full-on owner of Florida hotels could not have been worse timed. The terrorist strike and subsequent slide in Florida tourism hit hard.

But bad business decisions were only part of the problem. Jack Budrow remained in his father's shadow long after the old man rested in his grave. He was nervous and defensive. He hated to be told he was wrong. He found slight everywhere.

He also loved to spend.

Jack Budrow's first act as CEO was to turn half of Insignia's top floor into his own private fiefdom. The renovations cost Insignia almost nine million dollars. Insignia now had two private jets, an executive dining room that was staffed eighteen hours a day, a box at TD Waterhouse stadium, a box at Daytona, and another for the Buccaneers' home games. The outside shareholders might be screaming in protest, but Jack Budrow personally controlled over half the company's voting stock. Those who were close to Jack came to believe that the CEO took little pleasure in his lavish lifestyle. Jack Budrow spent to show the world who was king.

A couple more bad judgment calls, a few more real-estate deals that went south, and suddenly Jack Budrow was gasping for financial breath. Without his power cushion, life was proving a terribly rough ride.

It was Terrance who had discovered that Jack was using company accounts as his private source of funds. Some people might think a man earning a seven-figure salary and sitting on several hundred thousand shares would not require additional funds. But Jack could outspend the Pentagon.

Terrance had shown the good sense to come to Don Winslow. Already he and Don had been building a rapport of shared avarice.

Don had instantly agreed with Terrance that this was the venom they needed. Two days later, Don Winslow had walked into Jack's office and gently sunk in his fangs.

Don had gone to Jack with not an ultimatum but an offer. Look at these minor misdeeds, see the danger you're putting yourself into? The feds would love to nail you for things that five years ago would have cost you a slap on the hand. You know as well as I do how the atmosphere's changed. They'll nail your hide to the wall. We're talking twenty years, Jack. Which at your age is tantamount to life. Is that what you want?

Don accepted Jack's sweaty panic as all the answer he needed. Then he laid out the plan he and Terrance had cooked up. A way for Jack to gain so much money that not even Jack could run through it easily. Or so Don had claimed.

Which had led them to the day's events.

———

Terrance walked around the room, setting down his files with the solemnity of a mortician.

Don and Terrance played tag-team, laying it out. The seven visitors grew increasingly ashen. Jack Budrow did not speak at all.

Two and a half hours later, the company's outside counsel placed the call over the speaker phone. He was put straight through to the chief of the SEC's investigatory arm, an old golfing buddy. The SEC chief greeted him with, "I'm on my way out the door. I'm due at a reception the governor is hosting for—"

"You're going to be late," the attorney ordered.

Don and Terrance listened as the attorney put the news in perfect legalese, how an in-house investigation had revealed that two executives, Val Haines and an associate in the pension funds division, had embezzled funds. How the company's pension funds both in the U.S. and Great Britain had been systematically stripped bare. How yesterday evening Don and Terrance had finally uncovered both hard evidence of the theft and the scheme's outside partner.

"You got a name?"

"The New York corporate account manager at Syntec Bank."

The intake of breath was audible. "You can't be serious."

"Our two employees were apparently lost in the bomb blast. Since their disappearance this morning, we have been searching the pair's private files and confirmed they were indeed the perpetrators."

"You're telling me the two guys you lost—"

"Actually, it was one man and one woman, a Ms. Marjorie Copeland."

"Whatever. These two and a bank exec got themselves blown up so totally they can't even identify how many other bodies might be in there, and these are your culprits?"

"That is correct."

"Have you notified the authorities?"

"As I said, we are just now working through the ramifications of what we have discovered. You are the first person outside this room who is privy to the discovery."

"So it wasn't terrorists. Who planted the bomb, I mean."

"That's our reading as well."

"If the bank exec was culpable, as you say, he might have been scamming other corporate clients."

"That's a distinct possibility."

There was another pause. Terrance could almost hear the mental gears grinding in the Wall Street office. After all, this call was from a company they were preparing to investigate. The SEC man's tone grew harder. "There will be a formal complaint lodged about your attempt to keep this from the authorities."

"On the contrary." Their counsel was subdued, but equally firm. "No such attempt has been made. We are the ones bringing this matter to the SEC's attention."

"Only after the perpetrators have vanished."

"Only after they have been *identified*," the counsel corrected. "We could not discuss it prior to being certain who they were for risk of having the real perpetrators take notice and flee."

The SEC chief mulled that over. "All right," he sighed. "Let me have the bad news. How much are we talking about?"

It was the counsel's turn to take a very shaky breath. "It appears that there were two schemes, one relatively small and another that is, well, somewhat larger. We are uncertain that we have uncovered everything. We think so, but—"

"Ballpark figure."

The counsel shuffled through the file's papers, dragging out the moment.

"I'm waiting."

"Somewhere in the vicinity of $422 million."

The SEC guy groaned. "How much can you recover?"

The counsel looked at Jack Budrow. Terrance also risked a glance. The CEO was greyer than the counsel. Jack was apparently realizing just what this would mean, having such funds stolen under his watch. The board would search out a sacrificial lamb. Why not the founder's son, the exec most of them had come to loathe?

"I'm waiting," the SEC guys said. "How much is traceable?"

The counsel cleared his throat. But the obstruction was not dislodged. "None of it."

"What?"

"As I stated, all of the funds were channeled through the Syntec Investment Bank."

"And?"

"The bank is *gone*. Their entire records department was shredded by the explosion."

The SEC chief was shouting now. "What about backup!"

"That too. We have spoken at length with the Jersey head office. This was a quasi-independent arm." The counsel was visibly sweating. "Syntec operated like many small banks. Their home office maintained no detailed duplication—"

"A full investigatory team will be arriving on your doorstep tomorrow morning!" His rage had a scalding effect. "Heads are going to roll!"

———

Terrance stood in the boardroom doorway, watching Consuela usher out their guests. The auditors and outside counsel clustered like an anxious flock by the elevators. Their faces wore uniform expressions of sickly dread. They knew the score. A hit this big would strike their careers with the effect of wrecking balls.

"Shut the door, will you?" Don's attention was focused on Jack Budrow. The CEO had his head in his hands.

When the three of them were alone, Don walked to the front of the boardroom table and bent over. "Think, Jack."

"It's all I can do."

Don held his fingers a fraction apart and said, "We are *this* close to being rich for the rest of our lives. And we are *this* close to losing everything. Including our freedom."

Jack straightened. "Yes. All right. I see."

"You sure, Jack?"

"Yes. Yes, I understand."

"Good." Don straightened slowly, watching the CEO very carefully. "You've got to pull your weight from now on. Terrance and I are looking at dance cards that are full to the brim."

Jack nodded once, his pallor easing. "So what should I do?"

"You have contacts at the *Wall Street Journal*, right?"

"Of course. I partnered with the vice-chairman at last year's Bermuda golf tournament."

"Swell. Call the guy. Give it to him just like we've done with the SEC." Don's gaze was jury-taut. "Can you remember your lines, Jack?"

"Certainly."

"He'll most likely hear you out, then have a reporter join him and tape a second round. They'll listen to that tape about a hundred thousand times. If you leave a thread dangling, they'll pull it and they'll unravel it and they'll hang us with it." Don inspected their chairman. "Maybe we better let Terrance make the call."

"No." Jack Budrow rose to his feet. "I'll do it."

"Do it right, then."

Jack was at the door leading from the boardroom to the trophy hall and his office when he quietly observed, "I see the torch has already passed from my hands."

VAL HAINES ATE AT A NEARBY DINER. THE SUNSET WAS shrouded by city shadows and the diner's grimy front window. He sat on a stool at the counter, one of a dozen faces staring at nothing. He kept his gaze aimed at the *Times* laid out on the counter beside his plate. He forked the food into his mouth and tasted nothing. His actions were a calm lie. His mind remained as frenetic as the traffic racing beyond the diner's window.

Another memory had assaulted him just as his meal had arrived. In this one, he held a sleeping infant. The most beautiful baby girl in all the universe rested on his shoulder. Her breath came in tiny puffs he could feel on the nape of his neck. One hand grasped his finger. Val pulled out the hand far enough to look at the perfectly formed little fingers and even tinier nails. Her beauty was so complete he wanted to weep. Like all the other memory pulses, this one arrived with a ton of baggage.

It was the only time Val had ever held his child.

"You need anything else there, hon?"

"What?" Val jerked up. The waitress stood with one hand cocked upon her hip, the other holding a smoldering pot. "Oh. No, thank you. Just the check."

"Sure, hon." She set down her pot and scribbled on her pad. "Everything all right?"

Val pushed away the paper he had not really seen. The waitress observed him with the dull concern of one not able to offer anything to anybody. He dropped bills he could not see onto the counter and said, "Memories are a terrible thing."

———

The soft edges of another dusk gradually vanished, joining all the other pasts lost to him. He walked a street of New York nighttime energy. People hurried past and refused to meet his eye. Traffic shoved and blared. Vendors shouted back. Val turned away from his hotel, not headed anywhere in particular. Just walking. Caught up in the pressure of other people's lives.

Val was no longer certain how much he wanted to know. Uncertainty over what might strike next made his past feel very distant. He stopped before a shopfront window and stared at the stranger captured by the night. Maybe this was why he had gone into that bar in the first place. Just looking for a little distance.

Then he realized what he was looking at.

Val pushed through the door and entered the cyber café. It was empty save for the woman behind the counter. The woman had pink hair, two nose rings, and a wary gaze. The two side walls were segmented into semiprivate spaces, with scarred desks holding keyboards and flat-screen monitors. Hip-hop blared. Val approached her. "Can I use a terminal?"

"Why we're here. You want anything to drink?"

"Coffee. Black."

"I need a deposit. You got some plastic?"

"No. I left it . . ." He waved away the lie. "How about a twenty?"

"Works for me." She rang it up and pointed him midway up the left-hand wall. "Take number three."

The chair wobbled. The keyboard was filmed with other people's stress. But that was not why Val sat and stared at the monitor. He knew the computer was part of his former life. He based that on no specific memory, just an awareness that here before him was something vital. The question was, how much more did he want to discover? How much more could he take?

The woman called over, "That thing not working again?"

"No. No, it's fine." He sat and sipped his coffee. Passing headlights etched his silhouette into the monitor's surface.

The woman said loud enough to be heard over the hip-hop, "I got to charge you long as you're tying up the computer, whether you're using it or not."

Val waved without looking over. He sipped his coffee. He set down his cup and pulled out the two wads of cash, one from either pocket. Using the desk as cover, he counted it out. The money clip held eight hundred and sixty dollars. The roll bound by rubber bands was tight as a fist and held another fifty-four hundred-dollar bills. Six thousand two hundred and eighty dollars. What kind of person carried that much cash around with him for a night on the town?

He slipped the money back into his pockets. Everything he knew about himself suggested that he was not happy. A happy man did not go into the sort of bar where he would be drugged and arrested. A happy man did not rely on a false ID to mask whatever it was Val had been doing two nights back. So far his returning memories had been hazardous as grenades.

The young woman left her security behind the bar and walked over. "More coffee?"

He looked up. If he could ignore hair the color of cotton candy and the nose jewelry, she was actually very attractive, in a knowing New York sort of way. "No thanks. I'm good."

She stared at the blank screen. "Everything okay here?"

"Yes." He could tell she was making herself available. The smile was there in her eyes, just waiting for an excuse to break out. Was this part of what he didn't remember, a way with strange ladies? "I'm just trying to work up the nerve."

She wanted to ask more, but something in his face kept her silent. She picked up his cup and retreated.

Val pulled the keyboard closer. He had to know. He drew up the Google search engine and typed in two words: Valentine Haines. He put his name in quotes, so the engine would treat it as a single concept and not flood him with offers for romantic getaways. Then he hit Search.

The retrieval didn't take long.

Recovery from the shock, however, did.

Val realized the young woman had returned and spoken to him. He stared up at her. "Excuse me?"

"I was just wondering . . ." She seemed uncertain whether to stay or flee. "You went all white there."

He turned back to the screen. The blue headline across the top of the screen screamed so loudly at him he could no longer even hear the music.

"Right. Sure. Whatever." She went back to the counter.

Val clenched and unclenched his hand. He gripped the mouse and slid the pointer over to rest upon the first blue line. The arrow became stuck on the headline's last word.

Dead.

TERRANCE HAD PURPOSEFULLY KEPT THE AFTERNOON
and evening clear, a rarity. He normally liked to surround
himself with chattering faces. He found wry pleasure in
observing the human zoo at feeding time. Terrance considered himself a species apart. All proper Brits did, in his
opinion, whether they admitted it or not. Attitude and
power went hand in glove. The British Empire had not
been lost to armies but rather to a generation lacking the
will to rule. His own father was the perfect example of modern British spinelessness.

Though the sky was fiery with a patented Florida sunset, Terrance kept the top up. He wanted neither to see
nor be seen. His Lexus sportster bored a hole through the
violet dusk like a polished bullet, seeking only the target
ahead.

His home was a palace of creamy brick set on the
ninth tee at Isleworth. It had originally been built for an
Orlando Magic star forward, who had been traded to Los
Angeles just as the contractor was polishing the granite
master bath. The property was actually two houses connected by an ornate indoor-outdoor pool. Apparently the
Magic player had wanted his entourage close at hand,
but not actually sharing his home. Terrance parked the

Lexus beside his weekend toy, a classic Mercedes gull wing he had bought at auction after winning his latest promotion. He entered his house and listened to his footsteps echo off the atrium's forty-foot ceiling. Daily maid service left the place gleaming with a sterile air.

He lived alone, yet today he felt as though he were being observed by a thousand eyes. Terrance stripped off his jacket and tie, then opened the sliding doors leading to the pool. Steel girders supported a screened cathedral over the poolside veranda. A covered atrium contained an outdoor kitchen with built-in gas range and party-sized refrigerator. Ten imperial palms in giant wooden tubs marched down the pool's other side. A waterfall timed to come on at sunset poured musically into the Jacuzzi. Beyond the pool and the screen and his border of oleanders, a final trio of golfers raced the twilight.

As hoped, Terrance spotted lights gleaming in the guesthouse parlor. He crossed the mock Venetian bridge and knocked on the door. He heard a voice call from within and entered. "Mother?"

"Hello, darling. You're just in time." She appeared in a sweeping flow of silk and jewelry. "The hook on this bracelet is just impossible."

"Let me."

"You're a dear. How was your day?"

He pushed the catch into place. "Actually, it was rather horrid."

"Do I want to hear?"

"I'm not sure."

She turned and walked back to the second bedroom, now serving as her dressing room. "I suppose you'd best tell me."

Eleanor d'Arcy was a woman born to reign. She

deserved castles and private jets and servants offering the bended knee. She should have hosted monarchs for tea. She seated herself at the Louis XIV dressing table and used the silver-backed brush to bring her hair to perfection. Terrance said, "You look lovely."

"Don't vacillate, dear. The news won't improve with age."

"No, perhaps not. You remember Val Haines?"

"That dreadful man. I had hoped never to hear his name again."

"He's dead."

"What?" She stared at him in the mirror. "How?"

"Rather odd, that. It appears he was blown up."

"Don't joke."

"That is the farthest thing from my mind, I assure you." Swiftly he related the day's events.

"Do you mean to tell me he was in the bank when the terrorists attacked?"

"They don't know that it was terrorists. And his location has not yet been confirmed. All we can say with any certainty is that neither he nor his colleague have been heard from since."

She mulled that over. "I can't say I'll be sorry to see the back of that man. No doubt you feel the same."

Terrance was too aware of the thousand eyes to respond.

"Your sister was sweet on him, I suppose you know that."

"Yes." Which added a very special flavor to the moment.

She misunderstood the gleam to his eyes. "I would prefer that you maintain proper civility with your sister."

"Of course."

But she was not fooled. "Why do you despise her so?"

"I suppose there is too much of Father in her for my taste."

His mother started to respond, then let it slide. "I am hosting a charity dinner tonight at the club."

He accepted his dismissal and turned to go. His mother had been in Orlando for only seven years. Yet already she ruled the upper tiers of what passed for the social hierarchy. She was lithe and very fit and professionally slender. Her face and neck were miracles of modern surgery. Some people took pride in aging well. Eleanor d'Arcy had no intention of giving time's passage an inch.

Returning across the bridge, Terrance was halted by a sudden realization. He had mentioned his father. He never did that. Terrance could not remember the last time he had spoken about his father. Years. To bring him up now was a serious breach. To not even notice it at the time was far worse.

Despite the evening's closeness, a chill sweat pressed from his forehead. He could afford no such slipups. He must control everything. Right down to the smallest detail. Eyes would soon be holding them under constant scrutiny.

He entered the house via the kitchen and began warming up the meal prepared by his maid. He was not the least bit hungry. He had felt no craving for food since this critical phase of their plan had begun. He ate his meal standing at the granite-topped center console. He turned the pages of the *Journal* as he forked the food into his mouth. Nothing registered, neither the food nor the news. The television in the recessed alcove above the oven was tuned to MSNBC. Twice while he ate, the bank's charred image flashed on screen. The first time he used the remote to turn up the volume. The other time he left the image silent. The television was merely background activity for the theater he was shaping. The newscasters had nothing new to report.

He finished his meal and moved to the apartment he had fashioned from the house's far end. The first room opened both to the house and the apartment's private rooms. Terrance did not turn on any lights. The rooms were horribly bare. In the dim light that followed him from the living room, Terrance was able to reshape the rooms in his mind.

Terrance had always been alone. Even as a child, Terrance had known he inhabited a solitary universe. The tight core of seclusion never altered. Nothing could reach him. Terrance could stand in the middle of a dense pack of people and remain trapped within his interior void. Only one person had ever managed to pierce his shields and enter the hidden spaces. This room had been meant for her daughter. The next was a studio apartment for the nanny. After Terrance had secretly torn her former husband apart bit by mangled bit, Val's wife had finally agreed to enter Terrance's world. Then, at the last moment and without warning, she had fled to Miami. Terrance had gone wild with rage, smashing the handcrafted nursery furniture with a ball-peen hammer.

That night, after the fury had subsided, Terrance had confessed to his mother. How the core of his being was filled with a void. How he felt born to solitude.

Eleanor had patted his cheek, a rare show of affection. "My dear darling boy," she said. "Has it taken you this long to realize?"

"Realize what?"

"Kings are not merely born to rule," his mother told

him gently. "They are born to eternal isolation. It is their destiny."

———

Terrance made himself a drink, switched on the digital radio to a random channel, and pretended to read a book. Everything was merely theatrical moves for the hidden audience. Two hours later, his mother returned from the club. Eleanor tapped on the glass and waved him a goodnight. She did not ask if he was going to bed. Terrance had never needed much sleep.

When the guesthouse went dark, he turned off the downstairs lights and proceeded up the central stairs. He padded down the hall to his study. Across from his desk was a narrow cupboard for storing his personal tax records. The rear of the bottom shelf now contained a set of all-black running gear. He dressed in the dark. He hefted a waist kit containing a black knit cap, a penlight, a screwdriver, two keys in a manila envelope, and three sets of surgical gloves still in their sterile packs. Silently he went back downstairs and let himself out the back.

He left the house by the kitchen door. He stood by the property boundary and searched the night. When he was certain he was alone, he jogged across the golf course.

He exited the gated community by way of the golf course's maintenance entrance, which he knew from earlier reconnaissance was locked and empty after nine. The workmen's gate was easily scaled.

Don Winslow's Escalade was parked just down the highway. Don greeted him with, "Look at this traffic. You sit here long enough, the whole world goes by." Don wore a black sweatshirt with the sleeves cut off, black track pants, and black high-tops. A black headband held the graying hair out of his face. He looked like a killer ready for the night's rampage. As soon as Terrance shut his door, Don slapped the Escalade into gear. "Where are we headed?"

"Val's." Terrance did not need to think that one through. "We hit Val's first."

VAL LEFT THE INTERNET CAFÉ AND RETURNED TO THE hotel because he had nowhere else to go. He needed to retreat and work things out. But as he pushed through the outer doors and entered the lobby, memories buzzed about him like vultures over carrion. Retreating to his lonely room would only give them the chance to pick his bones.

The lobby was empty save for the dark-suited desk clerk. "If it ain't Mr. Smith. How we doing today?"

The lobby's only sofa was a brown as toneless as the clerk's gaze. The clock behind the clerk's head read a few minutes after midnight. Val could find no sense to the numbers. The hotel and the night had been divorced from life's natural cadence. Val took a seat and replied, "Not so good."

"Yeah? Sorry to hear that."

Val studied the ancient tiles at his feet. The hotel's name was inscribed in a mottled design almost lost to the years. The air smelled of cleanser and time distilled to a futile blend. Val sighed his way deeper into the sofa's lumpy embrace. What he needed was a way to shoot the mental vultures out of the sky before they could attack him again.

He realized the clerk was watching him and asked, "You mind if I sit here?"

"Do I mind?" The clerk showed genuine humor. "I been working this job, what, five years now. That's the first time a guest ever asked me permission."

"You're the boss here."

The clerk's reply was cut off by the ringing phone. He answered and began speaking in a low voice. But his gaze remained steady upon Val.

The Internet search had taken Val from the blue-flagged headline to an article in that morning's *Orlando Sentinel*. As soon as Val had seen the newspaper banner, he had known he was looking at his hometown. Not Des Moines. He lived in Orlando. The new memory and the newspaper article formed a heat pungent as steam rising from a lava bed. Val watched the clerk talk quietly into the phone and felt pummeled by the words he had read. According to the report, Valentine Haines and Marjorie Copeland, executives of a company called Insignia, had apparently been killed by a massive bomb blast. Terrorists were not believed to have been involved.

The blast had demolished the top two floors of a build-ing within the Rockefeller Center complex. The floors were home to the Syntec Investment Bank. The only rea-son there had not been a bloodbath was that the blast had occurred at six forty-five in the morning. The bank's prem-ises, however, had been completely destroyed.

The clerk set down the phone. His eyes remained upon Val's face, inspecting, gauging. "Looks like it's my turn to ask permission, Mr. Smith."

"What for?"

"See, there's some guys, they want to do a little busi-ness. Maybe you'd be better off heading upstairs."

The prospect of entering his solitary cell held no pleasure whatsoever. "Do I have to?"

The clerk's name tag read *Vince*. His eyes flickered through an instant's change, something that might have been humor. "There you go, asking me what I never heard before. Do you have to? That ain't the question. The question is, are you trouble?"

"Not for you. Definitely not." Val waved in the direction of the stairs. "I just don't . . ."

A pair of young men pushed through the outer doors. They crowded the lobby with uptown swagger and noise. The atmosphere palpably condensed. One of the men was rail-thin, dressed in a vest and no shirt, with a thick gold chain bouncing on his chest as he walked. "Man, this is some place, right, Jamie?"

"Sure." His partner was thicker in every possible dimension. He wore an off-white sweater and cotton boat pants. But his swagger was the same, as were the wraparound shades. "It's something, all right."

The thin man stalked to the counter. "Hey, Vince, my man."

"Long time, Arnold."

The desk clerk's tone stopped the slender man just as he was reaching out to shake hands. Arnold kept his hand moving up and swept off his sunglasses. "Jamie, meet Vince. As in, the man you need to know."

"Vince."

The desk clerk nodded once. Val felt as if he had aged into one of the old men normally dressing up the lobby. Pretending that by watching somebody else live the moment he could lay claim to a life himself.

Arnold went on, "I was just telling my buddy how midtown is moving into Harlem. The prices they're asking up here these days, it's unreal." He did a nervous feint in front of the counter. "A guy wants to do business, uptown is the place to come. Give you a for instance. How much you got out these days, Vince?"

The desk clerk scowled. "What kind of question is that?"

"Hey, we're all friends here."

"Correction. You I know." Vince turned to face the stockier man. "You can't be too careful these days. You got undercover cops dressed seriously street, looking to do business."

"I'm telling you, Jamie's a friend."

"That's not the issue here. Are you telling me you vouch for this guy?"

The dance grew more nervous still. "'Course I do. Why else would I bring him in here?"

"Stop this two-step you're doing and look me in the eye. I asked you a simple question. Do you or do you not vouch for this man I don't know?"

Arnold grew utterly still. Even time seemed trapped in the amber force of Vince's gaze. "Yeah, sure. I vouch for him."

"All right, then." Vince offered his hand. "Jamie, good to meet you."

"Likewise."

"Do me a favor. Lose the shades. I'm talking business, I like to look a guy in the eyes."

"No problem." Jamie used his sunglasses to point toward Val. "Who's the stiff?"

Vince's gaze shifted and drilled Val where he sat. A measuring instant, then gone. "Nobody. He's cool."

Val resisted the urge to probe his chest, see if Vince's gaze had punctured a lung.

Arnold asked again, much more subdued this time. "So how much you got out, Vince?"

"Not a lot." Vince looked back at Val again, communicating something Val could not understand. "Couple hundred, round there."

"Two hundred large, you call that not much?"

"It's nothing, compared to some guys I know. Keeps me under the radar screen of the big guys."

"You hear that, Jamie? Vince don't pay nobody but Vince."

"I go much bigger, I got to sit down with the man. He'd slap me around a little for working somebody else's territory. They'd shake me down, tell me they got to get a piece of everything I do."

"They slap *you* around?" Jamie tried an ingratiating grin. "Man, they must be some kind of tough."

"They're pros is what they are. I get any bigger, I got to sit down with them. These guys, a smack in the face is cheaper than a cup of coffee, and it wakes you up a lot faster."

Arnold was grinning now too. Eager to be part of whatever was going down. "Nothing personal, right?"

"Just making sure they got my attention. Just doing business. Speaking of which." Vince made a point of looking at the wall clock. "That about does it for the chit-chat, fellows."

The two on Val's side of the counter exchanged a look. "Jamie's looking to do some business, Vince."

"Yeah?" He showed no interest whatsoever. "You two want to rent a room?"

"No, man. Not like that. Tell him, Jamie." When his friend hesitated, Arnold hurriedly added, "He's good for it, Vince. He's an expert down at the phone company. What he does, I can't even explain it. But he's making good money, I know that."

"Wait a second here. You bring in somebody I don't know, tell me he's got a straight job, but somehow he's blown everything he makes, and I'm supposed to be impressed?"

Jamie cleared his throat. "I got this problem, see. My old lady—"

Vince sliced the air with his open hand. "You can stop right there. I don't know what kind of line you spent the trip over working up, thinking you're gonna walk in here and lay it out. So let me tell you up front. Your problem, it don't mean nothing to me."

"This is for real, what I'm saying."

"Maybe it is, maybe it isn't. I don't care either way. You could be the worst gambler to ever hit Atlantic City for all I know. That's your problem. All I want to know is, can you pay what you owe?"

"I'm good, man." He was visibly sweating now.

"Yeah, Vince, he's a straight-up guy."

"Straight, curved, crooked, looped like the Jersey Turnpike, it's all the same to me." He took aim with his forefinger. But he might as well have leveled a pistol at Arnold, the way the guy flinched. "You know what you're doing, vouching for this guy?"

"He's good, I tell you."

"For your sake, he better be. You hear what I'm saying?"

"Yeah, Vince. I hear you."

"Okay, then." Vince turned to the stockier guy. "How much you need?"

Jamie sniffed and backhanded his nose. "Twenty large."

"You want to get into me for twenty thousand dollars?"

"Yeah, see—"

"No. I told you. Whatever your business is, you left it outside." Vince tapped the counter once, twice. "Okay, here's how it's gonna play. I'll give you the twenty."

"Thanks, man. You won't—"

"Just shut your mouth and pay attention. You work the phone company, so your payday's Friday, right? Don't talk, just nod your head. Okay. So every Friday for the next seven weeks you're gonna be down here with forty-three hundred cash."

Both men gaped. Jamie recovered first. "You're charging me fifty percent for seven weeks?"

"That's the rate."

"You can't be serious."

"Oh really. Let me tell you why you're here in my place of business. You know other guys on the street, they'll give you the twenty large. But then they own you. They'll keep you paying for the rest of your life, which with a lot of these guys won't be that long. They'll get all you got, then take you out. After that they'll put your old lady on the street. Tell me I'm lying."

The two men were now very pale and utterly still.

"So you come to me. And I give it to you straight. Just like you heard before you got here. The twenty will cost you ten." Vince pointed with his chin. "You don't like it, there's the door."

Jamie's voice was down to a hoarse murmur. "No, no, it's good."

"Right." Vince reached under the counter, came out with a cracked leather pouch. He unzipped it and began unpacking banded notes. "Check it out."

Arnold tried for weak levity. "Hey, Vince, if you say it's good—"

"I'm telling you to count the bills."

Jamie ruffled the notes, but from his expression it was unlikely anything really registered.

"It all there?"

Jamie nodded.

"When am I gonna see you?"

"Friday."

"Right. Good doing business with you." Vince pointed at the door. "Stop by anytime."

After the pair left, the desk clerk refused to meet Val's eye. Which meant Val could openly study the man. He was fairly certain what would happen if he told Vince about the bar and the bomb and the attacking memories. "Deal with it," the guy would say, and shrug away the trauma.

He rose to his feet, driven by a restless urge to get on with doing just that. Vince gave him a single measuring look, then went back to his records. Val crossed the lobby and pushed through the outer doors. If only he could adopt a bearing so severe and cold nothing could touch him. A Kevlar vest to shield him from the next rain of mental bullets.

Val entered the night. He was filled with a bitter envy for the clerk and his world chopped down to emotionless little squares. A life spent running under the radar. Val understood him with unique clarity.

TERRANCE AND DON DROVE TWICE AROUND VAL'S neighborhood, an old development overlooking the Rio Pinar golf course. The night was utterly still. Live oaks formed a canopy over the road. Most homes were sprawling ranch-style, built when property was measured by the half-acre rather than the square meter. They parked a block away, just one more SUV in a world of minivans and tricycles. Don breathed heavily as they trotted down the empty street. This was the part Terrance hated the most, being out in the open and risking it all on a sleepless neighbor. But they needed to do this themselves.

While Don scoped the night, Terrance drew the manila envelope from his pack. Forging copies of the house keys had been easy enough. Like many commercial road warriors, both Val and Marjorie had kept extra sets of house and car keys with their secretaries. The lock turned easily. They entered, shut the door, and waited. Terrance had searched Val's desk and his secretary's and come up with no alarm code. As hoped, the old place was not wired. Terrance slid on a pair of surgical gloves and pulled the flashlight from his pocket. It was just like Val to hide in some old-fashioned neighborhood and pretend he was shielded from time. Sit behind his plate-glass armor and hope the world's changes afflicted everybody but him.

Terrance did a slow sweep of the front rooms. This was the first time he had entered the enemy's lair. Val's home had the impersonal nature of a hotel. There was nothing on the walls save bare shadows where pictures had once hung. The mantel and the window recesses and the side tables were empty. The living room carpet still had deep imprints where large pieces had once stood.

Don moved up beside him and studied where the flashlight's illumination fell. "Looks like the wife pretty much cleaned him out."

Terrance shook his head. "Stefanie only took what she brought with her."

Don aimed his flashlight into Terrance's face. "So how come you two aren't an item?"

"The clock is ticking, Don."

"This is not a difficult question." Don's tight grin was illuminated by the pair of flashlights. "You won the round hands down. Knocked the other guy out of the ring. So how come you and she aren't doing the happy couple thing?"

"She needed time alone." Terrance gave the room another sweep. "Stefanie was too good for Val."

"Yeah, looks like she'd agree with you on that one."

Terrance pushed Don's light out of his eyes. "Let's get to work."

They moved into their planned routines. Don hunted for hard evidence. Terrance attacked Val's home computer. He did not have Val's personal ID code. So he wiped clean all files dating from the past six months. Terrance did not need to know what Val had. He simply had to be certain nothing except the evidence he had planted would show up when the official investigation opened. Evidence that showed how Val Haines and Marjorie Copeland had stolen more than four hundred million dollars from Insignia's coffers.

Midway through his work, Don appeared in the doorway. "I think I found something."

Terrance followed Don back through the house. A narrow hallway opened at the rear of the kitchen, led them past the laundry room and into the double garage. One half was empty, Val's car no doubt still in the airport parking lot. The other half was a mess of woodworking equipment. Terrance steadied his flashlight on a half-finished cabinet. The work was good.

"Over here."

Don had shifted a long trestle table doing duty as a workbench. Thumbtacked to the wall was a world map. Terrance's flashlight picked up a number of underlined locales—Tahiti, Kuala Lumpur, Costa Rica, Java, New Zealand, Cape Town. With the table out of the way, a set of floor-to-ceiling doors to a recessed cabinet came into view. The doors were padlocked shut.

"Help me move this map." When that was done, Don gripped a set of heavy-duty shears and took a bite on the padlock. He grunted with effort and squeezed the handles shut. The padlock finally gave and rattled against the concrete floor.

Don twisted the handle, then gave a shout of alarm and jumped back. Books and boxes tumbled out, so tightly packed in the tall cupboard they might as well have been spring-loaded.

The two flashlights played over the pile. Don shoved an album of wedding photos with his shoe and said to no one in particular, "Do you believe this?"

Upended boxes revealed mementoes of a lost life. Dozens of music CDs spilled over a cedar chest of wedding silver. Dusty frames held the frozen lies of once happy faces. Terrance stared down at Stefanie laughing beside his enemy. His gut churned at the sight of her happy with the wrong man. "We can't leave it like this."

"It'd take us days to cram it all back inside." Don began cramming stuffed toys into the nearest box. "Stack the books that fit on that empty shelf."

The books were a mixture of marriage counseling, Bibles, and crisis resolution. By the time they were finished and the map repinned to the wall and the table moved back into place, both men were breathing hard.

Don stepped back, surveyed the blank space, and asked, "What happened to this guy?"

Terrance went back to Val's office.

When he was finished with the computer, Terrance opened the rear French doors in the living room. He stood listening to the night. The overcast sky was illuminated an orangish yellow by the city's false dawn. A rising wind blew in from the south. The palms rattled like angry observers, irritated by his calm. Terrance wondered if this was how triumph was supposed to feel. Like a barrier had been erected between himself and all of life. Perhaps this was why warriors of old paraded through the streets and danced around mammoth fires. They sought to create externally what they should have felt inside.

"Val doesn't even have a safe." Don came in with a trash bag full of papers. "All the interesting stuff was in a shoe box on the closet's top shelf. Have a look at this."

Terrance turned his flashlight onto the paper in Don's hands. "A false birth certificate?"

"Unless he's done a name change and forgot to tell

us." Don shook his head. "He'd use the birth certificate to apply for a passport, right? Looks like our guy was getting ready to fly."

Terrance read the name on the birth certificate. "Jeffrey Adams."

Don shone his flashlight down on the photograph dangling from Terrance's hand. The picture was of a laughing infant, held by an adult excluded from the frame. "That Val's kid?"

Terrance stared out at the night and declared, "Mine. The child is mine."

Saying it often enough almost made it so.

THE NIGHT ACTED AS AN AMPLIFIER TO THE STREET'S energy. Everything outside Val's hotel was louder, faster, harsher. He walked back the three blocks to the cyber café. Cars cruised the avenue, their salsa rock and hip-hop punching the air with pneumatic fists. Val was just another solitary guy walking the concrete in search of his fix. Just another mark.

Val reentered the café. A spiky-haired youth with spiderwebs tattooed on both forearms had replaced the young woman. The guy accepted Val's deposit and directed him to a computer without seeing him at all.

Val went to the Yahoo.com Web site. The screen address had come back to him while he had been seated in the hotel lobby. Just another shard of memory, another fleck of another guy's past. Val punched the button for e-mail retrieval, then typed in his screen name and password.

A long sweep of e-mails filled the screen. Val went through them carefully. The names and the messages formed imperfect mental fragments. Some e-mails asked him to get in touch with them if he was able. Most held the formal air of concerned business colleagues. After reading each one, Val hit the "keep as new" tab, so there would be no record of his having stopped by for a read. What he found there revealed no reason to go back.

Then a screen name leapt out at him. She used her own name, of course. Audrey d'Arcy. A very direct woman, surrounded in Val's mind by candlelight and sorrow of his own making.

Val hit the key to open her e-mail.

My beloved Valentine,

I can't believe this time you've left me for good. Now I'm alone and sinking inside the void where a heart used to be. Asking questions to a night that threatens to swallow me whole. I prayed for nothing more than to connect with you. Why was I doomed to fail with the one man I ever truly loved . . .

Val masked the letter and glanced around. No one paid him any attention. He stared at the front window and the night beyond, seared by her words.

He rose to his feet and went back to the counter. "Can I print something out?"

The guy still refused to glance his way. "Dollar a page."

"Fine."

The server keyed his register. "Just hit print. The pages come out back here."

Val returned to his keyboard and clicked on the print button without looking directly at the letter. He wanted to read the rest of what Audrey had to say. He had to. But not now.

Val stood by the register, keeping himself close enough to ensure the clerk would not take time to read. But the guy showed no more interest in the pages than he had in Val. Val paid and returned to the computer and began the process of shutting down.

The screen showed an instant-message e-board. The message struck him with five furious bullets.

You vile, despicable, evil worm.

The return address was the same as the letter stowed in his pocket. Before he could gather himself to respond, Audrey shot another assault.

Here, let me help. You stole Val's password in one of your nocturnal forays. And now you're checking things out. Making sure there's nothing to tie you to your appalling deeds. But I know. I know.

Val felt the yawning gap of all he wanted to leave behind. The prospect of becoming reconnected kept him unable to respond.

The screen blasted through one more blow.

Murderer.

Val took a sharp intake of breath. His hands moved from his heart's volition. He typed in, *It's me, Audrey.*

He sat and waited. He could see her now, the strong features and piercing ice-blue gaze. The hair of burnished copper, which she hated because of its impossible waves. The direct manner of speech, the overlarge mouth, the features that were sparked to animation by the slightest hint of emotion.

Like the anguish he had caused her any number of times.

The screen remained blank. So he typed in, *Really. It's me. Val.*

Another long pause, then, *You're not dead?*

The world thinks so. I intend to keep it that way.

The screen slapped him again.

Oh, Val, Val, you terrible beast of a man, I have wept for twenty solid hours. Couldn't you possibly have let me know? Is that so very much to ask?

Audrey, I've had an accident. I—

She broke through with yet another question. *Where are you?*

New York.

You can't possibly.

Yes.

Val, listen to me. Hide yourself.

You are the only person who knows I'm alive.

You have to get out of there. Out of the country, if possible. Come here, if you can, but don't travel under your own name. Can you do that?

Why?

The answer was slow in coming.

Because my brother thinks he has killed you. And if he learns you're alive, he will try again.

AS THEY DROVE AWAY FROM VAL'S, TERRANCE TURNED his cell phone back on. The message signal began flashing almost instantly. Terrance scrolled through a number of calls from financial players. He said, "Two o'clock in the morning and I'm still fielding calls from Wall Street."

"Bound to happen. People wired into breaking news want to check our pulse before the markets open." Passing headlights reflected off Don's face as if his features were sprayed with oil. "I'm thinking we should head back to the office, camp out there."

Terrance gave a mental shrug. He would not sleep much wherever he lay down. He continued to scroll through his messages, then stopped. He recognized the former policewoman's voice with the very first word. "I got something with explosive potential. Call me."

He pressed the phone to his chest. How should he play this? He had seen Don at work. But he was not Don.

"What's up?"

"Wally wants a word." He pushed the redial button.

She answered on the first ring. "Don?"

"No. Terrance here."

"A change like this," the woman declared, "is a very bad idea."

Suzanne Walton had been a highflier in the Baltimore police force until Internal Affairs caught her taking a bribe from a local vice czar. The woman loved to gamble beyond her means. The woman also lost. The money had to come from somewhere. Because she was one of the first women to earn a detective's shield, the force had let her quietly resign.

"We don't have any choice," Terrance replied.

"Explain that one to me."

There had been nothing the press could pin a story on. Which of course was what the Baltimore police had wanted. But they let word slip out quietly. When Don had come up with the idea of hiring Wally Walton, it had taken Terrance's sniffer hounds less than a day to come up with the goods. Walton was dirty. The Baltimore authorities had spread the quiet word far and wide. Walton was bad news.

Terrance replied, "Things are in motion now. The exec who actually pulls the corporate strings has to be the key player."

"Meaning Don Winslow."

Don stopped at a traffic light and stared at him. Terrance said to the phone, "That is correct."

"So he won't have time for me."

"Precisely. Plus, one of us must stand watch over Jack Budrow. I can't. He despises me."

"Why?"

"I've never quite been able to figure that one out."

"This way you're talking," Wally said. "Does this mean you're going to play it straight with me?"

"I can't think of any other way to work this through."

She mulled that over, then decided, "I guess I can live with that."

"So what do you have?"

"Maybe nothing. You haven't heard anything from Haines, have you?"

Terrance's chest was clutched by a titanium vise. "What?"

"Val Haines," she repeated. "Any word from the guy?"

"You have got to be joking."

Don was watching Terrance now more than the road. "What's going on?"

Terrance waved him to silence as the woman continued. "Like I said, it's probably nothing. But he didn't spend the night in the hotel."

Terrance turned his face to the side window, concentrating fully. "Are you sure?"

"I got a couple of friends on the force up here. You'll be hearing from somebody later today. The official word is, the guy is history. But they went into the hotel yesterday afternoon and found that the guy's bed wasn't touched."

The car turned into the office building's parking garage and halted in the executive space. Don cut off the motor. And waited.

Terrance was unable to move. "This is confusing."

"Maybe not. You told me the guy was a night creature."

"Yes." Terrance laid his forehead upon the cold glass. "Particularly when he's up there."

"Right. So maybe he got lucky. Found himself a more pleasant place to sleep."

His thoughts emerged in congealed lumps. All the documents had been structured to point at Val as the thief. Outside counsel and the auditors had been brought in. The files were now in the hands of the authorities. The scheme was in public play. Terrance forced himself to straighten. There was a damp spot where his forehead had rested on the glass. "We have to be certain."

"NYPD is setting up a citywide alert."

"They can't find him."

"Yeah, well, like I said. Most likely he's not anywhere to be found."

"No. You don't understand." Terrance's breath was so constricted he could only find air for one word at a time. "The authorities *cannot* find Val Haines."

WHEN VAL REENTERED THE HOTEL, THE CLERK
watched his approach with an impersonal gaze. Vince's
hair was cropped as close to his head as his graying
goatee. The bones of his temple, jawline, and cheeks
were as pronounced as his steely muscles. His skin was
pocked from beneath his left eye to his ear, like he had
been whipped with a chain or scarred by buckshot. He
wore a dark-gray suit and a white shirt, with a tie as
matte-black as his eyes. The muscles of his thick neck
formed a slanted decline to massive shoulders.

"Mr. Smith." Vince showed him nothing. Not in the
gaze, nor the greeting. "What's going on?"

Val forced himself to meet the man's eye. The walk
through the New York night back to the hotel had solidi-
fied his thoughts into a single focused objective. Val asked,
"Did you mind me listening to what went on earlier?"

"That depends. You a cop?"

"Definitely not."

"No, I don't think so. You come in here all beat up,
your clothes a mess. Only thing you're carrying is a
shopping bag full of new clothes. And you're wearing
those now."

"You're observant."

"Comes with the territory. Actually, you know what you look like to me? You look like a sucker."

Behind Val, the old man now camped out on the sofa wheezed a chuckle. Vince leaned to one side so as to look around Val. "Hey, why don't you take a hike upstairs."

"I ain't bothering nobody."

"That so? Well, I'm telling you it's time to hit the sack." Vince waited until the old man shuffled into the elevator and disappeared. Then he returned his attention to Val. "You were watching what went down with those guys."

"Yes."

"Tell me what you saw."

"You're a loan shark."

"Don't call it that. I'm a service provider. I've helped out a lot of people. They come to me when nobody else is gonna do a thing for them, except maybe break their legs."

"What happens if they don't pay you back?"

Vince did something with his eyes. The voice maintained its flat calm. But the eyes opened into bottomless pits. "Oh, they always pay me. Always."

"I believe you."

"Personally, I got a soft spot for suckers. I know what it means to be down and out."

"I'm glad to hear it."

"What I need to know is, are you trouble?"

"I told you, I'm not a cop."

"That's nice to hear and all. But I got to *know*. Somebody comes into my place of business, all beat up, pays cash, no plastic, no nothing, now he comes up to me like he's wanting to do business. I got to know what's going on with this guy."

"It's like you said, I got beat up and arrested."

"You got any ID?"

"All I've got is a driver's license. And it's fake." Val fished it out. "It says Iowa. But I'm from Florida."

Vince inspected it carefully. "Nice work." He handed it back. Vince moved like a boxer, his motions smooth and economical. Balanced constantly on his toes. His fingers rested lightly on the countertop. But he put no weight there. He leaned on nothing. "An honest out-of-town sucker. You get rolled?"

"Almost. I was in the process when the cops arrived."

"So why'd they arrest you?"

"They say I attacked them. I don't remember."

"You hit a cop? In this town? Man, you're lucky to be alive."

Val touched the bandage on his temple. "They gave me this."

"That ain't nothing. That's a love tap. Where I was brought up, that'd be a cop's way of saying hello." He cocked his head. "You know what I see? I see a clean-cut kinda guy, never been in trouble, never done time. No tattoos, am I right?"

"No."

"Show me your arms."

"What?"

"Roll back your sleeves. Yeah, like I thought. No tracks. Okay, you can roll 'em back down. People say they want some ID, what they're telling you is, show me you're street. You understand what I'm saying?"

"I'm not sure."

"Guys doing heavy drugs, they hear that every time they hit on a new source. Show me your ID. What they want to see are needle tracks. Undercover cops won't have tracks. They do, they're one step from turning."

"I told you—"

"I know, I know. You're not a cop. You're just a guy in trouble."

"Right."

"You're not street. You don't have idea one. And you're being straight with what you're saying."

"As much as I know how."

"See, normally to do business with me, you got to have an introduction. This ain't about, what you call it, a résumé. Somebody brings you in, tells me you're good for what you want to borrow, say you're after twenty thou like that guy. You don't pay, you skip town or get hit by a bus or whatever, this guy brought you in here? He's got to be good for the loan and the vig."

"That's hard."

"Welcome to life uptown." Vince turned away to deal with the phone. Back again. All business. As impersonal as a robot. "So what are you after, anyway? Money? Blow? Something special in the meat department?"

"A passport."

"You want paper. That's tough. Tough and expensive. Since the terrorist thing they been cracking down on the paper handlers."

"Can you help?"

"Maybe. Yeah, I might. Like I said, I got a thing for suckers." A flick of a smile. There and gone. "You got money to pay for the work?"

"Can you give me some idea how much it'll cost?"

"You want a new name too?"

"No."

"So this Jeffrey Adams you just showed me on the ID, it ain't real."

"No."

"For a passport, good work, I'd call it four, maybe five thou."

"I've got that much."

"Then yeah, maybe I can help you out. But I got to know up front, what's in it for me?"

Val wiped his hands up and down his trouser legs. What choice did he have? Vince simply stood and waited. Facing a sweat-stained man at the moment of decision was nothing to this guy.

Val unstrapped the watch from his wrist. "I can give you this."

Vince held the watch up to the light. Squinted and inspected carefully. "Cartier tank. Twenty-carat frame. With the alligator band. Nice. This hot?"

"Not to my knowledge."

"What, it was a gift? Got some sentimental value?"

"Not anymore."

"I like that. Cutting all ties. Neat and tidy." Vince made the watch disappear. "Okay, Jeffrey or whatever your name is. Let me make a few calls. I'll get back to you."

He stared at the pocket now holding his watch. "Can I wait?"

"Not a chance. I don't like the sound of heavy breathing when I'm working. Go do like the old man, use the bed you're paying for." Vince reached for the phone. "I'll let you know when it's time for round two."

TERRANCE WAS SO DEEP IN A MIDNIGHT COMA HE couldn't even tell if the pinging sound was a nightmare.

He rolled over and landed on his office floor. His eyes were open now. He crawled to the ringing cell phone perched on the corner of his desk. "What?"

"It's Wally."

"Wait one."

Terrance forced himself to his feet. He crossed the hall to the bathroom and washed his face. He had never slept in the office before. He had laid down thinking he could at least remain prone for the two hours until dawn.

Terrance returned to his office. His watch lay on the coffee table. He did not need to check it. He picked up the phone and said, "All right."

"What I've got, it's not the best news."

Terrance went from stupor to as awake as he had ever been in his life. Liftoff in three seconds flat. NASA should take lessons.

Terrance raced out of his office and down the side corridor in his T-shirt, pants, and socks. No belt. His front was still damp from splashing himself.

"Are you there?"

"Yes." He hit the stairwell door with his shoulder.

The steel handle struck the wall like an angry gong. "What do you have?"

"Like I told you earlier, I've still got some buddies up here in the force. I had them keep an eye out for me. Which has been expensive. You hear what I'm saying?"

"Spend what you need." He took the steps three at a time. Ripped the door open.

"I'm spending. Believe me. Spending isn't the question here. It's getting paid."

He sped down the hall. "We'll take care of you."

"You better."

"Haven't we always?" Terrance burst into Don's office. The man was dead to the world. Terrance kicked the sofa. Again. Don lifted his head but didn't open his eyes.

Terrance said to the phone, "You're telling me Val Haines is definitely alive?"

Don did a human catapult off the sofa. He crouched before Terrance, his face a rictus snarl.

"Not definite. Nothing definite about this case. But the evidence is definitely not in our favor."

"Tell me what you have."

"It occurred to me that if we couldn't get information on who got toasted in the explosion, we could at least find out who was still walking around. You with me?"

"Go on."

"I did a run through the local precincts. Just to be sure, you know, since your guy has a rep for going wild when he's up in the big city. I thought, okay, maybe he wasn't at the dance because he was held up somewhere else."

"You found something."

"A possible only. The precinct station in question is very far from the trail you'd expect a highflier to take. In the borderlands between Morningside Heights and Harlem."

Terrance huffed out each word separately. "Do. They. Have. A. Name."

"Jeffrey Adams."

Terrance staggered across the room and clutched the wall.

"I've never met Val Haines face-to-face. I been working from a company mug shot. And I couldn't be sure. But I thought, you know, it was worth checking."

"You were right."

"This guy Adams was comatose when they brought him in. Apparently he was in a bar that caters to the hard core. Carrying a wad of cash and a driver's license. No plastic. You with me?"

Terrance's senses were in hyperdrive, the same power he saw there in Don's gaze. "Using a fake ID to stay anonymous."

"Exactly. Some cops were there undercover. Apparently they saved this mark from a bad end. Only Adams took a swing at an undercover cop. So they brought him in. I'm not clear on why he wasn't charged. But they let him go. They've got a mug shot, the name I gave you, and a Des Moines address."

"Do you have a scanner?"

"Up and rolling."

"E-mail it through." Terrance watched as Don scrambled for pen and paper. "Use this address. And stay by your phone." He hung up.

Don powered up the flatscreen on the wall opposite his desk. He keyed in net access, watched the screen a moment, then said, "Here it comes."

They stood side by side. The download seemed to take eons. Finally front and side mugshots illuminated the office.

Don moved in close and intently studied the image. "I can't tell."

"It's him." Terrance pressed his fist to his gut, pushing against the nausea.

"You can't be positive. His own mother couldn't make a definite ID from this."

"I'm telling you. This is Val Haines. And his mother is dead."

Don slumped onto the sofa. "Tell me what you know about this guy."

"We've been through this before."

"It'll help me think."

Terrance walked behind Don's desk. The first time ever. He slid into the high-backed leather chair. Propped up his feet. Twisted the chair slightly so he was aimed at Don and not his nemesis. "Valentine Joseph Haines. Mother died when he was twelve. Father and he were very close. No other siblings. One aunt. They are not close. Father died, let's see, nineteen months ago. Val took it very hard."

"Get your feet off my desk."

Terrance remained as he was. "About a week after the funeral, his wife of four years filed for divorce. It becomes very messy here."

"Nineteen months, that's about the time you beat Val out of the promotion, am I right?"

"As I said. Messy. The divorce turned into a battle over a child that Val apparently did not know his wife was carrying."

"Your child."

"In court it was revealed she had been having an affair for some time. Val's lawyer demanded a DNA test to determine parentage. Which was when everything came into the open. Things became quite vicious."

Don's gaze could pierce Kevlar. "She was having an affair with you, and Val found out when the DNA test came back?"

"Val took this very hard."

"I can imagine."

"No, actually, you can't. In court that day, Val became unglued. We're talking totally insane. He accused me of everything except murder." Terrance's voice remained steady. But inside he felt the old acid biting deep. "He was yelling so loud guards showed up from three courtrooms away. He actually accused me of stealing his child as well as his wife by tampering with the DNA test results."

"Did you?"

"Don't be absurd. When they finally silenced Val, the judge handed down a restraining order."

"So Val loses his father. His wife files for divorce. He discovers she's carrying his child—"

"I told you. The child is mine."

"Far as Val's concerned, it's his. Am I right?" Don picked up the coffee mug from his desk and pointed with it at Terrance. "To top things off, he loses his place on the corporate ladder because he got stabbed in the back."

"That promotion was mine as well."

"What we're talking about is what Val thinks." Don smiled grim approval. "No wonder the guy went bad."

There was nothing to be gained from holding back. Not now. "I never expected Val Haines to steal. He was always one for the straight and narrow."

"That's simple enough. You pushed him over the edge."

"The plan had always been to snare Marjorie Copeland. Marjorie was a desperate woman who basically endured the corporate life only to get her pension. I left just enough of a trail for her to realize the pension funds had effectively been drained. If she went public, the company would be pushed to the brink. Whether it actually folded or not, Marjorie's pension was history. You know all this. We'd planned for her to steal what she could and disappear. Then we'd blow the story, only increase the amount she stole from a few million to half a billion."

"Then Val discovered what she was up to and went along as well," Don said.

"Which is the only item that has not gone according to plan."

"You mean, other than our Val missing out on the bomb." Don drained the remainder of his coffee like medicine. He said to his empty mug, "Remind me what your personal take is from this operation."

Terrance repeated the words, anchoring the moment, giving a solid sense of reason to what was about to go down. Which of course was what Don was after. "Eighty-three million, two hundred thousand dollars."

Don motioned to the image on the far wall. "There's no chance you could be mistaken about that being our Val?"

"None."

Don tapped the mug's rim on the desk. Slowly. Deliberately. In time to his words. "Do I need to tell you what has to be done here?"

In response, Terrance picked up his cell phone and punched in the number. When Wally came on the line, Terrance said, "We need to talk. I'm coming up to New York. In the meantime, see if you can quietly locate this Jeffrey Adams."

"I need something more to go on."

"He has to be sleeping somewhere."

"And if he's moved on?"

Terrance thought hard. "My guess is, he'll try to reach England."

"The precinct ID'd this Adams guy on his driver's license," Wally mused aloud. "It was the only form of identification he was carrying. If he's headed to Europe, he'll need a passport."

"You know where he would go to get fake papers?"

"Sure." Wally paused, then added, "My contacts at the precinct want to know if this is our man."

"I think it's safe to tell them," Terrance replied, his eyes steady on his partner, "that Val Haines is dead."

VAL LAY ON HIS HARD PALLET ON THE HOTEL ROOM
floor. He held Audrey's letter flattened against his chest.
Growing daylight filtered through slatted blinds. He
stared not at the ceiling, but at the images circling him
from all sides. Audrey's letter had released a hurricane of
fragmented memories.

Before his life had fallen apart, Val and his wife had
attended Orlando's Thirty-third Street Baptist Church,
which had moved to a new larger structure out by
Isleworth. It was a good place. Good people, nice social
life, growing fast as the city itself. His wife, Stefanie, was
involved with this and that. He had played in the church
basketball league. Their friends all went there. Which
made the gradual revelation that their marriage was falling
apart that much more public and harder to endure.

His father's death, the divorce, the revelation that his
wife had been having an affair with the same man who
then stole a promotion Val should have received—one
blow followed another with merciless consistency. Val's
days held to the same empty pattern, just going through the
motions, waiting for the next strike of life's wrecking ball.

Fourteen months after the divorce, a church friend
concerned about his lonely state introduced him to a

visitor from England. She was over to see her mother and brother. A wonderful lady. The friend failed to mention she was also sister to Val's arch nemesis, Terrance d'Arcy. If he had not been trapped by agony, Val would have laughed himself sick at life's awful irony.

The desire to use Terrance's sister as a means of revenge for her brother's actions had been strong as lust. But Val couldn't bring himself to do it. Audrey d'Arcy had been the one good thing in a dismal and storm-swept era.

Audrey was what in Britain was called a Christian counselor. She had both a private practice and a government contract to work with prisoners coming up for remand. She extended her stay in Orlando four times, not masking her growing love for Val. Audrey had accepted his tale of woe with the tragic recognition of her brother at work. Val had feasted upon a woman who wanted only to care and comfort and succor.

So why had he forced her to leave? Val searched and found nothing save a clearer recollection of their last day together. Outside the church, Audrey had held him for what had seemed like the lifetime he refused to share with her. The way she had touched his face, the taste of her final kiss, the soft sound of her broken farewell, all drifted now in the hotel room's dusty air. Val rose from his pallet and stared in the mirror as he dressed. Silently he condemned the man before him for ever sending her away.

Vince was not on duty when he arrived downstairs. Val left the hotel just as the sky overhead began going dark. The thunderheads rolled and boomed their way down, ready to devour the higher buildings.

Val entered the diner and took a booth from which he watched the first drops strike the glass by his side, big as bullets. They dimpled the glass and chased the pedestrians to an even faster pace. Further memories rained down, a jagged-edged deluge. Val could no more halt the torrent than he could the thunderstorm outdoors. He ordered the first thing that caught his eye on the menu and remembered how, four months earlier, he had caught one of his most trusted employees with her hand in the honey jar.

Marjorie Copeland was a single mom, abandoned by her former husband soon after she had given birth to a severely handicapped boy. The child was now ten. The day nurse cost almost half her salary. Marjorie clung to her job with desperate fervor because she needed the medical. Since his divorce, the two of them had shared a silent bond over life's raw injustice. That morning four months back, Marjorie had looked more rumpled and exhausted than usual. Val laid out what he had discovered, hoping against hope she could show how he had gotten everything wrong.

Instead, Marjorie had shut and locked his door, drawn the blinds over his inside window, and asked him to cancel his appointments and hold all calls. Then she laid it out for him. How someone had been dipping into the company's pension fund. Gradually siphoning off the employees' retirement money into a series of false accounts and dummy investments.

Soon as the shock had eased, Val had supplied the name behind the scheme. "Terrance d'Arcy. He did this."

Marjorie had nodded slowly. "You're probably right."

"No probably about it. I can smell his hand all over this." The certainty opened like a poisonous bloom. "I have to stop him."

"If you go public," Marjorie said, "I'll kill myself."

"Don't talk insane."

"Take that pension away from me, and I have nothing to live for." She had the fathomless gaze of one already dead. "I've checked carefully. The money is gone, Val. And there's nothing definite to pin it on anyone."

"That's still no reason to talk about suicide."

"Isn't it? I have *got* to keep my pension. Otherwise my boy is going to be imprisoned in some concrete cage for the rest of his life." Her eyes were so drained of hope their color was a lie in physical form. "I want to take what's mine. That's all. Not one cent more. Just let me get out and then you can do whatever you please."

"I can't believe you're planning to steal from our company."

"It's not stealing and it's not my company." Emotional exhaustion had pounded her voice to a toneless drone. "They *owe* me."

"How much are we talking about?"

"I've worked this out. If I live to the median age, my pension payment would be a million three. Down in Costa Rica that would take my son through a long, full life."

Then she waited. Not saying it. Just letting him taste the unspoken for himself.

Val tried to push the thought away. "I'll find a way to pin it on them."

"I don't think so. I'm good at my job. You know that. I've *checked*. All we've got is a drained pension fund and false trails that lead nowhere. So you get some minor evidence, so what? There will be a lot of suspicion and maybe some talk. They'll have four hundred million and change to hire the best lawyers. Sooner or later they'll skate." She let him mull that over, then added, "There is another alternative."

He glanced at his watch. Twenty-three minutes past nine on a Tuesday morning. Marking the time when he went from dedicated employee to criminal. "I'm listening."

"You caught me because I can't do this cleanly on my own. You sign off on all the transfers. You have connections with all our banks."

He nodded, but not to her words. The fact was simple and unavoidable. Terrance would walk. He knew this with the utter certainty of someone who had fought the man and failed. Terrance d'Arcy was a master of the dark arts. The only way to capture the man was to obtain all the answers. Which meant following his trail. Doing exactly the same. Then laying it out for the authorities. The bloom of vengeance sprang so easily from this putrid seed.

The second thought followed naturally on the first. What if he failed? What then?

The answer to this came just as easily.

Val refocused on the woman seated opposite him. "You've done the same calculations for me?"

"Yes."

"Assuming the same median age thing, what's my take?"

"Two million, two hundred and eighteen thousand dollars."

"You can get this out?"

"With care."

"You've tracked how they did it?"

"All the dummy fronts run through one guy at Syntec Bank in New York."

"We can follow the same pattern," Val said, thinking aloud.

The two of them realized together what he had just said. *We.* Marjorie's features crumpled. Val let her sob quietly for a time, then said, "How were you planning to disappear?"

"I found out how to obtain a false birth certificate on the Web." She took a handkerchief from her purse and repaired some of the damage. "I'm using a Des Moines temp office for an address and applying for a driver's license. After that, getting a passport is a breeze."

"Can you do the same for me?"

"Of course." Her mascara had run, leaving her face painted with the grief of ancients. "I never dreamed you'd go for this. I mean, I'm glad and all. But I just don't understand."

Val rose from his chair. "You don't need to."

———

When Val returned to the hotel from breakfast, Vince was behind the counter. The lobby was empty. Vince watched him approach the counter. There was a change to the atmosphere, a charged compression that signaled business about to be done.

Val walked straight up to the goateed weightlifter and demanded, "Where's my watch?"

"The watch is being checked out." Vince handled the question with his standard calm. "Forget the watch. Far as you're concerned, the watch is history."

"So you've found a guy who'll do me a passport?"

Vince did a thing with his shoulders. "Maybe yes, maybe no. Things are tough in this town. You hear what I'm saying?"

"I hear the words but they're not connecting."

"Especially since the Rico Act. I introduce you to somebody and you get caught, I go down with you."

"So how much will the passport cost me?"

"You need to focus here. We're not talking about the passport yet. We're not even close to that point. First you got to take care of me."

"You're telling me an eight-thousand-dollar watch isn't enough?"

"Forget the eight. Your watch is maybe gonna bring two-five on the street. So yeah, the watch makes for a nice down payment." He studied Val. "You don't get it, do you?"

"Obviously not."

He moved forward. It was a fractional shift, just a slight inching forward onto his toes. But the man's menace reached across the counter and gripped him hard. "Where'd you hide your stash, Jeffrey?"

"My money?" Val's voice sounded strangled to his own ears. "You know I can't tell you that."

"Tell me, don't tell me. It makes no difference." He did that thing with his eyes again. Opening them into a blank void. One large enough to swallow Val whole. "If I want it, it's mine."

"I thought—"

"You're in the city now. This means you got to learn a different way of thinking." Vince's words punched at Val with silken fists. "It cost you money to get into this town, right? It's gonna cost you a lot more to get out. You got no place to run, no place to hide. You're an easy mark."

"What are you saying?"

"You been straight with me. An honest sucker. So I'm gonna lay it out. I look at you, I know you're sitting on serious money."

"All I've got—"

"No, wait. Just hear me out. I'm not talking about what you're carrying in your pocket or got hidden away upstairs. Most guys in my situation, that's all they'd be interested in. How much are you carrying and how are they gonna take it from you? Gun, knife, alley, lobby, it's all the same."

"But you're different."

"We're standing here talking, aren't we?"

Val fought the words around the steel band constricting his chest. "So you're looking for a reason not to fleece me."

"See, I knew you were smart."

Val struggled to think beyond the world of trouble inside that guy's gaze. Things he had no interest in ever coming closer to than the other side of this counter. "Let's say you're right. Let's say we agree the watch is, what you said."

"Down payment."

"Right. And I accept what you're telling me. That I've got to pay you twice. Now I owe you for two services. Not one. First, I pay you for making the call. And second, I pay for you to keep me safe from everything bad out there I don't want to know about."

"Now you're talking." Vince eased back. The threat slipped a notch. "Now you're thinking street."

"Okay."

"Okay, what?"

"You get me the passport and you keep me safe. When I get where I'm going, I promise to wire you another ten thousand dollars."

"I'm thinking more like twenty."

There was no arguing with that face. "Twenty it is."

"You're asking me to take a serious risk here."

"Is that a yes?"

"You're asking me to make an investment in your future. Do I take you now, or do I take this chance you're an honorable man? I've done this before. Guys nobody else would've given a dime, I've loaned them a ton of money. Every week, I don't have to go looking for them. I don't have to call them on the phone. They show up. They appreciate what I've done for them."

Vince's gaze peeled away skin, bone, pulse. But Val did not look away. "I'll do what I say."

Vince must have found what he was looking for. He reached for the phone. "Don't you let me down, man. That's all I got to say to you. You better not let me down."

THE COMPLEX OF NARROW TOWNHOUSES OVERLOOKED the Intracoastal Waterway and one of Miami's millionaire islands. Terrance rang the doorbell and stared over the concrete balustrade at wealth on display. A twenty-five-foot Donzi powered past, the motor's rumble thudding in his chest. Across the waterway he could see gardeners working on an island palace's lawn. The island contained perhaps three dozen homes and two high-rise condos. The cheapest apartment went for two and a half mil. Terrance smiled into the sunlight and turned as he heard footsteps dance across the tiles inside. Stefanie deserved just such a place. And he was just the sort of person to give it to her. But not Miami. This town held too much baggage for them now. Bermuda, perhaps. Yes, that was just the ticket.

She opened the door, the shadow staining her face. As always. "Hello, Terrance."

"Good morning, my dear. How nice to see you." He kissed the proffered cheek. "Thank you so much for allowing me to stop by."

"Come in. You look exhausted."

"Yes, well, as I said, things are threatening to unravel at work."

A queen. That was how she had looked the first time Terrance had seen her. And a queen she remained. Even dressed as she was in linen shorts, sneakers, and a white shirt knotted about her tanned midriff. Even bearing the shadow of another man. "Would you care for coffee?"

"That would be splendid, thank you." He climbed the stairs behind her and entered the living room. Terrance pretended to take great interest in a sailboat beating upwind. But his gaze remained upon the island mansions. A year should be enough time for public attention to swing away from Insignia and focus upon whatever commercial disaster came up next. Then he would quietly slip in his resignation and depart. A waterfront palace in Bermuda and an elegant city estate on Eaton Square.

"Why are you smiling?"

He turned away from the future he was determined to give her. "Happy to see you. As always."

Her gaze flitted away, resting nowhere for very long. "Melissa is still asleep, I'm afraid."

"Ah, well, never mind." He accepted the bone china cup and sipped. Freshly brewed, a dash of milk, half a sugar. Perfect. "Excellent coffee, my dear."

Her eye caught sight of the Town Car parked across the street. A uniformed chauffeur leaned against the gleaming hood, staring out over the water. "Is that yours?"

"Yes. As I said on the phone, this is just a swift in-and-out."

"You didn't drive down?"

"No time for that, I'm afraid. I came by plane. It's rather an around-the-elbow sort of journey. I'm actually on my way to New York."

"You flew from Orlando to Miami to connect to New York?"

"I've rented a jet. Rather, the company did. Swifter, don't you know?"

"I suppose I could wake Melissa—"

"Don't be silly. I'll be quite happy to step in and have a glance."

He followed her down the hallway toward the bedrooms. "You look lovely, Stef."

She gave no indication she had heard him. Which was why he said it when he had, in motion, her back to him. He knew she was listening, taking in every word. He saw her steps falter slightly, then speed up. He was nothing if not observant.

And patient.

He had wanted her from the first moment he had set eyes upon her. A reception at the new art gallery. A gathering of Orlando's elite. Someone had pointed her out to him. Her father was an orthopedic surgeon who taught at the University of Miami and held a residency at the new Celebration hospital south of Orlando. Stefanie was an art historian and professional evaluator. She also consulted on rare porcelains to a dozen or so museums around the country.

But Val Haines had met her four months earlier. The night before she and Terrance had met, Val had proposed. And Stefanie had accepted.

By then, Terrance and Val were already corporate enemies. Val had beaten Terrance out of a major promotion, the first time anyone had ever managed such a victory at his expense. By the night he met Stefanie, Terrance had been smiling around bitter vows of vengeance for over a year.

Terrance had tried to break them up. Stefanie had been enormously attracted to Terrance as well. They had met several times at art events and charity functions, the sorts of affairs Val loathed. Terrance had tracked her movements and inserted himself where he knew Val would not show up. They had even met once for lunch, his mother in attendance for good measure, there to discuss an item that had been in Terrance's family for three generations. A Meissen vase. His mother had approved of this sloe-eyed beauty with the hair that was both brown and gold. Which was in itself a revelation. His mother approved of almost nothing and no one.

But Terrance had not managed to interrupt her marriage to Val Haines. So he waited. He was always there, never pressing. Just close enough to snag her attention from time to time, always there with a laugh, a friendly observation, a warm hello. Waiting.

When the fractures in her relationship with Val had started, Terrance was the first to know, because she had told him. How Val was so desperate to start a family. How he adored his parents and his growing-up years, and yearned for such a relationship with a child of his own. But Stefanie felt none of this. She felt like she had been put on a highly public and extremely traumatic treadmill, racing from doctor to doctor in a constant desperate search for what was wrong.

By then, of course, Terrance's corporate battles with Val Haines were public knowledge, at least among those who followed such goings-on. Which had actually worked in his favor. For as the fissures grew worse between Stefanie and Val, who better should she approach for comfort than her old friend, the man Val hated most in the world? It really was too sweet.

Then came their affair, followed by the very messy divorce. All according to plan. The fact that she had become pregnant was the perfect crowning element.

Only at this point, something went very badly awry.

Rather than move in with him, Stefanie had retreated to Miami and a rental property owned by her father. She needed time to sort things out, was the only explanation she had given him. They had had their only argument at this point. But thankfully Terrance had retreated before tearing everything apart. He had played the hurt but loyal friend. Who wanted to be more than friends, of course. Particularly because of Melissa. Or so he claimed.

Stefanie arrived at the end of the hall and opened the door leading to her daughter's bedroom. Together they padded across the carpeted expanse and stood staring down at the crib. Melissa had emerged from her baby-hood and was growing into quite an adorable little girl. Particularly when she was asleep. Terrance had no way with children. He found them odd little things, really. Particularly when they reverted to squalling bundles who could not properly communicate their needs. This was the time when it was good to have a nanny on constant call. Someone to take care of the nasty bits and return the child when it was freshly scented and smiling. But there were moments like now, when the little thing was bundled up in her flannel nightie, the hair soft as frost across her unblemished brow, and a pink tiger tucked snugly beneath her chin, when Terrance could imagine nothing finer than taking on the role of proud father.

He slipped his hand into Stefanie's, and counted it a minor triumph when she did not pull away. He had made no insistence upon seeing her. Instead, he had merely requested visitation rights to the child. Stefanie was far too much the lady ever to refuse him that.

As usual in such moments, Terrance inspected the little

face for any sign of Val. The light was too meager, however, and his experience in such things utterly nil.

One hundred and fifty thousand dollars. That was how much it had cost him to bribe the technician. It was not merely the matter of changing a name on a document. The young woman had needed to depart these reaches forever. Terrance stared down at the daughter legally declared his own, holding the hand of the woman who would soon bear the same title, and counted it the best investment he had ever made.

He sighed with contentment and turned away.

To his satisfaction, Stefanie kept hold of his hand back down the hall and into the living room. He pointed to an earthen vase occupying a place of prominence on a fairy-legged side table. "That's new."

"Ming. I discovered it at an estate sale. Quite a find, actually. I've already been offered twice what I paid by a local curator."

Of course his mother had approved of Stefanie. They were so much alike. With one crucial difference, of course. Terrance's mother was unapproachable on any terms but her own. Stefanie, however, would soon be his to possess.

She seated herself on the curve of the sectional sofa, so that she could both be beside him and look at him. She never let go of his hand. "You didn't come just to see Melissa."

"No, Stef. Of course not." The walls were decorated with the oils taken from Val's home. There were seven of them. Four here, one in the third bedroom she had turned into a private space, two in her own bedroom. The oils were all late Renaissance and worth more than the townhouse. They had been left to her by her grandfather, also a surgeon and a Beacon Hill Brahman. Which is from where Stefanie received her bearing and her poise. Her looks and the soft Southern lilt to her vowels came from her mother, an Atlanta socialite. Terrance knew all these things because he had made it his business to know. He knew a great deal about this woman and her life. Information was a vital part of tracking any quarry.

"No, Stef," he repeated. "I came to see you as well."

"I know that."

"I look forward so much to these visits."

"I know you do." She stared at him. "You are the most patient man I have ever known."

"I have great reason to be."

"I wish . . ."

He let it sit there between them. The air was charged with all the silent desires. "What do you wish?"

"Nothing."

"If you don't tell me, Stef, I can't give it to you."

She smiled at that. "You would, wouldn't you? Give me what I ask?"

"Anything and everything," he replied.

"Why do you put up with me and my mess?"

"You know the answer to that."

"It's not just Melissa."

"It never was."

"No. I know that also. I keep thinking if I just sit here long enough and take care of my daughter and get on with my work, I'll heal. Life is such a dreadful mess." She paused, then added more quietly still, "And lonely."

"Only because you insist upon it being so."

"I'm not seeing anyone. I tried. But it didn't work. So I stopped."

He knew that too. She had gone out twice, once with

the curator of a local museum and once with a University of Miami professor. Terrance continued to receive regular reports.

"I keep hoping one day I'll just wake up and things will be back to normal and I can start making a new life." She looked at him. Not saying the words out loud. But the message was clear in her eyes. *A new life with you.*

Terrance wanted to force her to speak the words. The desire was so fierce it must have blazed in his eyes, because Stefanie released his hand and rose from the sofa. She walked to the porch's sliding glass doors and stood there, her back to him and the room, hugging herself. "He was here."

The shock was a fist straight to his heart. "Val?"

"Last week. I came out of my front door and there he was. Standing across the road by the water. He looked awful."

Terrance did not recognize his own voice. "What did he want?"

Stefanie remained turned from him, hugging herself, silent.

Terrance clenched his entire body in the effort to keep himself from exploding. "You didn't. Stefanie, please tell me you—"

"He begged to hold her. Just for a moment. It caught me completely off guard."

He could not speak. To utter a single word would have been to unleash the beast. He envisioned a rage that left the entire room in shambles.

"Val wanted children so bad. You should have seen his face. He slipped Melissa from my arms before I could think of anything to say. The look he gave me, it was like he was being tortured." She stared out over the water, her back trembling as though sensing the emotion Terrance refused to let loose. "I took her back. He didn't object. He just walked away. I've never seen anybody look so totally destroyed."

The antique mantel clock struck the half hour. Terrance took a dozen slow breaths, forcing himself back to calm control. The so-called investigators he was paying a small fortune would reap the whirlwind. "Stef, please come over and sit down."

She relinquished her position very slowly. "What is it?"

"I have some rather dreadful news. And nothing's confirmed. I've spent two sleepless nights wondering whether it would be best to be the one—"

"What on earth are you talking about?"

"Sit down. Please." He snagged both her hands. "I fear Val is dead."

"What?"

"Nothing is confirmed. But it has been so long now, and the police . . ." He paused, released a hand, took a slug of cold coffee. "I can only tell you what I know. It appears that Val has been stealing from the company."

"That's impossible!"

"I know, it goes against the grain. But the evidence is rather compelling. A large amount of money has gone missing. The SEC has been called in. There is going to be a huge scandal."

Her mouth worked. "Val?"

"He, another Insignia employee, and a senior New York banker were apparently involved in perpetuating a massive fraud. The authorities think the bank might have bilked several major customers. Insignia among them. The bank was destroyed by a bomb. Val has not been heard from since."

There were tears, of course. Terrance held her and repeated the details, fleshing out the story. Being the bearer of bad tidings, the martyr. As he stroked her hair, he observed. He knew she retained some connection to Val, a few stubborn tendrils of affection. How exquisite it was to personally demolish them. Finally making room for her new future. Her destiny.

She gathered herself and asked the question he had known would come. "Why are you telling me this?"

"News about Val being lost in the bomb blast broke this morning in the local Orlando papers. Tomorrow word is bound to get out about the scandal. At that point it will be national news. This may not be as big as Enron, but it is by far the largest scandal to hit a Florida company."

"That's why you came?"

"In part. I didn't want this to catch you totally unaware. I had to do it in person. And it's like I said on the phone. I won't be available for a week or so. Perhaps longer."

"That's why you're going to New York?"

"Damage control." He glanced at his watch. "Speaking of which, my dear, I really must fly."

She rose with him. "I can't believe this. Val."

"Of all people. I agree."

"He hated you."

"I am well aware of that."

"You must be pleased." Her words crumbled wetly.

Terrance dropped his voice an octave. "I do not deserve that."

"I suppose not." But she was unconvinced.

"In all the time we have been together, I have never spoken a word against Val Haines. Not once." He made as to turn for the door. "I shall not start now."

"No, wait. That's not—"

"I know you're deeply upset. You have every right to be. I knew also I took the risk of being painted as a culprit by bringing you this news. But I had to prepare you, Stefanie. Even if it meant wounding myself. I had no choice."

"Don't go like this. I didn't . . ."

"You see, I love you more than I have ever loved anyone. That is why I came. And why I must now go." He bent over and kissed her tear-stained cheek. "Adieu, my dear."

He shut the door firmly behind him and hurried over to where the chauffeur was opening the door. He seated himself and kept his face pointed straight ahead. But out of the corner of his eye he saw Stefanie open the sliding glass door and call down to him. He gave no sign of having noticed. The car pulled away. He could hear her call faintly through the closed window.

He smiled. That really had gone rather well.

WHERE THE TAXI LEFT VAL OFF, THE SKYSCRAPERS
formed a steel-and-concrete noose. He was the only pedestrian who bothered to look upwards, searching out a glimpse of the dull grey sky. Val crossed the street and entered Grand Central Station. From where he stood on the upper veranda, the space looked larger than the outdoors that he had just left behind. The four-faced brass clock rising from the central information booth said he was five minutes late. He crossed beneath the distant ceiling's mythical star chart and asked directions from the hostess at the Michael Jordan Steakhouse above track thirty. He took the side passage to the western balcony and spotted the entrance to the Campbell Apartment. There he stopped.

"See, that's why I like this place for the meet-and-greet." A voice by his elbow said, "The first-timers, they come in here and do their gawk, and you know them straight off. You tell me you look like this or that, it doesn't matter. You need directions to this place, you know the fellow is going to come in here and freeze."

The man's hair was dyed a ridiculous orange. He had a crooner's voice. Everything else about him was mummified. He scarcely reached Val's shoulder. "You have also kept me waiting."

"Sorry."

"It's going to cost you." He pointed Val to a table opposite the bar. "The drinks in here are horrendously expensive."

The room belonged in a European palace, not a New York train station. The galleried hall was perhaps seventy feet long with a gothic fireplace dominating the far wall. The ceiling was thirty feet high and ribbed by hand-painted beams.

"Campbell was a man with power and an ego to match. He took this space because it was the city's largest ground-floor office. When he moved in, it was a barracks. He copied the salon of a thirteenth-century Florentine manor. He installed a pipe organ, a piano, and over a million dollars in antiques. That was back in the twenties, when a million dollars meant something." He held out his hand. "Let's have your ID."

"Excuse me?"

He gave a mirthless smile. "My, but we are new to this game, aren't we. The only ID that matters. Guess what that might be."

Val glanced around the room. No one seemed to be watching.

"Don't worry about them. This is New York, remember? Land of the professionally blind." He snapped his fingers. "The clock is ticking."

Val dipped into his pocket and pulled out his roll.

"Fan the pages just enough to show me this isn't a pack of ones I'm seeing. Okay." The man drained his glass. "You're after what, social security card, plastic, birth certificate, total makeover?"

"Just a passport."

"Expensive. What about the name you aim on using. Is it clean?"

"Yes."

"It better be. On account of the authorities, these days they do a computer search every time you pass through the border."

"It's clean."

"Sorry, I need a little more assurance than just your say-so." The scars where his face had been cut and surgically stretched ran from above his ears to his turtleneck. "See, if you're lying to me, they'll ask you where you bought your paper. They'll ask you very hard."

"I was arrested two nights ago. The police ran me through the national system. The name came up clean."

"Vince will vouch for that too?"

"Call him and see."

He tapped his finger on the glass, studying Val hard. "Nah. Like the man said, you got an honest face. So where did you buy your new tag?"

"My . . . I don't remember."

The surgical scars refused to move when he smiled. They formed two flat creases down each side of his face. Which was perhaps why his smiles came and went so swiftly. "Look there, you're learning. Okay, let's see what you got."

Val passed over his driver's license.

The guy pulled a set of reading glasses from a pewter case and lifted the card up to where it reflected the neighboring lamp's light. "This is good work. Almost as good as mine." He slipped off the spectacles. "Five thousand."

Val snagged the driver's license and stuffed it back in his pocket. "Four."

The man flashed his false smile. "Aren't we cute. Look, this is not bargain basement land. You want, you pay."

"All right. Five."

"My studio is just around the corner. Not nearly as nice as here, I'm afraid. The lighting's too strong and it smells like a lab. But you'll be in and out in no time. Me, I'm still looking for my ticket to paradise." The man rose to his feet. "Where did you say you were headed?"

"I didn't."

"No, silly me. Of course not." He pointed Val toward the bartender. "I should have said, five plus tip. Pay the man and let's do business."

TERRANCE MET THE EX-COP, SUZANNE WALTON, IN A Manhattan diner made for the blues. They sat in the corner booth. Beyond his grimy window, the street was a concrete canyon filled with grinding traffic and sullen faces and smoking vents. To his other side, the chef leaned against the kitchen windowsill and yelled at the lone waitress in some gutteral tongue. Terrance asked, "Why are we here?"

"You mean, so far from the parts of the city we all know and love?" She had a cop's voice and ate like a feral beast, watching him over her sandwich. "You sure you don't want anything?"

"I'll wait." His suite had been reserved at the Plaza. Their wine list was legendary.

"Number one, because up here we're faceless. Number two, I wanted you to see this terrain for yourself. My guess is, your man came in here and disappeared."

The woman's blunt manner helped enormously. Her attitude suggested that any problem could be handled and disposed of. "Which means he knows we're after him."

"Maybe yes, maybe no. I talked to a buddy at the precinct. This Jeffrey Adams character claimed to have lost his memory."

"What?"

"I'm just telling you what I heard. Jeffrey Adams was so drunk or drugged or both he took a swing at a cop trying to save him from getting rolled. The cop promptly clocked him. The next day Adams checked out of the holding cell claiming amnesia."

Wally Walton was not an unattractive woman. For someone fascinated by life's seamier side, she would even be classed as alluring. Terrance guessed her age at early to midthirties. She wore a jacket and skirt of midnight blue. A matching silk T-shirt did nothing to hide her feminine curves. She had mannish hands and strong wrists, but her nails were buffed and polished. Her dark hair framed a face of uncompromising angles. Her eyes were her worst feature, large and brown and utterly without bottom.

Terrance asked, "He doesn't remember? Not anything?"

"He didn't then. No telling about now." She used the grimy napkin to clean the sauce from her hands and mouth. She balled it up, dropped it in her plate, and pushed the plate aside. "I checked the neighborhood. They've pegged me for a cop. Probably vice, since I'm not showing them a badge. Which means I don't get much help. But he did check in at a local street clinic. That cost me a hundred, by the way. Head banged up, complaining of amnesia, everything checks out with what the cops said."

"They don't know where he went after that?"

"Either they don't know or they aren't saying. I've gone by all the hotels and boarding houses in the area. But these places, it's not like downtown. They play loose with the records around here, Terry."

"Don't call me that."

She caught the edge to his voice and smirked. "If you're

right, what you said about him wanting to leave the country, he needs a passport. The precinct shows him as only holding a driver's license. That won't get him far. Not these days. He's going to have to get hold of false papers."

"Can't you get flight records?"

"Not a chance. Since 9/11 you got to go through Homeland Security. My guys would face FBI scrutiny for even asking. Our best bet is to locate his source for false papers. There aren't so many of those around. I'm working on that as we speak."

A fist formed from the diner's grimy smoke gripped his gut. "So he might already be gone."

"Put that aside for a second and focus on what we know. The guy is alive, right?"

"Yes." Terrance swallowed against the bile being forced up his gullet. "Which is why we still need you."

"Let's take a look at that. You don't just want this guy dead."

"No."

"We're way beyond that now."

"Yes."

"You've gone public. Which means you need this guy to vanish. You need him to disappear so completely it's like he never came back from the dead in the first place."

"And fast."

"What do I call you? And don't give me d'Arcy. I can't say that with a straight face."

"Terrance."

"Okay, Terrance. This is going to cost you. This is going to cost you big."

"You're only being asked to do what you should have—"

"Stop right there." She planted an elbow on the table

and jabbed the air between them with her forefinger. Dried sauce from her sandwich collected around her fingernail like unnoticed blood. "I did the hit exactly as ordered. The bank is gone. Not just your guys. I was ordered to destroy the bank's records, computers, files, the works. Which I did, correct?"

"Yes." They had needed to destroy all banking records. The only ones that survived were held by the parent company on Jersey. The island was beyond U.S. reach. Jersey banks answered only to Jersey law. Jersey banking records were open to no one. The only records available now to the SEC investigators were those in Insignia's hands. Which contained some of Terrance's best work. "Why couldn't you at least be sure they'd actually entered the bank?"

"Come on, Terrance. Stay with me here. First off, the place is a warren. Rockefeller Center has, what, nineteen street entrances spread over two city blocks. Second, I had to set the charges after the cleaning crew had been through. Me. Working alone. Don was very clear on this. I asked for a team and he said this was to be a one-woman job. So you gave me the where and the when. And I followed orders, right?"

There was no way Terrance could hedge the facts. Not and meet this woman's gaze. "You did exactly what we asked of you."

She relaxed a trace. "So you're still playing it straight with me."

"We need you."

"I know that. But it's good to hear you know it too."

"I assume you've checked on Marjorie Copeland?"

"First thing I did after hearing about your guy. Night before the blast she stayed in and did room service. Hotel clerk noticed her leaving on account of the time, six in the morning sharp, and because she hung around the lobby for a while like she was looking for somebody. Used the hotel phone twice, paced awhile, then left on her own."

"Which brings us back to Val Haines."

"Right." She leaned forward. With him now. "The problem, Terrance, is your guy has probably left the country. Which means bringing in outside help."

"You can do that?"

"I know people. But it's going to be expensive."

"It already is."

"What you've paid so far, that's nothing. That's chump change. We're talking serious money now."

"This is your windup?"

"This is fact. There's nobody else you can turn to but me. So listen very carefully to what I'm telling you. First we've got to find the guy. Then we've got to make him disappear so there'll never be a trace he even surfaced in the first place. This means a lot of legwork. Especially if he knows we're after him. Does he?"

"Let's assume the worst."

"Which means we don't need a guy with a gun. We need an organization. Let's break this down. First you're going to have the upfront. Call it the conversation charge. Then there's the fee for finding this guy. And finally the vanishing act."

"You're forgetting your portion for all this extra work."

The first glint of humor he had ever seen entered Wally's eyes. "I haven't forgotten anything, Terrance. You have a clean picture of this guy?"

"In the car. You're sure you can get in touch with the right people for this work?"

"I already did. I figured if your guy was on the move, the faster we hit, the better. Right?"

"Yes. Definitely."

"So I contacted some people I know in England. I've done business with them before. They're tops. And connected. They're watching the airports. This guy shows up, they're on him. Any idea where he'll be headed?"

"Jersey."

"Where?"

"It's an island in the English Channel."

"But first he's got to go to England like you told me on the phone, right?"

"Yes. Or France. But he's been once before and went through London."

"Okay. So we'll stay with England for the moment, and if he doesn't show then we'll move to this island. It's really called Jersey?"

"Yes."

"You bring cash with you?"

"Yes."

"How much?"

"Enough."

"I doubt that, Terrance. I doubt that very much."

Here it comes, Terrance thought. He willed himself not to move a muscle.

She spoke the words almost lovingly. "A million dollars."

"What?"

"I'm not done. A million now. A million the day this guy disappears from the face of the earth. In return, I bring you in contact with people who can do this job. I make sure they take their money and vanish too. While all this is going down, I make sure the cops don't pinch you." She breathed the words in a soft murmur, her face inches from his. "Then I make like smoke and evaporate too."

He leaned back. Crossed his arms. She remained where she was, but there was a constricting about her. The muscles drew in tight around her eyes, her mouth, her shoulders. Her fingers looked ready to claw hunks from the table. Prepared for battle. Terrance said, "Here's my counteroffer. I'll give you two hundred and fifty thousand dollars in cash now. To spend as you see fit. A million dollars will be wire transferred wherever you tell me by the close of business today. From that you will pay the new hired help whatever you see fit."

"That's not—"

He raised his hand. "Allow me to finish. A million and a half more will be paid to you the day Val vanishes for good. Again, you pay your cohorts whatever is correct. They deal only with you. I am simply along as an observer."

Terrance leaned back over the table. "And another two million at the end of two years. Just to make sure you stay our very own silent lady."

The tensile power eased from her shoulders and neck and face. "I'm not a lady, Terrance."

"No. But the situation hardly requires one, does it?"

"This deal you've got going down." They might as well have been lovers sharing secrets across the scarred linoleum, they were that close. "It's very big, isn't it?"

Terrance just smiled.

"How—" She was interrupted by the pinging of her phone. She leaned back, checked the number on the screen, then flipped it open and said, "You got something?"

She listened intently, showing him the mask. "Give me a name." She made notes on her napkin, then slapped the phone shut and said, "I need to get moving here."

"Who was that?"

"Maybe a lead. Maybe nothing. But I got to check it out."

"I'm coming too."

"You sure?" She didn't quite smirk this time. Just a slight tightening to the edges of her mouth and eyes. "This is a long way from the Plaza, where we're headed."

"I'm ready," Terrance said. And he was.

Outside on the street she told him, "I need some cash."

"How much?"

"Ten grand should cover it."

Terrance stopped, ready to play the money guy and beat her down. It was his nature. He was good at this game. But again he caught the taut battle fire in her features. He gave a mental shrug. Why bother? He might as well get used to a little outgo. "My valise is in the car."

She slid into the back seat beside him. While the driver shut her door and went around to the front, Terrance flipped the locks on his briefcase and handed her two banded sets of hundred dollar bills. He gained a little satisfaction from her being disconcerted again by his ready agreement. Not ten thousand dollars' worth, mind. But some.

She stowed the money away before the driver slipped behind the wheel. She said quietly, "Five is for the information. The other five is to ease our way inside."

"You don't have to explain."

"That's right. I don't."

"But you do need to tell our fellow where we're headed."

She turned to the driver and said, "Find a place on South Park down by Murray Hill where you can pull over and wait." When the car pulled into traffic, Wally gave him that cop's smile. "You're okay, Terrance."

"From this point on, whatever you spend comes from your share." Terrance leaned back in his seat. He did so love the hunt.

THE CLOUDS WERE TOO LAZY TO HANG IN THE SKY ON their own. Instead, they leaned upon the highest towers, compressing the upper elevations and packing the city even more densely. There was no open space in any direction. No horizon upon which he could focus and find respite.

Val emerged from the subway and headed south from Douglas Circle. He turned left and walked to Morningside Avenue. The clinic was three blocks further north. In the distance the road dipped where the subway emerged from underground. The rail network rose to an overhead station, supported on painted steel beams. The sense of entering a man-made cavern was almost overwhelming.

The clinic's waiting room was empty save for a few mothers holding preschoolers and one ancient black man seated at the reception desk. He fiddled with his cane and watched Val's approach with rheumy eyes.

The receptionist asked, "Can I help you?"

"I was wondering if Dr. Martinez is working today."

The woman was the color of oiled ebony and very large. She spoke words that had clearly been said a million times before. "The clinic's doctors operate strictly on a rotating basis."

"Right. I understand that. But I saw her a couple of days ago—" "Your name?"

"Adams."

She tapped into the computer. "First name Jeffrey?"

"Yes."

"She left you a prescription for Percodan. Is that what you wanted?"

"No. Thank you, but I really need to ask her something."

The receptionist breathed disapproval. "Then you'll just have to wait. Dr. Martinez is out on break."

"When will she be back?"

She glanced at the wall clock. "Half an hour. But you'll still have to wait for her turn in rotation."

"Sure. That's fine. Thank you."

Val left the clinic and stood for a time on the street corner. The city's clamor held a New York air of uncaring hostility. He spotted someone entering the orange street-front church's doors and decided to follow.

Inside, however, Val was met by crowding thoughts, dangerous as any mugger. Val sighed his way into a pew at the back. Such places had once been a haven. But now he felt nothing. To pray for anything, even a return of what he could remember, would be a lie.

Here in this quiet space, Audrey's words haunted him like the hounds of heaven. Val drew the letter from his pocket. Holding it raised a paradox of comfort and silent keening. He ached for this woman. Yet he had sent her away.

Val unfolded the letter and read,

You are gone and still I cannot stop this empty dialogue. How often have I argued with the empty space where you should be standing? How many letters have I written and burned in the past six months? But this letter will be sent. I shall lie to myself the best I know how, and say this medium reaches even beyond the grave. I have so much experience at tear-drenched lies. After all, I almost convinced myself that one day you would return and grant us that most joyful of titles, a couple.

Life's wounds have never pierced me as they do this night. This dreadful, endless night, when I am reduced to writing to a past that no longer exists, a future that is now myth. Were it not forbidden me, I would use the dagger, I would drink the poison, I would join you. Wherever you are. Were it not forbidden.

Val folded up the letter and rose from the pew. The only answer that made sense lay with this half-remembered woman. That realization gave focus to his otherwise empty state. He looked inward now and took subtle comfort from the void. He had no interest in remembering anything more. Why bother with a man recently deceased?

He would go to England and rescue her. He had broken it off, no doubt for reasons that had made sense at the time. But that no longer mattered. He would get his money and steal her away. But not as Val Haines. That life was over. The world already thought he was gone. Why not make the vanishing act complete?

May the poor man rest in peace.

———

When the receptionist finally sent him back, Val found Dr. Martinez seated at a metal desk writing busily into a file. "Have a seat, Mr. Adams. I'll be with you in just a second."

"Thanks for seeing me."

"Any of the other doctors could have given you what you needed."

"Maybe."

She gave him a momentary inspection, then went back to her notes. "You clean up good, Mr. Adams."

"That's not my name."

This time she set down her pen and swiveled her chair around. "Say again."

"I was carrying a false ID."

"So your memory is coming back. Good." The doctor's air of unflappable weariness remained intact. The chair's metal rollers scraped across the scarred linoleum floor. "How do you feel otherwise?"

"I'm moving easier and I don't hurt so much." Val leaned over so she could pull off the bandage over his temple.

"You're certainly keeping your wounds clean. Let's have a look at the back of your head." Gently she swiveled his head around. "Things are looking good. So what can I do for you?"

"I want something to keep me from remembering."

She moved back around to where she could see his face. "Give me that one again."

"Is there a drug or something that can keep my memory from returning?"

She pushed herself back farther. "Look . . . What should I call you?"

"Do I have to tell you?"

"You don't want to tell me your real name?"

"Jeffrey Adams has worked well enough so far."

"Right. Okay. So you've started recalling certain portions of your past, and they have not been pleasant. Remember what I told you when you were first in here? The experience will be somewhat jarring."

"It's more than that."

She crossed her arms. "Correct me if I'm wrong here. But running away is what got you into this mess."

The air was thick with lemony disinfectant and the traces of all the reasons people like him came through those doors. "I asked you a simple question."

"And I'm giving you a simple answer. Are there drugs that can erase memory? Certainly. Most have a temporary effect. But just keep in mind, after your last bout you wound up in here with your head bleeding."

He was intensely aware of the gauzy curtain's inability to keep this a private conversation. "Could you lower your voice a little?"

"Listen, Jeffrey or whatever your name is. You're asking the wrong question. You don't want to erase your memories. You want to escape your pain."

His chest pumped as if he had entered the race of his life. "Whatever."

"Don't dismiss me here." A crucial intensity burned through her weary veil. "Knowing which question to ask is vital to finding the right answer. Think what would happen if a doctor inspected you for a cold when you had an intestinal problem. To achieve the proper solution, first you have to know what it is you're really hunting. Which in your case is a way to leave your pain behind. Not forget. Never forget. What you want to know is, how can you turn what you've been running from into something you can properly use?"

He was acutely aware of how quiet the chamber had

become out beyond the wraparound curtains. "Can we get back to my original question?"

"No problem at all. Here's what you do." The doctor rose, swept back the curtains, and pointed to the exit. "Head out that door. Go fifty feet in any direction. Find the nearest bar and fill your own prescription. Take up where you left off." She stepped away from him. "See you on your way back down, Jeffrey."

THEY LEFT THE CAR AT SOUTH PARK AND EAST THIRTY-
Sixth. The area was mixed, like a lot of Manhattan. Two
blocks further east, the air was concussed by traffic pour-
ing in and out of the Queens Midtown Tunnel. Their
destination was a decrepit brownstone poised above the
tunnel's maw. The fumes were worse than the din. The
building's front door was locked, but Wally pulled a
switchblade from her pocket and easily flipped the latch.

"A woman of many talents."

"Stay close."

Through partially open elevator doors emerged a
stench from garbage dumped down the shaft. Wally took
the stairs to the fifth floor. A chemical odor worse than
the garbage filled the corridor as they reached the top
landing. Terrance was about to complain when he
caught sight of Wally's smile. "What's that foul smell?"

"A good sign." She knocked on the door at the corridor's far end. "You mind if I run the show?"

"By all means."

The smiles came more easily now. "You married,
Terrance?"

"For all intents and purposes, I suppose I am."

"Shame." She knocked harder.

"I never mix business with pleasure."

"Yeah? Well, I do it all the time, baby." She pounded the door. "All the time."

A querulous voice said through the door, "Go away!"

She stowed the smile away and called back, "Horace, this door is coming down one of two ways. One, you turn the key. Two, I bust it down."

"Who are you?"

"We're people standing out here with your money burning a hole in our pocket."

A pause, then, "Who sent you?"

"Ben Franklin, Horace. Fifty of them. Five large. Now open the door."

Three bolts crashed back. The door opened the length of the final chain. "Show-and-tell time."

Wally fanned the bills, then pulled back when he reached through the crack. "You need my boot to help you with the chain, Horace?"

He studied the both of them for a moment, then shut and unlatched and reopened the door. "What do you want?"

"Five thousand buys us a minute inside, Horace."

A clown. That was Terrance's first impression upon entering the apartment and seeing the man clearly. A short, little clown with orange hair and a potbelly. A caricature who could only exist in a place like New York City.

"Shut the door." When Terrance had done so, the little man said nervously, "You're inside. So what is it you want?"

"A name, Horace."

"I don't divulge—"

"No. We give you a name. You give us either a yes or a no. If it's the right answer and you can back it up, we give you the five grand."

"What are you, a cop?"

"Come on, Horace. Does this guy here look street to you?"

"DA, then."

"We're not trouble, Horace. Not unless you want us to be."

"What I want is for you to get out of my life."

She did that thing with her face. From crudely feminine to wickedly severe without moving an inch. Her feral rage forced Horace back. He tripped over a lighting tripod and almost went down. Wally said softly, "I made the connection, Horace. I'm here. I'm offering cash. I could just as easily offer you something else. It's your choice. But you're going to tell me in the end." She lifted her hand. Horace flinched. "Which is it going to be, Horace? Rough or smooth? Your call."

The man quavered, "What do you want to know?"

"You're selling paper, right?"

His swallow was audible where Terrance stood by the door. "Yes."

"Passports?"

"Sometimes."

"See, we're making progress." She crossed her arms and leaned back a fraction. The room's fissured stress eased slightly. "Over the past day or so, have you done a passport for a guy?"

"Couple."

"One of them about the age of my guy here, name of Adams?"

His trembles formed a nod.

"First name?"

"I don't . . . Wait, no, I remember. Jeffrey. He was a mistake, right? I knew it the instant I laid eyes on him. I told myself he was trouble. But hey, a guy's got to make a living."

"Describe him for me."

Terrance had not moved. But Horace had somehow sensed his eagerness. Horace said, "For another thousand, I'll go one better and give you a photograph."

"Don't look at him, Horace. He's nobody. I'm the one standing here with your fate in my hands."

"An extra thousand's not too—"

"Thirty seconds, Horace. Then I'll assume you need a demonstration to understand we mean business."

Horace scuttled away. Or started to.

Wally was on him like a striking snake.

Terrance gasped. He had never seen anybody move that fast.

Wally's hand gripped Horace's wrist as he reached inside a drawer. "What you got in there?"

"Nothing!"

"You going for a gun, Horace?"

"Ow, you're hurting me! It's just a picture!"

"So open the drawer. Nice and slow. Okay. Good." She backed off. "What is this, your personal rogue's gallery? You do a little blackmail on the side, Horace?"

"What do you care?" The man's sullen tone was contradicted by a serious case of the shakes. He flipped through the pictures. "Here. This is the guy."

Wally took the photograph. She gave it a cursory examination. She flipped it onto the counter and said to Terrance, "It's not him."

Horace grabbed it back, studied it intently. "That's Adams! That's the man!"

"Sorry, Horace. Not our guy." She turned away. "Unless you got something else to show me, we're all done here."

He wailed, "What about my money?"

"What can I say? You didn't come up with the goods." But Wally stopped in the process of reaching for the door. She gave Terrance a look, then turned back. "You good at keeping secrets, Horace?"

"Like the grave."

She reached into her pocket, came up with the cash, and set it down on the camera. "We were never here."

———

Terrance waited until they were back on the street to say, "The picture you saw."

"Hmmm."

"It was our guy, wasn't it?"

"Yes."

"Val Haines. You're absolutely certain?"

"Positive ID, Terrance. Five by five." She reached for her phone.

"Alerting your friends?"

"Yes." Wally punched in the number, then gave him the eye. "The money better be there, Terry."

"I told you not to call me that."

"These guys, they may talk funny. But you don't want to mess them around."

"Soon as we return to the hotel, I'll arrange the transfer." He waited until she had finished her call, then walked with her back toward the car. "If they're anything like you, I don't need further convincing."

She gave him that smile of hers, the one that was equal measures feminine appeal and molten shrapnel. "You sure what you told me, about being tied up?"

THE TRAVEL OFFICE WAS LIKE MUCH OF THIS PART OF
the city, threadbare and grim and utterly lacking in frill.
The agent was Asian and proud of his ability to find Val the
absolute lowest price on a one-way flight to England. He
pushed Val to take a return ticket. The second leg was only
$119 more, plus taxes and fees. But Val was not listening.

Val returned to the Internet café and was directed to the
pay phone. He called the number in England that Audrey
had given him. But the phone just rang and rang. He
returned to the counter and paid his deposit to yet another
metal-studded attendant. This time Val was on and off the
Internet in a flash. It was not because of Audrey's warning
that her brother might be watching that he hurried. Val
had no interest in triggering further memory flashes. That
life was all but buried. He wrote Audrey a quick note that
he was coming and would call. Then he retrieved his
deposit and fled the café as he would a morgue.

He walked back to the police station and mounted the
precinct stairs. He pushed through the scarred swinging
doors and entered the front room's bedlam. He took a number and seated himself on the hard wooden bench running
down the wall opposite the reception counter. To his left, a
transvestite cuffed to the bench's arm rubbed toes blistered

by too-tight high heels. Val leaned his head against the wall and fingered the airline ticket in his pocket. Another set of unwanted memories began taking shape, these starring his nemesis, Terrance d'Arcy. Val fought them down and wondered why he had not disappeared long before.

"Number seventy-three."

"Here." Val approached the counter.

"Name?"

"Jeffrey Adams."

"ID?" The policeman reached over without looking up from his metal-backed pad. He copied down the false details, then handed it back and said, "Okay, what can I do for you?"

"I was arrested the night before last. There was a man in lock-up with me. Reuben somebody. An African American."

"You were locked up here?"

"Two nights ago."

"Charges?"

"Dropped." He found himself adopting the cop's terseness.

"And?"

"I want to know if he's still here."

"The reason being?"

"I want to bail him out. If I can afford it."

"Say again?"

"The guy probably saved my life."

"Probably?"

"Look. I don't know for certain what would've happened if he hadn't been there. All I know is, I owe him."

The cop turned to one of his own. "You believe this?"

The other policeman shook his head and returned to his paperwork.

The cop said to Val, "What's this guy's last name?"

"I have no idea. He just introduced himself as Reuben. He's probably six-seven and three hundred pounds. Heavier."

"Reuben James," said the guy working the files. "Yeah, he's still in the lockup. Couldn't make bail."

The cop gave Val a long look, then went back to a desk and tapped into the computer. "James is in on D&D. Drunk and disorderly. Bail is set at $900."

Val counted out the bills. His roll was thinned down to $470. It would have to be enough. He waited while the cop wrote him out a receipt, then moved back outside.

He stood on the precinct's front stoop, ignored by passing officers and offenders alike. An old woman made hard going of the six concrete steps, but fended away his offer of help with an upraised hand. Val retreated to his corner position and breathed the diesel-infected city air. Perhaps it didn't matter whether his memories fully returned or not. Maybe their imprint remained wrapped around his body tight as cellophane tape. There for all save himself to see.

Both precinct doors squeaked open and a hard, dark mountain came into view. Reuben James stood beside Val, blinking up at the sky. "Tell me that sight ain't sweet as heaven's glory."

Val gave the leaden clouds a cursory glance. He found nothing of interest.

The black man turned slowly. "I remember you. How's the head?"

"No concussion. Just like you said. Here, take this."

When he realized what Val held out to him, he showed two pale palms. "Man, that's your receipt. You don't want to be giving me that."

"It's yours."

"That's a ticket for nine hundred dollars, you'll get it back when I show up at court. Which I will. I'm good for what I owe you."

"You don't owe me a thing. I'm headed out. Take it."

"You're talking crazy."

"Look. You kept me safe in there. I just want to thank you."

"You bailed me out, that's all the thanks I need."

"I'm leaving the country tonight. I don't know when or even if I'm coming back. They may or may not mail me the money if I left an address, which I'm not." He pushed the paper into Reuben's hand. "So I want you to have this."

Reuben formed a massive fist around the receipt. "Why you doing this, man?"

"One more thing. There's a clinic three blocks away. Morningside."

"Like the street. Sure, I know it. Down by the church."

"They're looking for a nurse." Val turned away. "Ask for Dr. Martinez."

"Hang on a second. Ain't no place far enough away, you can run and leave the bad behind." He reached for Val, but missed. "Listen to me, man. I know what I'm talking about."

Val started down the steps. "I just want to do the right thing. That's all."

———

At the end of the block, Val glanced back to make sure Reuben wasn't on his trail. And collided with Vince's car.

Vince shouted at him through the open window, "What are you, drunk?"

"I haven't had a drop since that night."

"Like I care." He waved a hand like he wanted to punch a hole in the air. "Get in the car!"

Val opened the door and dropped into the seat. Vince hit the gas so hard the door slammed shut of its own accord. To his right a horn sounded ready to climb inside the car with them. "What are you doing?"

"Protecting my investment. What do you think?"

The car did a four-wheel skid around the corner and ran a red light. "Take it easy."

"I'll give you easy." Vince hit an air pocket and slid between a delivery truck and a cab. His feat earned him another horn blast. "I just left some old geezer who ain't got a brain sitting duty behind the desk. Promised him a week's free stay, I get back and the place is still standing."

"I don't get it."

He shot Val a look. "You owe me. That's all you got to understand."

"I know that already."

"This is new. This is add-on. I'm thinking another ten grand."

"For what?" Then he noticed the clothes piled in the back seat. "My flight doesn't leave for another three and a half hours."

"That's not the point. Unless they already got the airport covered, this way you're safe."

"Who's got it covered?"

"Now you're listening. That's good. You're hearing me when I say I'm earning this extra ten grand by keeping you alive." He squinted at signs zipping by overhead. "Which airport?"

"Kennedy."

"So it's Triborough to Central." He zinged around a limo, barely avoiding three pedestrians clustered on the corner, and zoomed away from the horns and the screams. "There I am, sitting behind my little counter, reading the *Post*, minding my own business. In comes this lady. Only she ain't no lady. She's trouble of the feminine variety. And she's looking for you."

"What?"

"Yeah. Imagine my surprise." He spared Val one quick look. "She knows your name, Jeffrey. And she's showing your picture around town."

"Is she behind us now?"

"For both our sakes, I hope not."

"Then slow down, will you?"

"Yeah, I guess I could do that." Vince eased his foot off the gas. "Look at me. Getting this worked up over a dame."

"Who was she?"

"The way she was asking her questions, I'd say a cop."

"You mean, from the precinct?"

"Nah, I know all of them. And she didn't flash no badge. So I'm thinking a bad cop." This time the look lingered. "Who you got after you, they'd go and hire themselves a rogue ex-cop?"

There was only one name. "Terrance d'Arcy."

"Who?"

"You don't know him."

"No, I don't. And seeing the company he keeps, I don't want to either."

"What did you tell her?"

"What do you think? That I never heard of you."

"Did she see you leave?"

"Nah. I waited 'til she got back in her limo and pulled off."

"She was riding in a limo?"

"Her ride isn't the problem here, Jeffrey." Vince pulled up in front of the terminal and stopped. "A limo is just wheels with a suit thrown in for good measure. Worry about how you're gonna stay alive long enough to send me my money."

Val stared out his side window. Passengers disembarked all around them, hugging friends and relatives, shaking hands, waving farewell. Val sat in a late-model sedan with a loan shark for company. Yet he made no move to leave. Vince did not press him. He seemed to be waiting as well.

Val turned around. "Who do you think my enemy is here?"

"You know this guy, not me."

"I'm not talking about the guy. I'm talking about the woman who's hunting me. You talked with her. Tell me what you think."

Vince gave his single nod, clearly approving of the question. He settled a fraction back into the seat. Probably it was as close to relaxed as this man ever came. He tapped his fingers on the steering wheel as he did on the hotel's countertop. Once. Twice. Even this simple gesture revealed Vince's quiet menace.

"A bad cop, like I said. I'm guessing early thirties. Dark hair. Everything about her very tight, you know what I mean? The lady stays in shape. Definitely somebody who'll never run from a fight."

"A bad cop," Val repeated, searching for a handle.

"Lot of them out there, believe me. Probably on the

job awhile. Got greedy. Might have a drug habit, but I doubt it. She don't have the look for that either. Most of your bad cops are heavy on the juice. But she didn't have the look. Probably got into a lotta trouble over something. Gambling, maybe. Or a scam that went wrong. End result, she tumbled."

"Sorry, I don't follow you."

"What, that she tumbled? Means she started off taking one wrong step, now she's dragged down so far she'll do anything, say anything, just to stay alive. You know what I'm saying?"

"I hear the words, but that's all."

Vince slowed down, giving it to him with patience. "We're talking street here. She slipped up. Maybe she thought she could get into the man for a taste. Needed some extra cash, liked the thrill, was angry with the boss over something, whatever. You remember what I told those guys wanting to do business? Most people on the street, you get into them, they *own* you. My guess is, she got into the wrong guy in a big way. This guy, he's keeping her on a tight leash, and it's killing her breath by breath. She's desperate and looking for a way out."

"What does this mean as far as I'm concerned?"

"Yeah, that's what you got to be thinking on." Vince gave him the gunslinger's grin, there and gone so fast it might never have happened. "If I'm right here, one thing you can say for certain about the lady. She thinks you're her meal ticket, you better watch out. This dame won't leave you breathing."

"You're about to get me very scared here."

"The people you got after you, fear's a good thing to have on your side. Help you grow eyes in the back of your head. Which you're gonna need." Vince took aim with his pistol of a forefinger. Cocked his thumb. "You see them coming at you, run."

———

Val bought a nylon duffel bag at an airport newsstand, then returned to Vince's car and packed up all his belongings. Vince drove away without a backward glance. Val checked in and went straight through security. He seated himself two stations down from his departure gate and watched the hustling flow. Val spotted no familiar face, nor anyone who paid him more than passing notice. After a while the faces became part of a half-seen collage.

A young woman took the chair opposite his. She held a young girl, scarcely more than an infant. The daughter fretted and kicked. Finally the woman let her child down onto the floor. The girl used her mother's finger as a support and rose unsteadily to her feet. Then she sang a child's laughter. Most of the surrounding travelers turned to smile with her.

Val should have walked away. There was no need to remain and be tortured by a fragmented past he was determined to leave behind. But walking away would make no difference. He ached for what had been denied him. He did not need a perfect set of memories to know he had never seen his daughter laugh. Nor that this life sentence was the work of one man.

Val had never known hatred before. He had never thought it was possible to want to murder another man. But Terrance d'Arcy had created in Val a rage of the lethal variety. The divorce, the revelation about Terrance's affair with his wife, the child, the stolen promotion—the body blows had almost destroyed him. One thing had kept Val intact. One thing had given a framework for his otherwise negated life.

Val knew his current rage was a mere shadow of what he had lived with for almost a year and a half. Which was as it should be. He was, after all, a different man.

A half hour before his flight was scheduled to depart, Val walked to the men's room and washed his face. He stared at himself in the mirror long enough for others using the facilities to glance nervously in his direction. Val paid them no mind. He was too busy searching for a future.

He was as free as any man could ever be. He did not even possess a decent set of memories. All he had to do was arrive safely in England, make it to Jersey, pick up his two million and change, gather up Audrey, and disappear before Terrance could destroy anything more. Simple.

Yet all he could find in his gaze was the same empty core.

When his flight was finally called, Val was first in line. But the questions barked at his heels. The bored New York attendant took forever to stop tapping into his computer and process Val's boarding card. Val scouted the hall a final time, seeing nothing because there was nothing to be seen. He found no comfort in that, however. The faceless crowd only amplified his own solitude. When the attendant wished him a good journey, Val breathed a silent farewell to all he hoped would chase him no longer.

The race was on.

THE SUN WAS AN INCH AWAY FROM MELTING iNTO
Orlando's western buildings. Don Winslow and Jack
Budrow ordered an early dinner and ate seated at the corporate boardroom, which was connected to Jack's office
by the Insignia trophy hall. Don had little appetite. Nor
was he all that keen to spend more time in the chairman's
company. But the day had been too full for them to speak
privately. Outsiders swarmed all over the company.
Reporters crammed the lobby and streets surrounding the
building. Even their homes were marked. Don pushed
food around his plate and watched a pair of thunder-
clouds mar the sunset. The coming tropical storm was a
fitting end to a torrential day.

Jack Budrow did not look well. Which was not altogether bad, since his face was the public image for
Insignia's gaping wound. Don might have worried about
the man's long-term prospects, if he could have spared a
thought. Which he couldn't. Not then. "Looks like we
might have a handle on Val Haines."

"You're absolutely certain this Haines is still alive?"

Don stared at his boss. The man shoveled prime rib
into his mouth like a demented robot. "We've covered

this, what, a billion times already. Yes, Jack. Val is above ground. But not for long."

"Where is he headed?"

"Terrance found the guy who supplied Val with a fake passport. So we assume Val's headed for Jersey and his stash. Our security lady put Terrance in contact with people over there. She claims we can trust them with this job."

"This job," Jack muttered around his next bite. "This *job*."

Don decided to let that one slide. "Right now Terrance is meeting New York's finest, giving them the lay of the land. Soon as we hear from the people over there, he'll wing his way across the Atlantic."

Jack dropped his knife and fork with a clatter. "I'm still concerned about trusting d'Arcy with this."

Don had played long enough with food his stomach didn't want. He pushed his plate aside. "Terrance is perfect as far as we're concerned. Those two guys have been enemies for years. Terrance and Val joined the company about six months apart. Val was dating a sweet young thing from Palm Beach. Terrance fell hard for her too, but Val won that round. Soon after he and the lady were married, Val beat Terrance out of a vice-presidency. Terrance doesn't take losing well, Jack. He just smiled and pretended everything was fine. And he waited. Then Val and his lady started having trouble on the children front. They went through all the doctors and clinics, apparently because Val was the one hot for a kid. He was desperate to be a dad. Don't ask me why."

"Terrance stole the man's wife?"

"About the same time he stole Val's promotion. Sweet, wouldn't you say?"

Jack hid his reaction by swivelling his chair around. "Which drove Val to steal from the company, something I never thought would happen."

"Two million and change. I've seen the records."

A bit of the acid emerged. "You're certain Terrance didn't doctor those books as well?"

"Ease up on your partner, Jack. We're not after a choirboy here." Don knew the real reason behind Jack's ire was that Terrance had caught Jack with his own hand in the till. But there was nothing to be gained from mentioning that. "You know who Terrance's father is, right?"

"Some employee of mine, you've already—"

"Arthur d'Arcy is a divisional manager. An engineer by training. Came up through production. Runs the facility we acquired a while back over in Hastings, England. Young Terrance, now, he and the old man don't get along. Not at all. We're talking about some serious friction."

Jack turned back around and gave Don his full attention. "You know why, don't you?"

"Makes for a fascinating tale. Terrance's grandfather was the real deal. A duke. Made a fortune in shipping. Some of it very shadowy, from what I hear. When Terrance was nine, his grandfather divorced Terrance's grandmother. Two days after the divorce was final, the old man married a twenty-four-year-old blond dumpling, then adopted her two-year-old son. Later blood tests proved the kid was his. The grandfather was apparently a real piece of work. The day Terrance turned eleven, the old man kicked the bucket. Problem was, the old man left everything to this young kid and the blond dumpling. Titles, lands, country estate, shipping company, London townhouse, money, the works. Not a cent to Terrance's father, or to Terrance. Who, by the way, was formerly listed as the old man's heir apparent."

"Is that legal?"

"Terrance's mother didn't think so. Her name's Eleanor, by the way. Lives here in Orlando now. Her house is connected to Terrance's."

"Eleanor d'Arcy. Of course. I've met her several times. Quite an impressive lady. But she's not British."

"Born and raised in Philadelphia. Old family. As close to aristocracy as America can claim. She pressed her husband, Terrance's father, to take the old man's estate to court. Arthur d'Arcy refused. Claimed it was a matter of principle."

Jack stared out over the dimming twilight, no doubt imagining the same happening to him. He said, "Eleanor did not take this well."

"To say the least. Divorced her husband, scooped up their son, and left. Bang and gone. Terrance did his studies here in the U.S. and joined us straight out of school. Never mentioned who his father was. Worked his way up through our ranks. Finally Terrance won promotion to VP and in-house auditor. Through some real shenanigans. Like I said, he basically stole the position from Val Haines, who's been his chief rival for years. He planted some incriminating evidence suggesting Val had botched a serious project and tried to hide it. Terrance was given the top slot and Val was sidelined in the pensions department. Left there to rot, basically."

"How do you know all this?"

"Because Terrance told me. I suspected. I asked. He makes no bones about it. Not between us. We're almost family now, right, Jack?"

The CEO stared out the window at the gathering night.

"Pay attention, Jack. It's important you understand how Terrance is earning his keep here. He hasn't just laid blame for this fiasco on our dear departed Val. He's also slipped in a hidden kicker. When the authorities start their investigation, they'll discover that Val managed to keep this from us because he had a secret partner in crime. One far enough away to hide his work from the U.S. authorities."

Jack was back to watching him intently. "Not Terrance's own father?"

"The very same. A careful investigation will show that Arthur d'Arcy was siphoning off funds from his own division's pension fund. Draining it dry, in fact."

Jack's face registered sudden shock. "Hastings. Now I remember. That's the plant—"

"We're scheduling for closure. Still very hush-hush."

"This was Terrance's idea as well?"

"It makes sense as a cost-cutting measure. But, yeah, he managed the study."

"So with the British pension fund raided . . ."

"The laid-off workers won't get a dime. And it'll all be Arthur d'Arcy's fault. He'll spend the rest of his days in prison. A guest of Her Majesty's government, is what they call it. With his good name in tatters." Don let that sink in a moment. "Whatever it takes, Jack. That's what we can expect for our boy to do out there in the field. Whatever it takes."

WALLY RODE WITH TERRANCE TO THE ROCKEFELLER
Center but declined to accompany him farther. Her presence at a meeting with the police would accomplish nothing. She slipped into the crowd and vanished with a professional's ease. Terrance told the driver to find someplace to wait, smoothed his jacket, and entered the fray.

The combined pressure of events coming together worked to Terrance's advantage. He was clearly exhausted, harried, and needing to be elsewhere. Which was what everyone would have expected. And they were watching. He could already feel the spotlight swiveling his way. He had played many roles up to now. But none so critically scrutinized as this one.

Terrance slipped through the army of reporters and photographers and gawkers bound behind the yellow tape. Rockefeller Center was a series of nine buildings covering two city blocks. The blast was high enough for Terrance to spy the gaping hole in the easternmost pinnacle. He heard footsteps approaching, but remained as he was, reviewing the role ahead. He was the executive in to make a cursory visit, do his best for his company, and worried sick over what was happening.

"Mr. d'Arcy?"

"That's right."

"I'm Detective Harris, homicide." He gestured to the grey-suited man hanging two steps back. "This is Agent Frost, FBI. We're expecting an investigator from the SEC, but she's hung up in traffic. She's bringing one of the bank execs with her."

"Fine. Can we go on up?"

"Are you looking for anything in particular?"

"I want to know about our people." Terrance was already moving.

The detective hastened to keep up. "We've talked to your security chief about this. What was her name?"

"Suzanne Walton."

"Right. Like I told her, there's nothing to go on."

"I want to see."

"Okay. Sure." They followed him toward the entrance. "Your security chief, she's ex-cop?"

"I believe that's correct."

"I made a couple of calls. Walton left Baltimore under something of a cloud."

Terrance pushed through the doors. "If you know all this, why are you asking?"

Harris flashed his badge at the security guard. "We have three people missing and presumed murdered, Mr. d'Arcy. It's my business to ask. So this Walton, how did you manage to find her?"

"You'd have to ask our executive vice president, Don Winslow."

The elevator pinged and they stepped inside. The FBI agent tracked Terrance's movements like a grey wraith. Harris asked, "Where is he?"

"Keeping his finger in the dike down in Orlando. Don is also chief in-house counsel."

"We have to get off two floors below and walk up the rest of the way. We're lucky the bank occupied the top-most floors. The rest of the building appears intact. The blast was directed up and out." Harris punched the button for the fifty-second floor. "So there's nothing you can tell me about Walton?"

"That's not what you asked me, Detective. You asked how she was hired. If you want information about her current status, you need to inquire more specifically." Terrance rubbed his forehead, pleased to see his hand shook. His senses were on hyperdrive. Every second was sliced into microscopic bits, so fine he could be utterly involved in the moment and yet able to expend his awareness out in a thousand different directions. He wondered if this was how it felt to be on stage. "Two years ago, Insignia acquired six hotels that were going under. In my first inspection of the books, I uncovered evidence that the hotels were being ripped off in a highly organized fashion."

"You hired an ex-cop to hunt down some missing towels?"

Terrance cut him a single look. "I said organized, Detective. Initial estimates put the losses at a quarter of a million dollars annually. Per hotel."

The FBI agent spoke up for the first time. "That's a lot of little soaps."

"We found evidence of rooms being rented and showing no revenue."

"How'd you do that?"

"I measured the outflow of laundry, bed linen, food, everything. I compared it with other hotels in similar categories. We were using between a quarter and a third more resources than the billable rooms and restaurant takings required."

The doors opened. Terrance followed the detective into the lobby of an empty law firm. A chandelier had fallen from the ceiling, leaving a hole now covered by cardboard. Two recessed fluorescents had shattered and not yet been replaced. One part of the ceiling and the Persian carpet below it were both badly stained. The left-hand wall of glass bricks bore a sizable crack.

The detective led him to a steel door flagged with yellow police tape. The stairwell smelled of water and oily smoke. There was noise from below. Nothing came from above them except a thickening of the air with each step. Terrance went on, "I discussed the hotel problem with Don, my boss. I needed someone who could identify the thieves without alerting the guests or the press. This needed to go away quietly. Suzanne Walton did an excellent job. Within three months of her hiring, the problem vanished."

There was no door. Terrance halted on the landing because there was nowhere further to go. The blast had wrecked the steel and concrete structure overhead. He stared out across a blackened expanse. Plastic sheeting replaced the former floor-to-ceiling windows. They billowed slightly in the evening breeze.

Harris pointed at the plastic sheeting. "The engineers tell us that's why the building didn't suffer any real structural damage."

"The blast focused upwards, like you said."

"Right. But it pretty much destroyed everything on these two floors, as you can see. We figure it for eight charges, all timed for just after half-past six. Which suggests they aimed to take out your people, Mr. d'Arcy."

"Or the banker they were here meeting," Terrance said.

"What do you know about the banker?"

"Nothing except the name. Which we lifted from Val Haines's calendar."

"How well did you know the victims?"

"Val Haines I thought I knew well. Marjorie Copeland less so. She was an employee of long standing in our pensions department." Terrance shook his head, apparently distracted by the chaos. "What a calamity."

"And Val? That's his real name?"

"Valentine Joseph Haines. He was previously in my own department."

"So you've known him for how long?"

"Five years, almost six."

"And you guys were friends. He never mentioned any anger at the company, any desire to—"

"You misunderstand me, Detective. Val and I were not friends. Far from it. You're going to find out sooner or later. Val Haines hated me."

"Why is that?"

"First because I won a promotion he thought was his." Terrance grimaced. "Then he and his wife divorced. I was named in the suit as his wife's lover."

"Yeah, I'd say he had probable cause. What about you?"

Terrance turned from the ruin. "Me?"

"I'd say you had reason to hate this guy. Want to see him destroyed."

"Most certainly," Terrance replied. "Only there's one thing missing from the equation, Detective. With Val and Marjorie gone, we have no chance now of recouping our losses. Or, for that matter, bringing them to justice."

"What about . . ." The detective halted at sounds rising through the stairwell.

They were joined by a wiry accountant-inspector from the SEC and the U.S. director of Syntec Bank. The bank director looked as if he had been hollowed by the incomprehensible. His corporate world stretched out before him, utterly destroyed.

Terrance suffered through a second series of questions, many of which returned to the same ground all over again. He answered with the same weary strain he saw in the banker's features.

Terrance had spent his entire life assigned a part that was not his. Forced into a role meant for someone else, stuffed into a cheaper set of costumes because his father had refused to do his duty. His own father, the man he should have always been able to rely on, had shown all the backbone of a jellyfish. That was how his mother had described Arthur d'Arcy on the day she had told her son the news. There had been a great deal for a nine-year-old boy to take in. How his own grandfather had willed everything to a floozy and her illegitimate offspring—his mother's words again. How Terrance's father, her husband, had refused to fight the decision. How they had been left with nothing. How Eleanor was divorcing her husband. How Terrance was never to mention his father's name again. Eleanor had cried as she had told him, the only time Terrance had ever seen his mother weep. He had promised her in as manly a voice as he could manage that he would take care of her. She had smiled through her tears and called him her little king. But Terrance had known even then that the title did not fit. From that moment, as he danced his multiple roles upon stages on the wrong side of the Atlantic, he had known that someday he would return and claim what was rightfully his.

All his life he had been preparing for the big role. Life

was, after all, just theater. Nothing more. Most people thought actors were remarkably adept at impersonations. This was ludicrous. The champions of stage and screen were people who had learned one simple truth.

All life was false. There was nothing at the core of existence save death and despair and an endless unfillable void. Most people spent their entire lives running from this inescapable reality. Actors were unique in that they had *embraced* this. They utilized the fear and pain by *confronting* the void. By *mastering* the power of their sorrow and anguish. Just as Terrance had.

Either people got the big roles or they didn't. Terrance was born to be a star. Anyone who stood in his way became dust and fond memories. As his wretched father soon would discover.

But Val Haines was more than just another unfortunate. Terrance had savored taking Val down in stages. When Terrance was ensconced in his Bermuda palace or his Belgravia townhouse, sated from a lovely meal, watching his daughter play with his lovely wife by his side, he would look back on Val's demise as one of life's sweetest triumphs.

———

Terrance decided to dine in his suite. He loved the Plaza's dining room, with its palatial surroundings and impeccable service. But he felt drained, as exhausted as he had ever been in his life. The previous day's work, the travel, the visit with Stefanie, meeting Wally, confronting the counterfeiter, the cops, the shattered bank. He needed time alone to unwind.

And the news about Insignia was breaking. Terrance

dined on rack of lamb au jus with a rosemary and Dijon mustard topping. He had the waiter set up the table where he could eat and watch the television. MSNBC was giving Insignia the lead position. Between the on-site reporter and Insignia's building, Terrance counted eleven other television vans. And these were only the ones he could see.

He waited until he had poured his second cup of coffee to call Don. "How was your day?"

"Brutal. Where are you?"

"Plaza. Dining in my suite, watching the bomb go off."

"Bomb is right. Any word on our guy?"

"He's left the country."

"You're sure?"

"Fairly. Wally says we can handle it."

"If Wally tells you that, you can take it to the bank."

"That's my impression also."

"What's next at your end?"

"I've got the plane on standby. Soon as he's found, we move."

"You want to be there for the kill, is that it?"

"We have to be sure this time, Don."

"Yeah, I guess we do."

"I'll go by the Jersey bank afterwards, make an appearance, ask for our money back. Hire a lawyer, that sort of thing."

A burst of noise poured through Terrance's cell phone from Don's end, loud as static. Don's voice turned edgier still. "Got to go. Stay in touch."

Terrance disconnected, rose from the table, and headed for the bedroom. He doubted he could sleep. The internal circuits were jammed on high. But he needed to stretch out, try and get his taut muscles to unlock. He pulled off the covers and sprawled on the bed. His joints felt connected to a power source, jerking in tight spasms. He shut his eyes.

The next thing he knew, his cell phone was ringing. Terrance lay as he had fallen, his legs dangling over the edge of the bed. He fumbled in his pocket. "What time is it?"

"Late. You awake?"

"Barely." Terrance rolled over. "Where are you?"

"Idlewild. Planeside. Waiting for you." Wally's voice carried the taut eagerness of a pack leader on the scent of prey. "I just heard from England."

Another day began with an adrenaline jolt. "And?"

"Your man has been spotted."

"I'M VERY SORRY, MR. ADAMS. BUT THERE'S NO WAY WE can fly you to Jersey until late tomorrow." The Gatwick check-in attendant tapped on her keyboard. "No, I lie. All those flights are fully booked. You'll have to wait until the day after."

Val's hearing was impaired by jet lag and the disorientation of arriving in a new country with nothing to claim, not even an identity. "Why so long?"

"This fog is not expected to lift until tomorrow midday, if then. Flights to Jersey do not have the instrumentation required to land in such conditions." The British lilt added a courteous smile to her voice that was not reflected in her features. "The first flights out are already fully booked."

"I've just come in from America. I really need to get over there."

"You could take a ferry. There's a new high-speed service." She pointed him to the concourse's other side. "Take the escalator down to the railway terminal. Trains for Portsmouth depart from track four."

The one known as Matt made the call. "I've got the mark."

"You sure it's this bloke Haines?"

Matt caught sight of his reflection in the vending machine and stopped to preen. Black lace-up boots met skin-tight black jeans that joined to a black silk T-shirt. Matt liked to think of himself as a human stiletto. The other blokes who worked for Boss Loupe, the ones who fitted into their Cerutti suits like muscular sausages, called him a weasel. But not loudly. Matt was too good at his work.

"You there?"

"The face fits the photo you gave me. I've tracked him out of customs. Bang on time from the New York flight."

"Where's your mate?"

"Jocko's tailing the guy."

"So what is Haines up to now?"

"Made a beeline for the Jersey flights. Isn't having no luck there, though."

"Why's that?"

"Weather. It's a right mess."

"So what's his option, then?"

"Wait the night or take the boat, far as I can see. Can't drive to Jersey, that's for certain."

Matt's wit was lost on the other end. No surprise there. "Stay close. Find out where he's headed."

"And then?"

"Do him like I told you. Nice and clean."

"No worries."

"The boss is watching this one."

"Yeah?" Matt tried to keep his voice light. "That translate into a little extra dosh for us?"

"Just do your job. Keep it simple. The boss wants this one put away where nobody will ever find him. Clear?"

———

Val used a pay phone by the checkout counter and called Audrey's number. This time a man answered. Val held the phone an inch or so from his ear, caught utterly off guard. The man had a gentle sounding tone, even when speaking to dead air. Val hung up.

Val replaced the receiver, hefted his nylon duffel, started for the escalator, then was snagged by the smell of fresh coffee. He stopped so abruptly the man behind stumbled into him. "Sorry, mate."

"No problem." Val would not have noticed the contact except that the guy was so solid. It had felt like backing into a brick wall. Val stepped into the newsstand and bought an *International Herald Tribune*, then joined the coffee line. He shoved his satchel forward with his foot, idly scanning headlines.

Then he froze.

"Sir? Did you want to place your order?"

Val looked up at the cashier. Neither the place nor the words registered.

"Can I get you something?"

Wordlessly, Val hefted his case and stepped away from the counter.

In the terminal Val returned to the paper, futilely hoping the words would have rearranged themselves on the page.

Insignia, his former company, was front-page news.

Val turned to where the report continued on the first business page, then returned to the front page and started over. The words did not sink in until the third read.

He refolded the paper and scanned the terminal. No

one appeared to be paying him any great attention. But there was no way he could be certain. There were too many faces. Too many strangers. The threat could be anywhere.

Val hefted his satchel and ran.

THE TWO-HOUR TRAIN JOURNEY TO PORTSMOUTH COM-pacted Val's thoughts into lines of determined panic. Everything had finally come together with lethal force. The ease with which he and Marjorie had extracted what they claimed as their due, the bank explosion back in New York, Audrey's warning, his returning memories—everything meshed together now.

Portsmouth station was the next stop, and the train's remaining passengers were already collecting their belongings. Val glanced out the window. A dreary grey landscape came and went as the fog drifted and condensed. Val spotted a few buildings, cars racing by on a neighboring highway, a world washed of all color. He returned his attention to a newspaper article he knew now by heart.

He had been set up from the beginning.

Knowing Terrance, the man had probably left clues in clear enough fashion for Marjorie to have realized the pension fund was being stripped to the bone. Terrance had used Marjorie as he had used everyone else. People were nothing to Terrance unless he wanted them for some purpose. Then they became fodder for his plans. Nothing more.

Unless they got in his way.

The train pulled into the station and halted. Val rose and joined the other passengers flowing through the doors. He stepped onto the concrete and tasted air far too metallic for late April. He spotted the ferry-port sign and joined the throng. Val stumbled over the curb as he tried to read and walk at the same time. The newspaper article feasted upon the lurid details of the corporate thieves being killed in a bomb blast. Syntec Bank U.S. was also under investigation for its hand in draining Insignia's pension funds.

A theft of $422 million.

Val stuffed the paper into the satchel's side pocket and hurried. The walkway was crowded with other passengers whose flights had been cancelled. By the time Val arrived at the ferry terminal, the grayness had condensed into something too thick to be called fog and too fine to be rain. It felt like he was breathing cold diesel tea. The waiting room was a linoleum-lined warehouse with industrial lighting, filled with echoes. Val headed for the bank of phones lining one wall. He dialed Audrey's number. The same man answered. Val hung up and stood with his hand poised on the receiver. Had she found someone else since he had sent her away? If so, why had she written as she had, then urged him to come? Val turned away. His next step remained perfectly clear. Go to Jersey and grab the money. He would call her again from the bank. If the man answered again, Val would forge ahead regardless.

Val purchased his ticket, tried to make himself comfortable in a molded plastic chair, and hid behind his paper. He reread the story and added what the paper could not supply. Terrance had let him get away with the theft because Terrance had always been in control. Terrance had needed a fall guy. In order to make a clean sweep of the larger theft, Terrance had let Val and Marjorie and their tame Syntec banker get away with pocket change. Two million dollars had seemed like the world to Val. But to a guy planning the theft of four hundred million, it was nothing. Val started to wonder who else at Insignia had been in with Terrance on the grand scheme. Don Winslow, for starters. He was the man who had cast the deciding vote against Val and for Terrance in their latest bout. Val wondered if Jack Budrow, the spineless son of a great and good man, could have stooped so low. Then he decided it didn't really matter. Whoever thought they were controlling this particular dance, Val knew Terrance d'Arcy was the one really calling the tune.

———

Matt made the second call while standing in line to buy ice cream. Two young children at the front of the queue couldn't make up their minds. The ferry's waiting room was large as an airplane hangar and all hard surfaces. Outside, the fog had condensed into drifting rain. Six kids ran in tight little circles around the chairs and played like fighter planes. A mother screeched at them to give it a rest. Matt could have discussed the crime of the century and nobody would have noticed.

Matt's contact at head office demanded, "Give me the good news."

"Don't have none, do I. There's been no chance so far to do it clean like you said. Haines has stayed in crowds every step of the way."

"So what's the bloke doing, then?"

"He's going for the boat."

"You're certain of that?"

"I'm standing in the Portsmouth terminal with him now."

"Follow him."

"I never been one for water. Not even in a glass."

"I didn't ask that, now, did I? Matter of fact, I don't give a toss. You do what you're told."

Matt swallowed against a nervy stomach. He could handle most things. But watching a ship go up and down on the telly was enough to have him shutting his eyes and humming a little tune. He glanced over to where his mate stood in line at the ticket counter. "You want this bloke clean away, not seen away."

"That's the ticket."

"Like an accident at sea, maybe."

"Nobody's meant to notice a thing. Do him quiet and do him fast. You got that?"

"I heard you the first time." Matt swallowed against the dread of his first journey ever on a boat. "Bad weather, no sky, he'll never be missed."

"Where's our lad now?"

The loudspeaker blared overhead, announcing that the ship was boarding. Matt stepped from the line. "He's headed for the gate."

"Hang on, the boss wants a word."

If Matt had not already been green, this would have done the trick. In all the years he'd been on the old man's ticket, Matt had only spoken to Boss Loupe twice. Even so, he instantly recognized the old man's voice. "Matthew, is that you, lad?"

"Yes, Mr. Loupe. Sorry about the din."

"Never you mind. Listen carefully, my boy. Word is, the gentleman you're tailing is headed for the Syntec Bank on Jersey." The old man spelled out the name. "Above all else, your job is to make sure he doesn't arrive."

"I'll do him on the boat, just like you said."

"Nice and quiet, mind. Not a soul's to notice. Leave it for the island if you must. So long as he doesn't enter that bank."

"He'll be gone like smoke, sir. You can count on me."

"I am, my boy. We all are."

Matt shut the phone and swallowed hard a second time. Messing up a job the boss was watching didn't bear thinking about.

If only it wasn't going down on a poxy boat.

VAL COULDN'T BE SURE. BETWEEN THE JET LAG AND the newspaper article, his senses were jammed on overload. Not to mention the disorientation brought on by this featureless grey day. His world had been jarred too far off its axis. Nothing was registering with clarity.

But he was fairly certain he was being followed.

The two men back in the terminal had been noticeable by their size. One rose almost to Val's height but was cadaver thin. He wore skin-tight clothes that only accented his narrow frame. The other was a bullish giant with a shaved head and a tattoo on his neck. Both had been watching him as he went through the boarding process.

What was more, Val feared he had seen that same tattoo on the guy who had bumped him in the airport. But he could not be certain.

The departures terminal was connected to the boat by a covered walkway. This led to a sloping ramp rising to the middle-deck entry. Val's heart drummed in time to rain striking the walkway's canvas cover. At the gangplank Val slipped the duffel bag to his other hand, gripped the rail, and turned as if to give England a final glance.

The beefy guy was just slipping past security. His narrow-faced mate was nowhere to be seen.

The vessel's entry hall was crammed with excited passengers and squalling kids. Val slipped around a bustling tour group, crouched, and scurried down the main hall. He entered a largish chamber done up as a ship's salon from a bygone era. A café stood at one end and a bar at the other, with circular brass-rimmed tables and wire-backed chairs and Tiffany lamps and polished wood flooring. Val stepped into the bookstore by the opposite wall and slipped behind a revolving magazine stand. He crouched almost to his knees.

A massive pair of Doc Martens boots hustled by, stopped, and turned back. A few moments later they were joined by a set of black lace-up boots with pointed toes. The two stood there together for what seemed like eons. Then they split up.

A young woman with an olive complexion approached Val and asked hesitantly, "Are you all right, sir?"

He made a very feeble pretense of searching the bottom rack. "Do you carry *The New Republic?*"

"Is that a journal?"

"No, never mind." He raised himself up in stages, checking carefully. The pair were nowhere to be seen. "Thanks anyway."

He had to find someplace to hide.

MATT AND JOCKO HAD WORKED TOGETHER ANY NUMBER
of times. There was little chatter, or need for it. Jocko
joined the queue of foot passengers jostling good-
naturedly toward the gate and the gangplank beyond.
Their mark was about fifty feet ahead.

The metal detectors and security inspectors were
trouble. Matt always preferred to carry a full set of tools on
him. Today he'd just have to rely on Jocko. He slipped
back to the gents' and pulled his knife from the special
sheath tucked in the small of his back. The handle was a
lovely set of brass dusters made special to fit his undersized
hand. He wrapped the knife in paper towels, climbed onto
a loo, and stored the bundle up top of a cistern. He
dropped down and surveyed his handiwork. He would so
miss that knife. It was like parting with his best mate.

When he came back into the terminal, Jocko was
already through customs. Matt rejoined the queue,
passed through the metal detectors, handed his false ID
to the coppers, then headed for the boat. It was raining
harder now, really coming down in buckets.

The high-speed craft was one of those new jobs, lifting
up on an angled V like something off the telly. There was
limited car space. The entire ship could have fitted into a

larger ferry's main hold. Which made their job all the easier. Matt slipped around the crush of families milling about the entry, telling himself there was no need for the way he already felt. Not while they were still tied up at the dock.

Jocko waved him over. The big man was looking none too pleased. "I've lost him."

"You can't have."

"He's not here, I tell you."

The boat's turbines chose that moment to rumble awake. Matt leaned against the side wall. "You're sure he came on board?"

"I walked the plank right behind him. I'm telling you, he's done a Houdini."

"He must've made us."

"That's what I reckon as well." Jocko looked more closely. "What's the matter with you?"

"I don't like boats."

"So what's the plan?"

"We find him, is what." Queasy or not, Matt had no choice in the matter. "Where do you think he's gone?"

"He don't have all that much space to maneuver. This boat's tiny. There's the level below us for cars; it's locked tight as a drum. There's these four great rooms and whatever they got up top, and that's the lot."

"So you have a gander around this level." Matt kept one hand clamped to his gut. "I'll go search up top. Keep your eyes peeled."

"And if I catch him, what then?"

"We got to do this one clean. That's the word. Don't do him if there's anybody about." The motors rumbled and the boat slipped away from its mooring. Matt swallowed hard. "The boss spoke to me personal."

"When was this?"

"Back in the terminal. We don't do this job right, we never go home. That's as plain as it gets."

Overhead the loudspeakers started up their cheery hello. "You're not having me on, the boss gave you the word?"

"Mr. Loupe himself." Matt forced himself off the side wall. The boat was already pitching. "We find this bloke, and we do him."

———

The boat was claustrophobic. And fast. The rain was a solid sheet of water upon the forward facing windows. To either side, spumes flew up high as the third floor where Val now stood. Below him was the boat's only car deck, now locked. He knew because he had tried both doors. Below that, he assumed, was the engine room. Above him was the observation deck where people huddled in protected alcoves and enjoyed the sea air.

Val took a chair in the central salon between the two passenger compartments that ran the entire length of the ship. His table was by the wall, which gave him a view of both entrances. But he was totally exposed.

The ship's motors sounded a single deep note, thrumming in his body. Val needed to rest. Despite his adrenaline-stoked fear, he could feel the jet lag and the missing night's sleep deep in his bones. Val leaned his head against the rear wall. The soothing vibrations carried through his temple. He blinked slowly. Then he forced himself to his feet. If he stayed there, sooner or later he would doze off.

The problem was, the boat was constructed to do away with all blind corners. Val stationed himself at the opening to the crammed luggage rack and searched the forward compartment. The boat was all noisy crowds and rain-swept glass and open spaces.

Val retreated into the bathrooms, one after the other. But the places were crawling and the stall doors were symbolic at best. Every new face threatened to become the mammoth bruiser with the tattoo.

He hesitated in the doorway leading back into the hallway. As a trio of beery louts shouldered past, he spotted a door marked "Staff Only." Val watched as two officers passed through. They remained deep in discussion. The younger of the pair used a key connected to his belt by a silver chain to open the door.

Before the door could lock shut, Val slipped across the hall and caught it with his heel. He waited through a pair of breaths. Then he pushed the door open a fraction and glanced inside. The doorway opened into a short hall, which then descended down a series of steps. Val heard the sailors' voices disappearing into the distance. He saw no one. What he could see of the hall was narrow, windowless, and empty.

He stepped inside.

———

Jocko knew full well what the world thought of him. He was the silent muscle, not meant to have even half a brain. Nobody expected him to speak. Which suited Jocko just fine. He had no time for idle chatter. He wanted a bloke's attention, he clapped him one. That always worked.

Problem was, Matt was always telling Jocko what to do. Even when Jocko had his job down cold. Like now. It was simple enough, really. Clean was clean.

Yammer, yammer, that was Matt in a nutshell. But Jocko was the one seeing to what needed doing. When time came to shut the gob and act, Matt played like smoke. Just like now.

This guy was such an easy target. That was Jocko's first thought when the bloke popped back into view. Haines was already injured, his head patched. Jocko slipped back a notch, to where the coffee bar met the side wall. One little tap and Haines would be laid out clean as you please.

Haines hovered in the doorway leading to the gents'. His eyes were doing the dance, seeing danger everywhere. Jocko snorted quietly. Matt thought he was the brains? So what would he be doing this minute? Telling old Jocko to sort this bloke out, that's what. Give the word and take a giant step back.

Jocko was watching this Haines. Oh yeah. Watching him make all the mistakes.

And he had just made a big one.

———

Val spied the rushing hulk a split second before impact. The simple fact that Val's senses were on hyperalert granted him just enough time to step back from the door. Or try to.

The attacker's strength was shocking. Clearly he had intended to pin Val between the steel door and the bulkhead, breaking Val's ribs and halting him in his tracks. Instead, the door's glancing blow blasted Val back three paces. The door struck the side wall with the force of a cannonade.

Val could have caught himself on the top stair with the

railing for a brake. But he let himself fall. In fact, he used
the railing as a slide, stumbling backwards down the nine
steps. He hit the bottom landing and sprawled. But the
guy was already thundering down from overhead. Val did
a crabwise backwards crawl down the corridor.

His foe leapt down the final three steps. The narrow
passage made his bulk even more monstrous.

A side door opened. A woman in uniform peered out.
She gaped at Val's panic-stricken crawl, then spotted the
massive intruder. She started to scream.

The attacker heaved her back with an open-palmed
punch to her chest. His strength was such that he cata-
pulted her across the chamber and slammed her against
the far wall.

The attacker peered in the open door, a single instant
to ensure she wasn't able to give him trouble. Val took
this as his only hope for escape. He clawed his way to his
feet and raced down the hall.

The thunder behind him added wings to his flight.

The door at the hall's end opened. The young officer
stepped into view. Val ducked down and slipped past the
man and through the doorway.

On the other side was open space and noise. The
landing was metal and about four feet square. A spiral
staircase headed downwards. Val ignored the shout
behind him, gripped the rails with both hands, and hit
every fifth step.

Above him, the officer's second shout cut off abruptly.
Val leapt over the railing and dropped the final ten steps.
He landed upon a catwalk that ran the entire length of
the ship. To either side roared a giant pair of turbine
engines painted a monochrome green. They bellowed a
constant note.

The metal catwalk bounced like a trampoline beneath Val's feet when the attacker landed. Val did not risk a glance backwards. He knew the man was closing. Val pounded down the metal road.

Up ahead, a mechanic in greasy overalls talked to the senior officer Val had seen by the upstairs doorway. They peered at some valve or meter. The mechanic looked up, spied Val racing toward them, and shouted a warning.

These men were far more experienced than the younger officer. They spread out in a flanking pattern, barring his progress.

Val leapt up and over the metal railing. He hit the lip of the motor, a narrow ledge running down the entire side with bolts protruding like painted traps. The machine's vibrations almost knocked him off his feet. Val could not maneuver on that tight strip. He did the only thing that came to mind, which was to climb the motor's rounded hump to the top.

The motor's tremors traveled up through his hands and legs. They rattled his vision. The two crewmen yelled at him and at the bruiser who was scrambling across the catwalk railing.

The mechanic raced forward and grabbed the attacker's leg. The bigger man kicked him, a casual motion as if he were shaking off a pest. The mechanic went down hard.

The senior officer turned away from both Val and the bruiser and raced down the catwalk. Val kept going in the same direction, hoping for a diversion. The vibrating motor felt like a galloping metal horse. He was threatened with falling into an abyss of pumping iron and oily darkness.

Behind him, the bruiser hesitated in the act of climbing onto the motor's ledge. The ship's officer was headed for a red alarm box. The attacker shouted an oath and clambered off the barrier. He raced after the officer.

Val turned and did a monkey scramble in the opposite direction. He slid off the motor, leapt over the railing, and raced back down the catwalk toward the stairs.

The oil on his hands and feet and knees turned the curving stairs into a nightmarish assault on a slippery metal mountain. Val clawed his way up. The young officer sprawled on the upper landing, moaning and moving slowly. Val leapt through the doorway, left an oily stain on the opposite wall, and plunged down the hall. The young woman in the office-cabin called weakly for help. Val scrambled up the final stairs and reentered the ship's public space. The antechamber was full of passengers astonished by his sudden appearance.

Only then did Val realize that his head was bleeding again.

Val took the most likely avenue of escape, which was up. The stairs ended in a small antechamber with a door to either side. He flung one open and entered the rain-swept maelstrom.

The rain was turned into blinding pellets by the wind and the vessel's speed. To his left, a few passengers huddled within an open-ended chamber and shouted against the din. Ahead, the grey hulk of Jersey emerged from the storm.

Val could not risk becoming trapped in the passengers' steel-sided alcove. He gripped the wet rail and started around the back of the central smokestack.

Val turned the corner and came face-to-face with the second man.

The attacker gripped the railing with one hand and

his gut with the other. He gaped in utter shock at Val's appearance, then reached below his jacket and shouted a name, or started to.

Val did not think. He roared his anger and his fear and raced forward until he slammed into the thin man.

The attacker slid backwards until he rammed the opposite rail. Val continued pushing, trying to fling the man into the flying spray and the slate-grey water. To his left, the passengers huddled within the second metal-walled alcove gaped in shock at their struggle.

The man was smaller than Val, but he was streetwise and vicious. He was also fighting for his life. The first punch connected with Val's leaking temple and almost blinded him with the pain. Val hung on and struggled with all his might to shove the attacker over the railing. Below them, the vessel's wake was a constant roaring wave.

Voices shouted and moved toward them. But Val did not loosen his grip until the hands forced him. Countless hands. Too many for him to fight against. The pain in his temple was a great booming force, stronger than the thrumming motors. His vision leaked with the spattering rain.

Val shouted against the wind and other voices, "Who sent you?"

The man struggled against other hands gripping him. He stared at Val with a manic gaze and said nothing.

"Who sent you?"

The boat slowed as it passed through the Jersey harbor entrance. Somewhere overhead a horn blasted.

The door behind Val blew open. The bruiser from downstairs shoved his way forward. He reached over the knot of people surrounding Val and grabbed for him.

"Jocko!"

The bruiser hesitated.

"Move it!"

The brute flung aside the other passengers and freed his mate. The two of them raced toward the stern. Val watched the pair slip down a ladder, then another, until they stood on the lowest open deck. They stripped off rain-washed jackets, then waited as the boat slowed further. The smaller of the pair turned and looked back up at Val. He leveled a finger and took aim. Then the bruiser gripped his arm.

Together the pair dove over the side.

"SIR, THE PORT AUTHORITIES WOULD VERY MUCH LIKE to have a word with you."

"Fine. I'll talk to anybody you want." Now that the battle was over, he had to fight the words out around chattering teeth. "But they've got to come here."

"I'm afraid that's not possible. This boat keeps to a very tight schedule."

"I have no problem with that." He nodded his thanks to the orderly who brought him a cup of strong black tea. Val needed both hands to bring it to his mouth. He blew, sipped, said, "Let's take off. Now works fine for me."

The officer wore short-sleeved whites. They were seated in a room across from where the woman now lay being tended by the ship's first-aid officer. Val's temple throbbed beneath his new white bandage. His duffel had been located, and he wore a dry tracksuit. A blanket was draped over his shoulders. His tremors rocked the cup he held. He did not feel cold now so much as utterly drained. His voice sounded raw and empty to his own ears.

The officer had the no-nonsense air of former navy. He was seated upon the fold-down desk opposite the bunk where Val sat. "You're saying you do not wish to disembark on Jersey?"

"You kidding? Those brutes are out there waiting for me."

"I presume you mean the pair of men who reportedly attacked you over football."

"Crazy, isn't it? I had no idea they were that drunk." Every word needed to be pried from a brain that felt gummed solid with fatigue. He named the only British team that came to mind. "Or Manchester United winning some cup was all that big a deal."

The officer crossed his arms. "Indeed."

A young sailor knocked on the open door. "Customs says his documents are in order, sir."

He reached over and accepted Val's passport. His eyes never left Val's face. "Thank you."

Val hid his relief at having his passport back within grabbing distance by sipping from his cup.

"My officers confirm that you were the victim and the large man the attacker." The officer tapped Val's passport on his thigh. "What I fail to understand, Mr. . . ."

"Adams."

"Is why you felt it necessary to go after the man on the deck."

"I saw he was going to attack me," Val said, still examining the dregs of his teacup. "I didn't want to give him a chance."

"And yet the passengers claim the man had spent the entire voyage being extremely ill."

"Like I said, none of this makes any sense to me."

A young woman tapped on the door frame. "Master's compliments, sir. We're ready to begin boarding."

"Carry on."

"Sir." She departed.

"I agree, Mr. Adams. None of this makes sense." The

officer pushed himself off the desk. "But I have no reason to deny you passage home, much as I might like. I can, however, insist that you spend the journey isolated in this compartment."

"Could you have someone bring me a sandwich?" He tried futilely to dredge up a smile. "I missed lunch."

———

Val woke to the drumming of the engines and the motion of a ship at sea. The vessel did not rock so much as slice the waves. It buffeted, but not harshly, like an ax cleaving the sea's surface. Val struggled to sit upright. He glanced at his watch. But he could not recall what time it had been when the ship's officer had finally left and he had lain down.

A tray had been brought in and left while he was asleep. He reached across the narrow cubicle and pulled out the stool hidden beneath the desk. Val seated himself and ate with ravenous appetite. Val's temple throbbed and his body ached. His shoulder throbbed from being struck by the door, his hands from abrasions as he flew down the stairs, his knees and ankles from scrambling along the motor.

A mirror was embedded in the alcove wall. He finished eating and stared into his reflection. The face looked flaccid with exhaustion, the eyes cavernous. Val examined his features, seeking a simple answer. What was he to do? And once he knew, would he have the strength to do it?

He lay back down. In an instant he was asleep once more.

The boat's altered motions woke him. This time he felt far more alert. He glanced at his watch. He had been asleep for almost two hours. The motors were rumbling at a lower pitch now. Val rose and entered the cramped washroom. Whoever had brought him lunch had also left a disposable razor and a small bottle of mouthwash. The motions helped loosen the muscles still cramped and sore from the attack. His mind was sluggish, however. There was still a sense of being disconnected. Whether this was from jet lag or the attack, he could not say.

The young male officer who had returned Val's passport unlocked the cabin door. "Ship's docking, sir."

"Thank you." Val stuffed his wet belongings into the duffel bag and headed out. The officer refused to meet Val's eye. "Just up the stairs ahead of you."

"I know the way."

"Certainly, sir." There was a toneless etiquette to the young officer's voice. Like a prison officer on public view. He dogged Val's steps, hanging just far enough back to keep from tripping over Val's feet. At the top of the stairs he said, "To your left, sir."

The entry salon was empty save for three cleaning staff. They did not look up at Val's passage. He had the sense of being officially declared a leper. To look was to risk infection. Unclean, their silence shouted. Unclean.

The officer halted at the gangplank. No farewell word. Nothing. A pair of customs officers awaited him at street level. They had clearly been forewarned. Their search of his bag, his passport, and his body was extremely thorough. Val maintained his story, and kept his tone mild. A day trip to an island he had read about but never visited had been disrupted by two drunken louts. He was terribly sorry for all the trouble he had caused, and extremely glad to be back in England. He gave as his address the West End hotel where he had stayed the last time over.

The customs officers had no reason to keep him, and finally let him go.

Val crossed the ferry port's vast parking area, taking great draughts of free air. The evening smelled of sea and salt and rain. Trucks passed in a slow convoy, headed for the continent. He was soon drenched. He did not mind in the slightest, though he had no more dry clothes. The rain helped wash away the mental fog. He left the port area and headed down the main road. There was bound to be a nearby bed-and-breakfast catering to the trucking crowd and accustomed to admitting bedraggled men.

Mental gears meshed begrudgingly as he walked. Clearly his attackers were still on the island. The bank was definitely going to be watched. Which meant he could not access his funds. He and Marjorie had arranged the numbered accounts so that their money could be withdrawn only in person.

Which meant Val was now extremely stuck.

He had less than three hundred dollars to his false name. He was as incognito as he could have asked. A nameless man, unloved by all, seeking freedom from a stranger's past.

TERRANCE AND WALLY JOURNEYED ACROSS THE
Atlantic in a Gulfstream IV outfitted like an elegant hotel
suite. Wally tried hard to pretend it was all part of the
game. But the private steward and the crystal decanters
and the kid-leather seats and the walnut burl table and
the filet mignon with fresh truffle sauce left her gaping.
When they finished dinner, the steward turned the seats
into two beds with Sea Island cotton sheets behind hand-
painted privacy screens. Five hours later, they were awakened by coffee served on a silver tray and fresh-baked
croissants.

The bathroom was cramped but contained a miniature shower. Wally came out toweling her hair and
announced, "I'm busy making a list of everything I
didn't know I needed until right now."

They landed in a fog so thick they saw nothing until
touch-down. Terrance peered through the soup. Waiting
upon the tarmac was an elderly gentleman standing
beside a vintage Bentley.

The old man stepped forward as the steward released
the stairs. Only then could they get a clear look at his
face. Wally halted Terrance with a hand to his arm.
"That isn't my guy."

Terrance waved the steward away. "What are you telling me?"

"The suit. He's not who I called." Wally took another worried glance beyond Terrance. "My guess is, we're looking at our guy's boss."

"So? This is good, isn't it?"

"I don't know what it is. I don't like changes in plan. Especially not this one." Wally had the tight look of taking aim. "This deal is my ticket out. The score that is going to get me out of the hole once and for all."

The gentleman halted at the base of the plane's stairs and called up, "I'm looking for a Mr. Terrance d'Arcy."

Terrance asked her, "Aren't we overreacting a little here?"

"Maybe." Wally squinted through the grim day. "But where's my guy, that's what I want to know."

The gentleman called, "I say—"

Terrance ducked under the doorway. "I'm d'Arcy."

"And right on time. How splendid." The man's smile was far brighter than the overcast day. "Josef Loupe, at your service."

The air was heavy with a chill foretaste of rain. Terrance met the outstretched hand as he stepped off the bottom stair. The skin was papery with age, but the muscles underneath were firm. "How do you do."

"Such an honor, Mr. d'Arcy. I have so looked forward to this encounter." He bowed slightly over Terrance's hand, in the manner of bygone courtiers, then indicated a uniformed gentleman waiting two steps back. "If I might trouble you for your passports, we can make your arrival official."

As the customs officer leafed through their passports, Terrance inspected their contact. Josef Loupe wore a camel-hair overcoat draped across what once had been very powerful shoulders. Now he had a scarecrow's frame and a face to match. Up close, the smile revealed capped teeth so white they appeared painted. The man's age was impossible to tell. Somewhere between sixty and eighty, with a calculated tan and eyes dead as cold tar. He chatted lightly through the process. "Such is the pleasure of private aircraft these days. No queues, no intrusive inspections. One lands far from the tourist hordes and is treated with proper respect. You cannot put a price on such items. Either you can afford it, or you cannot."

The officer demanded, "What is the purpose of your visit to England?"

"Just a quick stopover before continuing on to Jersey."

"How long do you intend to remain in the United Kingdom?"

"Not long. A day."

Loupe cleared his throat. "Regrettably, events might require you to remain here a bit longer."

Behind Terrance, Wally huffed as though taking a blow to the gut. Terrance glanced over. Wally refused to meet his eye.

"I should think three days would be more than adequate," Loupe went on.

The officer stamped both passports, then nodded at the cases that the steward had set on the tarmac. "Anything to declare?"

"Nothing."

He handed Terrance both passports. "Enjoy your stay."

Terrance waited until the officer was well away to say, "We were expecting to be met by someone else."

"Your contact is seeing to matters in Portsmouth."

"Matters?"

"A temporary setback, nothing more." Loupe indicated the waiting limo. "I shall endeavor to explain everything once we are underway."

The car was a vintage Bentley with a front end long as a polished blue locomotive. Terrance let the elderly man settle him into a seat soft as rarefied butter. Loupe slipped the overcoat from his shoulders and handed it to his aide. The attendant was neither tall nor big, but carried himself with a pent-up menace. His face was professionally blank, his motions as tightly silent as a panther. Wally watched while Loupe's man loaded their bags, then climbed into the front seat. She never looked directly at Loupe. The old man did not seem to register her on his radar. Terrance heard Wally sigh as she shut her door. Her disengaged attitude was more irritating than worrisome.

The Bentley's rear compartment was so spacious Terrance could stretch out his legs and still not touch the front seat. Terrance faced a triple set of television screens set in sterling silver frames, with clocks to either side. A bar extended to form a tongue of walnut burl. On it rested a coffee service and a silver tray holding magazines and the day's *Financial Times*. Loupe indicated the coffee service. "May I offer you something?"

"It's not necessary."

"No, please. I insist." The faintest tremor touched his hands as he filled the delicate porcelain cup.

The Bentley pulled through the airport's security gates and powered away so smoothly the coffee did not even sway in the cup. "Where are you from?"

"Ah. The accent. Over fifty years in this country, and still I talk like an immigrant."

Terrance leaned back and took a sip. Perfect. "On the contrary, your English is better than mine."

"You are too kind. I came to England in 1947. Before that time, I carried the same name as the town where I was born. Josef Lubavitch. You have heard of it?"

"No. Sorry."

"No matter. It was a place of mud and misery. Stalin should have destroyed it. He started to, then stopped. Don't ask me why." He gave an old man's smile this time, a thinning of his lips. Perhaps the first genuine gesture Terrance had seen from him. "When I was fourteen I began fighting in Stalin's army. Just another child soldier meant to feed war's ravenous maw. We all were given different names, part of building camaraderie in the face of coming defeat. I was known as Loupe, French for *wolf*."

Loupe opened the door beneath the coffee service and offered Terrance a linen napkin. There was an elegant servitude to his gestures, a subtle layer of messages. He unpacked sandwiches and set two on a bone china plate. The bread was white and cut very thin and the crusts had been trimmed away. Terrance was not hungry. But he did not refuse. The old man's actions were not about food.

"My battalion commandant was a rarity, a nobleman who had survived Stalin's purges by being the most fervent Communist alive. As a youth he had spent his summers taking the waters at Cannes. He returned to fight alongside his Russian brothers. As I said, a genuine fanatic. He liked to sprinkle his addresses with French. He said it added a certain dignity to our cause."

Loupe placed a pair of sandwiches on a second plate and settled back into his seat. He did not touch the food either. "He was an absurd figure, no doubt. Standing in a wilderness of mud and death, draped in a tattered uniform and waving a bayonet because his saber had been broken on a helmet or a rifle or a tank. We were all dressed in rags. Our boots we had stolen off the bodies of fallen comrades. We were starving, of course. That is what I remember most about my war years. The hunger. That and the smell. The odor of a battlefield is so fierce it leaves you unable to taste anything fully ever again. I was always famished. When I arrived in London I weighed one hundred and nine pounds. I was twenty-three years old."

Terrance leaned forward far enough to set the plate down on the newspaper. Wally stared straight ahead, apparently blind and deaf to all that surrounded her. In a flash of insight, Terrance understood her disconnectedness. This was no run-down tenement in a city she knew. They were surrounded by an alien level of luxury, hosted by a gentleman of the old school. The woman was utterly out of her element. Which, truth be told, suited Terrance just fine. He was the master performer when it came to power and privilege. This was his realm.

"Newly arrived in England," Loupe continued, "I assumed I was invincible. After all, I had survived the Nazis and the Reds. But Stalin was not my worst enemy, Mr. d'Arcy. Time is such a subtle foe. You think you have mastered everything. But in the end, time always wins. Look at me. Seventy-four, no sons, no one I can trust with my business. So a mistake has been made, and I must personally travel out to meet you, and apologize."

Terrance set his coffee cup down. "Tell me what happened."

"I assure you, Mr. d'Arcy, we took your request most seriously. I sent two good men to cover this job. I had formerly considered them to be some of my most reliable people."

Loupe's accent was such a subtle shading it was almost lost behind his careful diction. Clearly the man had spent a fortune on elocution. "They failed?"

"An utter shambles." No amount of plastic surgery could fully hide the creases of concern. "Your man is alive and back in England."

Rain began falling heavily. The only sounds inside the Bentley were the gentle thunking of the wipers and Loupe's recounting of the foiled attack. The two people occupying the front seats remained motionless. Wally might as well have been turned to dark-haired stone.

"The only bit of good news is that your man has not come close to the Jersey bank. My men are now stationed there twenty-four hours of the day." Loupe mused to the side window. "I am thinking that perhaps I might leave them there on permanent assignment as punishment for having failed us."

The Bentley pulled through an arched stone gate and entered the grounds of a palatial hotel. "Where is our man now?" Terrance asked.

"We are doing our utmost to determine that, Mr. d'Arcy. And I can assure you that there will be no second failure. I intend to personally ensure that everything is done according to our agreement. And done swiftly." Loupe nodded as the bellhop opened his door and bid them welcome. "We'll give you a night to recover from your journey, and tomorrow we shall go on the attack."

VAL PLACED THE CALL FROM THE CHEERLESS FRONT
room of a run-down guesthouse, just another weary brick
rowhouse in a street by the port. The front room had a
small television set by the windows overlooking the
street. The program was something about gardening. A
trio of truckers snored beerily from the sofa, the grime
and fatigue of constant travel a stain as deep as their tattoos. The wall clock claimed it was only nine, but the
night felt eons old. Val sat in an alcove formed by remov-
ing the door from a rear closet. The walls were carpeted
and smelled of ten thousand cigarettes. The telephone
was brown plastic and had a counter that counted down
the seconds remaining before he had to feed in more
coins. Val unfurled the rumpled page with Audrey's
number and dialed.

"Hello?"

"It's me, Audrey. I'm sorry to be calling so late."

Her tone instantly went frigid. "Did you do it?"

"Not the four hundred million like they're saying."

"That's not what I asked. Did you or did you not steal
money from the company?"

"This is not the sort of greeting I was expecting."

"I take that as a yes."

Her voice was so arctic Val felt it necessary to beg. "Don't hang up. Please."

"You of all people. Never in a million years would I have thought you capable of such a thing. Why ever did you do it?"

"I don't remember."

"Hardly the most brilliant of excuses."

"I was sort of hoping for a different reception. You know. After your letter."

"Forget the letter, Val. That was before."

"Before what?"

"Just put the letter down as the ramblings of a distraught woman. Pay it no mind."

Val's pay telephone beeped a warning signal. The slot where he fed in coins was stubborn, as though even the apparatus was trying to tell him it was a mistake to have called. "How did you know? About my taking the money, I mean."

"Don't be daft. Terrance is my brother, remember? His forte is finding another's weakness and going on the attack." She paused, then asked, "Where are you?"

"Portsmouth. The Seaside Bed and Breakfast on Wyckham Lane." Val felt her uncertain silence compress and squeeze. Leaving him no way out. "I really need your help, Audrey."

"You're stubborn enough to think you're doing the right thing when you're only causing further harm. Which is precisely why I have to see you, I suppose. To ensure you don't make matters worse than they already are."

She hung up on him then. A new first. As far as he could remember.

The street held the night in a narrow embrace made slick by rain. A car coughed apologetically as it passed, the tires slicing dark rivulets along the asphalt. Val could have remained inside. But the guesthouse stank of the landlady's constant cigarettes and the guests' bleak weariness. Val had no idea whether Audrey would show up. He decided to wait for a time before letting the bed claim him. He extracted Audrey's letter from his pocket, his movements slow. It was not that he wished for more of her instruction. He simply found comfort in unfolding the well-creased pages. The words revealed a woman who thought well of him. The knowledge of love, even one now past, warmed his bones.

Val raised his gaze to find Audrey leaning against a car. She observed him with crossed arms and a hostile expression. The truth was, whatever she wanted to hit him with, he probably deserved it. He showed her the pages and said, "Your letter has meant an awful lot."

Audrey bit off the words very carefully. "I suppose it's my nature to reach out. Even when the cause is utterly lost."

Val was determined not to offer her a reason to rage. He stowed the letter away and rose to his feet. "I just want you to know how grateful I am."

She stabbed the air between them with a blade of a hand. "I want one thing understood right here at the outset. You are not to try and draw me back in again."

Val remained mute, while his heart keened at her closeness and the distance between them.

Audrey opened her door and slipped behind the wheel. "I suppose you'd better come along."

"Where are we going?"

"Home."

"Are you sure that's—"

She started the engine and jammed down on the gas pedal, drowning out his protest. "Just get in the car."

———

Her automobile was a vintage Rover, a boxy vehicle turned an indeterminate grey by the night and age. Val felt as though he knew the car, which was impossible, for he had never seen Audrey in England before. Of that he was certain, and little else. "Why did you come for me?"

"You'd prefer I leave you for my brother to devour?" The car had an oversized steering wheel of hard plastic, which Audrey constantly kneaded. When Val did not respond, she finally said, "The police came by."

"Why would they want to talk with you?"

"Not me. My father. This could not have come at a worse time for him."

Val took this for the male voice on the phone, and breathed easier. "Is he sick?"

"Dying, actually." The words caught in a throat clenched taut. For the first time her stern facade cracked slightly. "The cancer has spread to his lymph nodes."

"I'm so sorry, Audrey."

"Everything that is good in me I owe to him." She spoke with determined matter-of-factness, and patted the steering wheel. "Even this old dear of a car."

"You went back to care for him?"

Her tone hardened instantly. "I left because you ordered me to go."

Passing headlights painted her in brief flashes. She

looked so strong, so vibrant. Val could see so much of Terrance in her, the same determined set to her features, the same brilliant luster to the hair. But in Terrance everything was tainted. Never was Terrance's twisted state more evident than now. "Tell me about the police."

"They came with some dreadful man in grey from the American embassy. He had some official title, I don't recall what." Audrey's gaze reminded him of a lifetime seafarer. Her eyes appeared focused upon some infinite horizon. Even when she was looking at him. Like now. "They claim Pop was behind the theft."

"Why would Terrance take aim at his own father?"

"You've forgotten all our discussions?"

"I don't remember a lot of things."

"In this case it's perhaps for the better. My family's history no longer concerns you. You're here because we have to stop him before he does further damage to a fine, dear man."

Hastings preserved its medieval village charm even at night. Gas lamps lined the thoroughfares rising from the rocky beach. Tudor houses marched in complacent camaraderie up the steep slope. Beyond the market square and the ancient church tower glistened a holiday port. The sea had the radiant quality of oiled silk. The rain had stopped. Audrey waited until she parked in front of a thatched-roof house with walls of wattle and blackened beams to ask, "Did Terrance do that to your head?"

"Not directly, no." He did not hurt in any particular place so much as throb in general. Residual jet lag mixed with the day's battering to form a potent mixture. "Where are we?"

"My father's house."

"This is a terrible idea, Audrey. Terrance's hired goons

attacked me on the boat to Jersey. They're probably still on the island hunting for me. But there could be others."

She said in a tightly compressed voice, "You were just going to sail away, weren't you?"

"I was hoping you'd . . ." The closed door behind her eyes stopped him in midflow. He changed direction to, "Terrance has muscle on my trail. I don't know how they tracked me to the boat, but they did. This wasn't just some random attack. They wanted to kill me."

"I should have known. This is what you were planning all along, wasn't it? This was why you stole." Her face took on the pinched quality of having received the worst possible news. "Val, there is only one way to die to the past and all its burdens and mistakes. Stealing money and running away is not it."

"Please, Audrey, listen to what I'm saying. Terrance knows about us. Sooner or later they'll come here looking for me."

"Oh, why on earth do I bother? You wouldn't listen to me then. Change was your worst enemy. Why should now be any different?" She rose from the car and slammed the door. Her shoes clicked an angry pace up the stone walk. She unlocked the door and entered without a backward glance.

Casting worried glances behind him, Val followed her inside. The home's interior was as charming as outside. Beams thicker than his chest laced overhead. The floor was polished tongue-and-groove planking two hands broad. Val guessed the wood was oak, but centuries of polish had masked the grain. Antique brass candelabra had been refashioned to hold lightbulbs. The windows were squared with lead, the panes hand-blown and so old they had run like clear honey. Lamplight danced a soft tune upon antique furniture and a stone fireplace large enough to contain a bench and cooking station. The rooms smelled of beeswax and a roast.

She was already busy in the kitchen. Audrey said through the framed partition separating her from the living room, "Do you think you might possibly delay running away by a few days?"

"First I need to find someplace where you won't be endangered."

She waved at him with the carving knife. "Let's move beyond that, shall we? Are you or are you not going to help us stop Terrance?"

"Who is we?"

She finished slicing a lamb roast into thick slabs and began slapping hot English mustard on fresh bread. "Answer my question."

Val felt something ugly and unwelcome crawl around in his gut. Terrance had outmaneuvered him very badly. The attackers on the boat had terrified him. His entire focus had been on one single tactic. Cut and run.

Audrey's attitude became clear to him now. His conception of this woman and her state were entirely wrong. She was not pining away for him. Nor was she planning to help him escape. She had brought him here with the exact opposite in mind. And she was worried he would let her down.

Again.

The kettle whistled behind her. She moved with the efficient motions of an experienced chef, drawing out plates and saucers and cups, fixing a pot of tea, slicing fresh lemon, squeezing it into one cup, stirring in two heaping spoonfuls of sugar. Reaching through the partition and setting it on the counter for him. Val stared at the steaming mug. He was far less sure what he wanted than Audrey was.

"Go tell Father his tea is ready. No doubt you'll find him in the garden."

Nighttime had been banished from the rear of the house. Spotlights were fastened to the back wall, and others embedded in the garden soil. A postage stamp of a lawn was rimmed by flowers that sparkled from the recent storm. The perimeter wall was fifteen feet high and made from brick so old it was crumbling. The garden was on fire with color.

Arthur d'Arcy puttered by the back wall and hummed a single faltering note, a soft message that his entire universe was bordered by these brick walls. Val stood in the doorway, breathing in the scent of tilled earth and an evening stolen from some softer season. Overhead he spotted a first star.

"Mr. d'Arcy?"

"Eh? Yes?" The old man slowly rose from his stoop. "Ah. You're Audrey's young man."

Val watched him ease up in very gradual stages. The hand holding the trowel was slightly curved, like a bird's claw, and pressed tightly against the base of his ribcage. "Audrey says your tea is ready."

"Splendid." He set the trowel down by the flowers he was planting and stripped off his gloves. "The weather has been positively atrocious, wouldn't you agree?"

Val pointed to where roses the size of pink dinner plates climbed the rear wall. "Those are some amazing flowers."

"Yes, my high walls trap the spring heat. That is, when there is any sun at all." His walk was not quite a limp, but he carefully favored his left side. "But those roses have very little to do with me, I'm afraid. I trim them back each November and till in a bit of bone meal every spring. The rest is up to God and nature. Have a look at the stems where they emerge from the earth. Thick around as your thigh, they are. I wouldn't care to hazard a guess how long they've been standing sentry there by my wall, doing their proper duty each and every spring."

D'Arcy smiled at Val as he took the back steps one at a time. "Pity not all of life follows such a proper course, wouldn't you agree?"

Val matched his pace to the older man's and followed him back inside. The home's ease relaxed him so thoroughly that, in his already weakened state, he had trouble lifting his feet over the top step.

Arthur d'Arcy washed his hands in the kitchen sink and asked his daughter, "What has he determined?"

Audrey kept her gaze on her work. "Val hasn't said."

The two of them stood by the back window, eating their sandwiches and sipping tea in the companionable silence of people who had long since left behind the need for empty chatter. Val's provisions were stationed on the kitchen's other side, a silent message that he was relegated to the fringe.

Arthur reported to his daughter, "Gerald phoned you."

"What did he say?"

"That he was back and he had your message." Arthur held his cup out for refilling. "He said if you were absolutely certain, he would go along."

Audrey cut Val with a glance, but said nothing.

Val stared through the partition to the empty living room. An ancient anger barely managed to flicker up through the blanket of fatigue. But he knew it was there, banked up and hidden behind the same walls that kept out most of his memories.

Val turned around. He could hear weariness gum up his words, but could do nothing about it. "What exactly is it you want?"

Arthur smiled slightly, then buried it in his cup.

His daughter replied. "Terrance drained the British company's pension fund. He has blamed it on my father. Now we learn that the plant is due for closure."

"Spun off, I believe is the word they're using." Arthur shrugged. "The employees will be left penniless. This simply cannot be permitted."

"They're going to blame it on Dad. They've said he might be brought up on charges."

"Hardly a major concern," Arthur replied. "Given my current state."

"I won't let that happen."

Val stared down at his hands. He knew what the next step should be. Not even the weight bearing down on his eyelids could keep that out. He told them, "I need access to a computer wired into the company system."

"Listen to you," Audrey said. "You're asleep on your feet."

Arthur drained his cup. "Gerald should be able to arrange that."

"Who's Gerald?"

"A chief engineer at the company," Arthur explained. "Splendid chap. My former protégé."

"You'll be staying at his place." Audrey slipped her keys off the counter. "Safer for us all."

Arthur went on, "I won't have this turned into a vendetta against my son."

"Pop, please."

"This is about saving the livelihoods of hundreds of good men and women. People I have worked and lived with for years. People who trust me. I can't let them down. But I will not be party to a lynching of my firstborn."

Audrey slipped by Val without actually looking his way. "We've been all through this."

Arthur waved that away. "Mind what I say. This can't be about attacking Terrance. No matter what he's done. Two wrongs have never been known to make a right."

THE NEXT MORNING'S HIGHWAY WAS A SWIFT-RUNNING
trench six lanes wide. The weather made no difference to
British driving patterns. The Bentley kept to the middle
lane and drilled through the dismal day at a steady eighty-
five kilometers per hour. The spray formed sheets higher
than the car. The car behind them was less than five feet
back. The Bentley was even closer to the one ahead.
Trucks hemmed them to the left, a Porsche hammered
past on their right. Inside the Bentley, it was so quiet
Terrance could hear the clock ticking in the distant front
dash, the chunking sound of the wipers, the quiet hum of
the bar's refrigerator.

Terrance knew he should be highly worried about
this turn of events. But he could not get beyond his
sense that he was seated by a true professional. Loupe's
features were mottled with age spots, but he handled
himself like a prince. His voice was as solicitous as it
had been the previous day. Loupe inquired if Terrance
was hungry, if there was anything further that might be
done for his comfort. Terrance knew he was on the
receiving end of a charm offensive. And did not mind in
the least. Wally remained stonelike in the front seat.
Terrance did not mind this either. He was in control

now. Let her play the dutiful servant until her skills were required.

Portsmouth struck Terrance as the epitome of all that was wrong with England's towns. The highway clogged as it fed into a frenetic ring road. The rain was blowing in hard off the sea now, dissolving colors and turning the town a shade of industrial grey. The driver's phone chirped as he maneuvered through a traffic-snarled roundabout. He raised his voice to announce, "They might have found something, Boss."

"Ah, a welcome gift for our arrival. Don't you agree?" He flashed the chalky teeth. "Take us there."

The street was a weary Victorian hedge against the tides of upward mobility. The houses marched down either side of a narrow lane, each with a front garden the size of a welcome mat. The houses were all brick, all leaning tightly against one another, with cars crammed down the road almost as firmly as the homes. A pair of hardfaced professionals left their sentry duty by the front door of a bed-and-breakfast. They stepped forward and did homage to Joe Loupe, giving little bows and deferential murmurs. Wally rose from her car seat but did not move forward with the others. She stared at nothing, was recognized by no one. Just a hard-faced woman standing at the edge of the action.

An older woman appeared in the bed-and-breakfast's doorway. She greeted all this commotion with a raspy cough and fished in her sweater for a cigarette. "Any you gents spare a light?"

The driver flicked open a gold lighter and held it for her. She thanked him with another cough. Ashes formed intricate grey swirls on the front of her cardigan, surrounding a multitude of burn holes. The woman was

greasy and unkempt. Up close, Terrance could see the
pink bald skin beneath hair of woven glass. "Like I told
the gents, your honor, I didn't see a thing."

"But surely you must recognize one of your own
guests."

"The blokes that come here, they ain't after being recognized. They want a stroll to the bar, a quiet kip, a slap-up
breakfast, and they're off." She dragged in about a third of
her cigarette. "The less I ask, the more they'll come back.
That's the way it is these days, your honor."

"Of course, my dear lady. You do what you must."

"The only reason I noticed him at all is on account of
how he's taken a room and dusted off already. Didn't take
no breakfast."

The muscle confirmed, "His room's empty."

Loupe lifted one hand. Instantly the muscle passed
over a photograph. "Just have one more look at this,
would you please?"

She reluctantly glanced over. "Like I told your blokes,
they come, they go. It mighta been him."

"I find a bit of cash can do marvels for the memory. A
veritable wonder drug, don't you agree?" He pressed the
photo closer still. "Say, a hundred pounds?"

The woman had clearly been waiting for this. "Said
his name was Adams. The bloke sounded American."

"Did he, now? How very splendid." He motioned to his
driver. "Pay the dear lady. Now then, you see? We have
established a line of communication. Might there be anything else you could share with us?"

"For another hundred knicker?"

"I pay for what I receive, dear lady. You bear witness to
that."

"He made a call."

"From your own line?"

"Separate. Got it set up in the front parlor for my guests."

"A pay phone, is it? And you receive a list of all calls made, don't you?"

She pretended a casual shrug. "I suppose I could print you out a page."

"How very splendid. Michael?"

When the money was handed over, she extracted a well-creased page from a pocket big as a pouch. She pointed with a yellow-stained finger. "That's the one. Down there at the bottom. Last call but one going out."

Terrance craned forward, though he already knew what he would find. One glance was enough. "That's our man." He turned and stamped away. A dozen paces beyond the Bentley, he pulled out his cell phone and dialed.

Don came instantly on the line. "What?"

"It's me."

"And?"

"Val is still on the loose."

Don huffed quietly. Again. Then, "This cannot be happening."

"He took the boat to Jersey. They had two hit men stalking him. Val got away. He hid on the boat, didn't get off at all, and returned to England."

Don's voice kept to a light musicality. Despite the late hour, Don must have already been on public display. "Let me get this straight. We're down here spreading out all our evidence, which they are all taking as solid gospel, let me tell you. We're claiming Val Haines has managed to slip away with $422 million. Boom. He's gone. They are raking through this with electron microscopes and

SEC sniffer hounds, looking for some way to tie us in and drop us in the pit."

"The inspectors are with you now?"

"Inspectors, auditors, external counsel, we have an army of suits in here. The entire office building is smelling blood. Their own. So my job is to walk around pretending that everything is just fine. Which they know is absolute fabrication." His breaths were tight little wisps. But his words kept coming out light as air. Terrance could imagine the rictus grin he was wearing. "We're spinning our tales and they're swallowing our bait. I'm singing and I'm dancing and I'm lying with every breath. And everything depends on this one thing going down. Everything. Our lives, our futures, our money. And you're telling me this guy is *on the loose?*"

"I know where he is."

"So tell."

"Hastings."

"You mean, he's headed for our plant in Hastings?"

"That would be my guess."

"What for?"

"He'll try to access the company system. Break into our own files. See what's up."

"Can he do that?"

"Maybe."

"This is not the answer I need to hear."

"He oversaw installation of the system related to the pension department. People have always liked Val, you know that as well as I do. It's possible our in-house nerds told him about a backdoor."

"A what?"

"Software engineers often insert hidden entries into their systems. They're called backdoors. Supposedly they can be used for ongoing repairs. Often it's just to show how smart they are. If Val was told about one, he could use it to access our data no matter what firewalls I insert around the standard entry points."

"That *cannot* happen."

"You need to have our IT people cut Hastings off entirely. The computer system needs to be completely disengaged. No interoffice traffic in any guise."

Don's pause was microseconds long. "Done. Now what are you going to do about the crisis?"

"I'm on it."

"Hastings is a town, right? There's a lot of places where he can hide in a town."

Terrance pushed a fist into his gut, trying to still the churning nausea. "I know where he's headed."

"You're sure?"

"He's had a thing with my sister."

"If we weren't talking about our collective futures, I'd be laughing out loud." Don paused a long moment, then, "What I need to know right here, right now, is this. Can you handle what needs handling?"

"And I'm telling you I am on top of this."

"What if he gets to the bank? Can he access the funds?"

"His, yes. But not ours."

"You're sure of that? Absolutely certain? I'm asking, you know, on account of my neck is on the chopping block here."

"You have a set of access codes. I have the other. Yours are in your bank's safety deposit box. Mine are in the microcomputer in my briefcase. Those are the only sets. Nobody else has any connection whatsoever. So that is not the problem here. That is not what we have to be focusing on."

"Val."

"If he shows up at the bank, Syntec will inform New York, New York will go ballistic, and we are *dead*. Josef has two men stationed permanently on the island to see that doesn't happen."

"Who?"

"Our ally over here. Never mind."

"This the same ally who didn't get him like he was supposed to when he arrived? This is a reason to trust him?"

Terrance cut the connection and stalked back to the car. The rain was so light as to drift in the air, settling on nothing, drenching everything. Josef stood smiling slightly and smoking a cigar. He waved it in Terrance's direction. "Would you care for a panatela?"

"No. Thanks." He panted from the strain. Don's frantic state had seeped through the phone like a viscous acid. Terrance hated this day. This place. This seedy district of weary houses and rain too disdainful to even fall correctly. People with worn-down faces. Air that smelled of sea and industry and dense hopelessness. Terrance wiped the moisture from his face. "You just better not fail again."

Wally was leaning on the Bentley's front end. She rolled her eyes at Terrance, shook her head, and slid into the seat. Taking up the position again, eyes front, seeing nothing.

The boss casually rolled his cigar's glowing end around his fingernail. Terrance saw how the repeated act had charred a slender half-moon, staining it like a blooded talon. Josef asked, "Shouldn't there be an 'or else' after that little statement?"

"I need this job done."

"Of course you do. But it seems a bit odd, a gentleman like yourself taking such a tone with the only man in England who's able to offer a helping hand." Loupe gave Terrance a look, his eyes holding nothing at all. Just dead air.

Terrance sensed something behind him, like an unseen furnace door had opened. He knew without turning that the driver had stalked up with a predator's silence, moving in tight. He resisted the urge to glance back. "I need this man to vanish immediately."

"That's why we're all here together, now, isn't it? To make sure I live up to my part of the bargain." The man dropped his half-finished cigar to the road, where it sizzled and died, and reached for Terrance's arm. "Shall we continue with our little journey?"

Terrance let Josef steer him around. To his astonishment, the driver was by the car, holding open the door, giving him that same blank mask. Only now there was a different face to the day, as though he could peel away the soft, rich facade and hear a faint scream. At least it was Val's pain he was hearing. He was fairly certain of that.

AN HOUR AFTER RISING WITH THE DAWN, VAL KNEW HIS
plan was futile. Even so, he remained where he was, isolated in his host's home office, listening to the house come
alive around him. Gerald was a production engineer working the line at Insignia. Like most engineers, his home
computer was hardwired into the company system. Even
so, Val did not have a chance to even try his backdoors.
The UK computer system had effectively been frozen out.

Sunlight pierced the house with an unfamiliar tone.
Val took his empty mug back to the kitchen. Three men
sat at the table, their morning chatter silenced by his
appearance. The atmosphere was stale as the over-
cooked coffee. Val poured himself a mug and retreated
to the office.

He stood by the side window and sipped at coffee
stewed to its bitter dregs. He watched as Audrey's dilapi-
dated Rover pulled up to the curb. Val found himself
unable to walk out and greet her. Instead, he touched
Audrey's letter through the fabric of his shirt, as he would
a talisman.

When the doorbell rang, a burly middle-aged man
emerged from the kitchen. He opened the front door and
greeted her with, "All right, love?"

"Hello, Bert." Audrey's voice held to a comfortable burr. "Everyone behaving themselves?"

The big man liked that in the manner of old friends. "Looks like we should be asking you that one."

Gerald walked down the hall from the kitchen. He gave Val a single glance through the open office doorway, then bussed Audrey on the cheek. Gerald was lean and taut in build, with hair one shade off blond. He had pianist's hands, long and supple and very strong looking. He wore a button-down Oxford shirt of pale blue and had three pens in his breast pocket. Everything about him shouted engineer.

Audrey said quietly, "Thank you, Gerald."

"Glad to help," he said, but he cut Val another look that suggested something else.

"Have you discussed things yet?"

"We decided it was best to wait for you."

"All right." Audrey finally acknowledged Val, but showed him nothing. "Did you sleep well?"

"Fine, thanks."

"Perhaps we should get started."

Val felt Gerald's gaze steady and hard on him as he followed the others into the front parlor. A third man entered through the kitchen. Dillon was younger than the others but bore the same scarred rigidity as Bert. Val stationed himself by the doorway, giving himself an out in case the natives turned hostile.

Gerald's home was a bachelor's sort of place—monochrome carpet, bare walls, functional furniture. A pair of mismatched sofas were permanently reshaped by the bodies lodged there. Pastel drapes framed windows pleading dustily for a good cleaning. Val saw a lot of his own dwelling space in how Gerald lived.

Gerald selected a hard-backed chair by the empty fireplace and asked, "Is it true what they say, that they're closing us down?"

Audrey replied, "I don't have anything definite. But the rumors seem pretty conclusive."

"What about our pensions?" Evidently Gerald was their appointed spokesman. "Is that true?"

"Yes. I'm afraid it is."

"Someone has stolen from them?"

Audrey gave Val the resigned expression of one knowing it had to come out. Val said, "Not someone. Terrance d'Arcy."

Gerald asked Audrey, "Your brother has tapped into our pension fund?"

She nodded at Val, who replied for her, "Not tapped. Drained. Terrance has effectively stolen it all. Or enough so that everything else will go to the company's creditors."

"What about us?"

"There are always other liens and priority claims on a pension fund. Legally, pension holders are the last in line. They have no secured interest. It's wrong, but that's the way it is."

"You're telling me that Insignia is going to shut us down and we won't have any pension to tide us over?"

"That pretty much sums it up."

Audrey nodded at him once more. Val took a very hard breath and added, "I stole from the fund as well."

Gerald looked at Audrey again. His voice was perplexed. "You've been keeping the torch for a thief?"

"Val isn't a thief."

"Excuse me, love, but you heard him the same as I."

"I know what he said." Audrey met Val with an unwavering gaze. "But Val Haines is not a thief."

Gerald crossed his arms across his chest. Holding himself back bunched his shoulders and corded the muscles in his neck.

The large man seated on the sofa asked Val, "What'd you do that for, mate?"

"I don't remember."

Gerald snorted. A quiet puff of sound, there and gone. Like a coiled spring wound tight for far too long.

"I had an accident. I suffer from amnesia. I remember parts now. But not everything. I know I stole from the fund. Maybe it was just to get away. I remember telling someone that. But it doesn't fit. I can't figure out why I'd go against everything just to . . ."

The gazes around the room and the struggle to remember felt like fists squeezing his head. Val knew the reason was there. He could almost fit the pieces together. He pushed at his temples with the palms of both hands, adding to the external force. He lifted his gaze. It wasn't coming. He said, "I'm sorry."

Gerald snorted again. He jerked his chin at Val. "This is the best we've got?"

"He's our only hope," Audrey replied.

Gerald kicked at the wall behind him with one heel. Softly. Just releasing a bit of the excess steam.

Bert said from his place on the sofa, "Well, all right, then."

Gerald wasn't ready to let it go just yet. "What chance do we have of getting back what's owed us?"

"Slim to none." Val was not going to lie. Not anymore. "But I think we should try."

"Oh, and it's 'we' now, is it?"

"Gerald," Audrey said quietly.

The taut man looked down at his floor and went back to kicking the wall.

Audrey rose and gave Val a fraction of a head motion. The two hard-faced men watched him depart with blank stares. She exited the house by the front door and started down the street. As Val fell into step beside her, Audrey took an intense aim at something on the far horizon. She cupped her elbows with her palms and walked stiffly. Their footsteps formed the only discordant note to a lovely sunlit lane.

The previous evening, Audrey had driven him up the steep lane leading away from the medieval town and the sea. She had driven west about twenty minutes, to where a housing estate sprawled around an aging industrial park. Gerald's unassuming house was made spectacular by its setting. Two dozen modest homes fronted a narrow lane marking the industrial township's outer boundary. Behind the houses stretched an expanse of English myth, a great bowl of highland pasture shining in pristine splendor. Rising in the far distance was a steep-sided hill with veins white as old bones.

"Where are we?"

"The border to the downs." But Audrey paid no attention to her surroundings. "Your plan failed, didn't it? I can see it in your face."

Val explained what he had tried to do. "I should have known Terrance would have shut down the company's systems."

"What can we do?"

"I'm working on that." He gestured behind him. "They don't want me here."

"What do you expect? A stranger from head office declares they're about to lose their jobs and that he's stolen from a pension fund that won't pay them a farthing?" She took hold of the fence. "Those are good men, Val."

"The two guys look like they've had a hard life."

"Bert and Dillon have both done time, yes. I met them through my work. They're friends now." She leaned heavily upon the words. "Good men, the both of them."

"Gerald thinks a lot of you."

"It seems like the entire town is busy making sure I am fully aware of that. We met in an Alpha course I'm teaching at the church. You've heard of Alpha?"

"I don't—"

"Remember. Of course. How convenient."

"It's the truth."

More than the morning light tightened her gaze as she inspected him. "Did you truly believe you could actually leave it all behind?"

The pressure mounted again, her words squeezing at him, working to dislodge what he could not quite grasp. "I thought . . ."

"Yes?"

"That you might come with me."

The message was clear in her gaze long before she spoke. "What tore us apart before is still there between us now."

There were a hundred things he could say. But he remained trapped in the moment, staring at someone who had once cared for him deeply. Despite all the worries and unanswered questions, he felt his life constrict to this lane, the rusted old fence fronting the downs, the birdsong, the sunlight that turned the pastures into a green mirror, these words, this love. How could he have ever left her? "Audrey—"

Whatever she saw in his gaze was enough to make her grateful when someone called from the house. Audrey stepped away. "We'd best go see what's got them stirred up."

The men said nothing to Val as he entered. But the way they watched him was clear as an oath. Bert said, "Something's happening inside the town, love. Something bad."

"Is it Terrance?"

Bert motioned to his younger mate in the doorway. "Tell her."

Dillon carried himself with the hardness of streetwise life. "A mate's just come off the hotel's early shift. These men show up, not your basic run-of-the-mill toughs."

"What do you mean?"

"He means trouble, love." Bert was a hard man with the grime of years ingrained in his gaze and his voice. "Trouble that don't bear thinking about."

"One of them was an older guy with a funny sort of accent." The young man looked pained by his news. "Another was a Yank."

"Terrance?"

"My mate says he looks a lot like you."

Gerald added, "Word's come down from the works. There's been visitors in and out, talking to the dodgy blokes on the shop floor."

"I heard the same." Bert aimed his thumb at Val but kept his gaze on Audrey. "They been asking for the bloke here."

"Did they name him?"

"Not in so many words. But it's him they're after, all right."

Gerald directed his words to Audrey, not Val. "What about the plan you told us he had?"

Val replied, "I can't access headquarters. They've locked the system down tight."

Audrey said, "We'll just have to think of something else."

The room's silence gradually condensed around Val.

Bert was the one who spoke aloud what the men were all thinking. "Say we was to let them have the bloke."

"No," Audrey replied. "Val is our friend."

"He's a thief, Audrey." This from Gerald. "He said it himself."

"No."

"What if . . ." Bert looked at the others, drawing support from two stone-hard faces. "What if they was to offer to give us our due and return the pension money? What then?"

"You don't know Terrance. He'll promise you whatever it is you want to hear. But he'll give you nothing. He'll take what he wants and disappear."

"But if we was to get a guarantee, like."

"Val knows the system. Val is our only hope of making things right." Audrey gathered up her purse and keys. "I have to go see to Father."

"Audrey . . ."

"I'm telling you that we need Val."

The others parted to let her through, but Gerald remained where he was, blocking the hall. "*We* need him, or *you* do?"

"Val has told us nothing but the truth since he arrived. He came up with one possible option. He'll come up with another." She turned to look at him. The others followed her lead. "Won't you?"

Val confirmed, "If Terrance is in town, there is definitely something we can try."

"There, you see?" Audrey started to force her way past, then caught herself. "Terrance is here, Gerald. Father is by himself. I must go."

"Perhaps I should come with you."

"Stay and work out the next step. I won't be long."

Val felt the eyes rake him as he moved down the hall behind her. He waited until they were outside to ask, "You're leaving me here?"

"I told you before, Val. These are good men."

"They'd like to feed me to the wolves." When she continued her march to the car, he asked, "Don't you want to hear what I'm thinking?"

"I'm not the one who needs convincing, Val." She slid behind the wheel. "Go in there and talk with them. I'll be back as soon as I can."

Audrey did something then, a gesture that pained him like a hook through his heart. He realized he had seen her do it many times before. She lifted her chin with a determined jerk and shook her hair back. It tumbled over her shoulders in a burnished cascade. The lines of her face and the cast of her eyes were caught clearly by the sunlight flooding through her open door. Her lips were a translucent wash of palest rose. A determined woman, bearing the weight of so many different things that were both out of her control and not of her liking. Val knew that he looked upon someone far stronger than he would ever be, and far better. The reasons he had insisted upon leaving her were lost. Even worse, they were meaningless. He loved her. He had lost her. The knowledge rocked him forward just as she restarted the motor and shut her door.

He called through her open window, "Audrey . . ."

But she was gone.

WITHIN AN HOUR OF THEIR ARRIVAL IN HASTINGS, THE band of people surrounding the boss had swelled to eleven.

Hastings's finest hotel rose like a grey Victorian wedding cake where the old town met the port. Foppish towers and curlicues adorned the roofline. Flags made a colorful row beneath the second floor window. A doorman in maroon uniform with gold braid stood sentry outside the grand entrance. Josef Loupe had taken the two-bedroom penthouse suite as well as rooms to either side. Sunlight flooded the suite's parlor like a persistent intruder. Terrance stood by the bowed portside windows and observed families at play on the rocky beach. The children raced through the sunshine, chasing seagulls and each other to the water's edge. Many adults still wore street-clothes, their pants legs rolled up and their pale heads covered by handkerchiefs with corners tightened like four white pigtails. A pair of merry-go-rounds with diesel-driven calliopes stood at either end of the beach. Gaily colored stands sold Italian ices and grilled spicy sausages and draft beer. The benches lining the streetside sidewalk were jammed with old people. Families carrying buckets walked along the southern rock wall, searching among the seaweed for cockles. Terrance felt he had entered a time warp where there was no place for him or his ambition.

He turned away. Let the peons have their day in the sun. He was hunting bigger game.

The area around Arthur d'Arcy's home had been staked out, as had the two entrances to the Insignia factory. Insignia employees who pilfered components or sold drugs on the factory floor or shook down the unions had all been contacted. Bribes had been offered. People came in and out of the hotel suite in a fairly constant stream. A house a quarter-mile from the hotel had been rented for Loupe's men. It stood on a cul-de-sac, well removed from its nearest neighbors.

The boss sat in the center of his parlor suite like a cashmere-draped tarantula. He smoked his cigar, talked on the phone, and greeted each of the shadowy newcomers as brethren. Terrance felt encased in an exquisite tension. He observed Loupe's face as through a magnifying glass, seeing every pore, all the avarice hidden beneath that genteel calm. He glanced at Wally, sitting in the far corner by the door leading to the bedroom, smoking a chain of cigarettes and staring at nothing. Terrance found himself pitying her in a mild way.

Loupe turned to him. "Are you sure I can't offer you anything, Mr. d'Arcy? A fresh pot of coffee, perhaps?"

Terrance knew the old man shared his enjoyment of the mounting tension. "I think we should hit the house."

Loupe nodded thoughtfully, as though considering this for the first time. "There are problems. It is a busy street. Your father's home is connected on the south side to its neighbor. Any disturbance is bound to draw the wrong sort of attention. You said yourself we must act with discretion. I assume that has not changed?"

"There is a way." He could feel the words linger on the tongue. Each held a distinct flavor.

Terrance found himself recalling a meal he had once had. A New York waiter had brought a fresh white Italian truffle big as two fists. Using a silver cheese serrator, he had sliced off paper-thin wedges. The truffle had filled the entire restaurant with its perfume. The flavor had been unlike anything Terrance had tasted before. A superb nuttiness, almost musky in texture. An essence as strong as now.

Loupe watched him with eyes of wet agate. "Yes?"

Terrance realized that the man had known all along, and had been waiting for Terrance to make the move. Commit himself. He was, after all, the key. "No one would suspect a son coming to visit his own father."

"You would do this thing?"

"I'll need help."

Loupe smiled benevolently. "You are a man after my own heart, Mr. d'Arcy."

Terrance was almost sorry to draw the moment to a close. "We had better get moving."

———

The air in the town held the same condensed ambiance as the hotel suite. The early wind had completely died. Every sound carried for miles. The sun pounded with uncommon strength upon Terrance's head as he stood on the sidewalk before his father's house. He had never been here before.

The place was exactly as Terrance had envisioned. A proper little slice of England, a miniature castle for a man who had never dared think big. The home was bordered by a front garden the size of a throw rug. Rose petals, the color of dried blood, were scattered across the flagstone path. Terrance turned the polished brass handle. His father had never locked the door to any house they had ever lived in. It was one of the many things that had driven Terrance's mother insane. And rightly so.

Instantly the scents threw him back to the impossible years when he had been young and helpless. Back when his father had elected to destroy Terrance's life. He heard a scraping sound in the kitchen. His nerves began to crawl under his skin like angry electric worms.

His father shuffled into view. He was far older now, yet unchanged. The core of this man was exactly the same. A man who had never known the exquisite thrill of going for a kill. A stranger to his own son.

"I should have known you would come." His father shuffled forward. He favored his right side, as though winded by a long run. "Perhaps I did, and tried to hide it even from myself."

"Where is he?"

His father made no pretense of hiding his knowledge. "Not here."

"That's not what I asked."

"You won't find him."

Terrance glanced at Loupe's driver, standing by the open front door. Wally had elected to stay out front on guard duty. The driver wore his dark hair in a bowl cut plastered tightly to his skull, such that Terrance could see a shallow indentation at its center. The well-cut suit did nothing save accent his wiry strength. "Shut the door."

The man slipped to one side and closed the portal. When Terrance turned back to his father, he saw fear in the old man's gaze. The worms beneath Terrance's skin thrashed about more wildly, feeding upon a lifetime of futile rage. "You think you can save him, is that it?"

In response, his father pulled out a dining room chair and slowly sank down. His gaze went to the floor by his feet and remained there.

Terrance's movements were jerky as he crossed the front room. He could feel his muscles hungering for motion, a driving force to tear and rip and flay. "My entire life has been shaped by your spinelessness. Your futile yearning to avoid conflict of any kind is despicable. You cared so much for your rigid peace, you would sacrifice anything to keep it. Even me. Isn't that true? Isn't it?"

His father said to the floor by his feet. "They tell me you're a thief."

"Who says that—Audrey? Your dear self-righteous freak of a daughter? Why should I care what she says?" Terrance laughed, and to his own ears it sounded like the baying of wolves. It was beyond delicious, this ability to finally release a tiny shard of the loathing for this man he had carried for a lifetime. "What if I am? Who do you think brought me to this point?"

"No one is responsible for your actions but yourself."

"What an utterly typical response. You let your own son languish in poverty rather than stand up for what was my rightful inheritance. You let *my* titles and *my* estate go to the offspring of the *real* thief. And you did it without raising a finger! Why? Because nothing mattered to you except maintaining this figment of your own imagination, this ridiculous sham of an existence."

"That's not true."

"What nonsense." Terrance's panting breaths seared his throat. "Of course I steal! What choice did I ever have?

I steal because I've been stolen from! Not by my grandfather and his floozy. By you! You wanted peace at all costs. You wanted calm. You wanted a myth of an English country life. Even if it meant sacrificing your own son!"

Arthur sighed and slumped further still. He might have said something. He might even have mentioned Terrance's mother by name.

"This whole rotten mess comes down to your failure to be a father!" Terrance felt himself standing outside the situation, as if the years and his success and his power all had been stripped away in a single instant, by this man who was incapable of any response. Terrance was both the raging banshee and the invisible observer. "You are going to tell me what I need to know."

The front door crashed back. "You!"

Terrance whirled about. And smiled. "Hello, sister."

She was taller than Terrance recalled, or perhaps it was merely her ire that added stature. She vaulted into the room, screaming as she raced for him. "You get *away* from him!"

Loupe's driver moved like a cat. He came up behind her and pressed something to her neck. There was a soft zapping sound. Audrey jerked into a full-length spasm, then sighed quietly and came crashing to the floor by her father's feet.

"No, please." The words carried no strength, as though Arthur knew they were futile even before he uttered them.

The moment was just too delicious. Terrance touched his father's shin with the toe of his shoe. "Look at me, Father."

Arthur locked gazes with his son. Terrance opened the hidden door, the one he had revealed to no one before this moment. And showed his father the full extent of his rage-driven ferocity. Arthur flinched and looked away. "I don't know where he is. They took him away somewhere. I can't tell you anything."

"Ah, but for your dear daughter's sake, you must. You cannot possibly imagine what they will do to her if you don't." Terrance signaled to the silent man. The driver lifted Audrey as easily as he would an empty set of clothes. Terrance drew out pen and pad and wrote down his cell phone number. He dropped it into his father's lap, between the unmoving hands. "Just give me Val."

Terrance crossed to the front door. "I sincerely hope you find a way to help me. For once."

THE HOME'S ATMOSPHERE WAS POISONOUS. DILLON glared at him from the hallway, Gerald did sentry at the kitchen doorway. Bert stood by the sink and measured him for a coffin. Val forced himself to reenter the kitchen and sit at the table.

"I have an idea," Val said. And waited.

Bert finally said, "Let's be hearing it, then."

Val did not respond. He remained as he was, crouched over the table, staring at his hands.

Finally Bert sighed and dragged out another chair and seated himself. Val kept to the same position. Waiting.

Dillon slipped past Gerald and joined Bert at the table. Bert said, "All right, mate. Let's hear what you've got."

Gerald remained leaning against the kitchen door frame, arms crossed over chest, gaze heated. Val turned his attention to the men seated at the table. Given the circumstances, two out of three wasn't bad.

"Terrance will be carrying the codes with him," Val began.

"Codes," Bert repeated.

"To access the bank funds," Val explained.

"This is the money he stole we're talking about," Bert said. "Our pension money."

"Right. The newspapers are onto this theft. Which means the SEC has been called in."

"Official government investigators," Gerald supplied from his position, speaking for the first time since Audrey departed.

"Right. Terrance wouldn't dare go hunting for me without keeping tabs on his money. He would never trust his partners. And he's definitely not in this alone."

"How can you be sure of that, mate?"

"Because if he was, he wouldn't be free to come over here now. He's needed back in the States to handle the inquiry into the disappearance of the funds. There's someone else on the inside, someone high up enough to cover for Terrance." Val rocked back in his seat. "Don Winslow."

Bert asked, "That name's supposed to mean something?"

"Executive vice president," Gerald said. "I've seen his name on documents."

Val explained, "Don backed Terrance's hand when he stole a promotion from me."

Gerald said, "I thought you had amnesia."

"My memory was a total loss right after the accident." Val forced himself to meet the man's gaze. "Things are coming back. But it's patchy. And most of what I remember are things I'd just as soon forget."

Gerald snorted quietly. But he subsided.

Bert refocused the discussion with, "So you've got a history with Audrey's brother."

"Six years."

"Bit of bad blood there, I take it."

"About a year and a half ago," Val replied, "Terrance seduced my wife. Then he stole a promotion that should have been mine by falsifying documents, pinning a series of losses on my watch. That I know for certain. He bribed a lab or a doctor to alter a DNA test so he could steal my child as well."

"You got proof?"

"No. No proof. But I'm sure it happened."

Bert looked at Gerald, who said, "You have quite a way with the ladies."

To that Val had no response.

Bert continued playing the moderator. "So Terrance is going to be carrying the codes with him."

"These days, access to a numbered account can be as simple or as difficult as you want to make it," Val said.

"Know this from personal experience, do you?" Gerald said.

Val lifted his gaze. "That's right. I do."

Gerald shook his head. Pushed off the doorjamb. Walked over to the window. Gave his attention to the green vista out back.

Val waited until the others' gazes had returned to him. "Knowing Terrance, there will be a series of very complicated maneuvers required to access those funds. Something that has to be done in strict order. He'll have part of it in his head. The other part will be in a computer. Terrance has always loved his toys."

"You're thinking he's carrying this computer with him," Bert said.

"That or something else."

"Something we can lift."

"Right."

"Something we can use to renegotiate our position with."

"That's my thinking."

The youngest of the trio spoke up. "They've taken the

grandest suite in the hotel where I work. I could get in and out, no problem."

"Not you," Val said. "Me. There's no need to get anybody else in trouble. And I'd have a better idea what to look for."

"Just whose position would you be after saving here?" Gerald asked the window. "Yours or our pensions?"

Val decided he'd had enough. He rose from the table and walked outdoors. Clouds were piling in from the north. The afternoon sky contained a riot of tainted moods. The narrow strip of shadow between cloud and hill was shot with silver where sunlight struck the falling rain. Val futilely searched the horizon for a single shred of the confidence he had exhibited inside.

His mind returned to the same unanswered dilemma. Why had he forced Audrey away? The incident in New York might have scrambled his memory, but something far earlier had tainted his heart. How could he have felt something this powerful and still made her leave? Val pounded the post marking the boundary between city and verdant fields, convicted anew by all he could not remember. There was no escape. It was not the exterior that trapped him. It was everything inside. All the things he could never let go.

A siren sounded far in the distance, so faint it should have been possible to let it flow into all the other city noises and disappear. Yet this one rose and fell with the strident force of an alarm meant exclusively for him.

Then he heard the shouts rising from inside the house. One word was cried in anguish. A woman's name.

———

Dillon said nothing as they walked down the alley leading to the hotel's rear entrance. The lane held a sickly sweet odor of rubbish bins and coming rain. Dillon ducked inside the metal "Employees Only" entrance, then swiftly reappeared. "Ready?"

"You can wait out here if you want."

"If I'd wanted to wait I'd still be in the van with the others." Dillon led Val down a concrete hall painted a grim yellow. He pushed open the door to the gents'. "Stay put till I come for you."

The room was cramped and lined with rusting metal lockers. A shower dripped. Machinery clanked overhead. Val moved to the sinks and pretended to wash his hands. The mirror revealed the same helpless fury that knotted his gut. It was no longer the past only that held a blank void. Audrey had been kidnapped by Terrance. That Terrance had gutted Val's future once more was irony at its most vile.

After Arthur d'Arcy's panic-stricken phone call, Bert and Gerald had gone into town and fetched Audrey's father. The man had been so distraught his words had emerged only half formed. They had learned what they could, then tucked him into the bed last used by Val. Afterwards they had regathered in the kitchen and grimly run through Val's strategy. Doing nothing was not an option.

Bert had toyed with the salt shaker, the glass pyramid tiny in his hands. "I know what the dear would be telling us just now."

Val asked, "How do you know Audrey?"

"The lady managed to drag me and Dillon here out of one truly dark pit. You know she works as a prison counselor?"

"We don't need to be going there. Audrey was there when our trouble was at its worst. That's all you should be telling the bloke." Dillon rounded on Val. "This plan of yours. Is it going to work?"

"You can use me as a trade if you think that has a better chance of success."

"That's not what I was asking, mate."

"Yes it was."

"All right, then," Bert said. "Straight up. Tell us why that's a nonstarter."

"If you give me up, we're empty-handed. They have all they want. They have no reason to give Audrey up."

The men studied him intently. "Know what I think, mate? There's more to your plan than just stealing the bloke's phone."

"Computer."

"Whatever. You're after more, aren't you?"

"I'm just thinking ahead."

Bert's gaze was hard as his tone. "You're out to shut him down."

"If I can."

"And restore our pension fund?"

"I'd like to."

Gerald remained against the doorway, arms crossed, voice an iron rod. "What about the bit where you stole some for yourself?"

Val had nothing for them but the truth. "I don't understand why I did it. Money's never been all that important to me. Before, I was working for a wife and the children I hoped we'd have. Now I don't have either."

Bert looked at the others. "I say let's do the job."

———

Dillon returned in uniform, bearing a second maroon-and-yellow outfit in a plastic cover. He was nervous but bearing up well. Clearly he had been in tight spaces before. The only real sign of his fear was the way his eyes tightened and his cheekbones pinched white against his skin. "I can tell you already this is too small. But it's the only one I spotted."

The uniform was scarcely better than a clown's outfit on Val. The trousers were a full four inches too short, the waist impossible to fasten. The jacket's wrists and shoulders were scarcely better. He did all of the jacket's gold buttons up the front except the one at his collar, which would have fitted him like a noose.

Dillon set a matching maroon-and-gold pillbox hat on Val's head and grimaced. "All you need is a tin cup, mate. You'd be ready for the monkey's dance down the boardwalk."

"If I bunched my shoulders I bet I could split this thing from top to toe."

"We'll move fast, hope nobody gets too good a look. Ready?"

They took the service lift up to the top floor. Over the clanking lift motor Val could hear the same sibilant noise he had been catching ever since news had arrived of Audrey's abduction. The sound was somewhere between a drill and a very shrill scream. The fact that the sound had traveled with him left Val in no doubt of its origin. The day was being ground down to a raw and fiery edge.

They came out of the elevator and started down an empty corridor. Val was consumed by how little chance they had of succeeding. He should never have sent Audrey away. Val no longer cared what his justification might have been at the time. It was insignificant now. He followed Dillon into the pantry. His body was a shell encasing nothing more than a void. A fragmented past and no future. And it was all his fault.

Dillon piled his arms high with terrycloth robes and fresh towels. When he was done, Val was masked from his waist to his chin. Dillon looked down at Val's exposed ankles and shook his head. "Nothing to be done about that."

"Except move fast," Val said. Forward motion of any kind gave him at least a shred of hope.

Dillon's gaze tightened further, as close to a smile as the guy could manage just then. "You're all right, mate."

Val replied, "Let's do it."

THEY FINALLY LEFT AUDREY AT THE HOUSE RENTED FOR
Josef's thugs because Terrance grew tired of wasting his
time. Audrey might know where Val was, but they could
roast her over live coals, plug her with arrows, and she
would give them nothing. Audrey would relish playing
the martyr. Terrance ordered them to cuff her to the
radiator in the smallest of the upstairs rooms. Her
mouth was taped, but nothing could be done about the
daggers in her gaze. As usual, his darling sister refused
to let him have the last word. Even when she couldn't
speak.

The driver had already returned to the hotel, and
Loupe's men did not want to leave without word from the
boss. Which was fine by Terrance. He felt enclosed
within a cage the size of this proper little English town.

Wally spoke to him for the first time since their arrival.
"I need to walk, get a little air."

"My thoughts exactly."

The muscle protested, "We can't raise the boss."

"Stay here," Terrance replied, already moving for the
door.

"The boss—"

"Your boss," Terrance corrected.

The senior man said to one of his men, "Make sure they make it okay."

"It can't be more than ten blocks." Terrance protested. "Hastings hardly looks like a dangerous place."

Loupe's man said nothing, merely walked a few paces behind them. Wally remained the silent wraith throughout. The sky was split so definitely in two they might have been witnessing a schism of the universe. To the west and south was an aching empty blue. To the north a storm approached, strong as night. Thunder rolled across the vacant reaches, bringing expressions of real fear to the scurrying tourists. Only Wally seemed unfazed by the squall. By the squall, by the day, and by the fact that they were walking down Hastings' main street, six thousand miles from where they needed to be, and still minus Val Haines.

Terrance pulled out his cell phone and checked for messages. Nothing. The action had become reflexive, something he did every few minutes. He had tried Don repeatedly for hours with no results. Not even on what Don called his red line, the number only a few people knew and one that Don had promised would lift him from the grave. Terrance had left five messages there and still had not heard back. Being this far from his home turf and not being able to contact his chief ally left Terrance extremely unsettled.

He could sense Audrey's helpless fury like smoke rising from a branding iron. He should be feeling some sense of vindication, having trapped her and isolated her and finally left her helpless and silent. But the day was not working out as it should. Terrance snapped his phone shut as the hotel doorman greeted them and held open the portal. They had to find Val. Find him and finish him. Fast.

When they entered the hotel lobby, Terrance realized that Wally was watching him. "What?"

"I didn't say anything."

Terrance turned to their shadow. "Go on up to the suite."

The muscle glanced uncertainly around the reception area. Clearly there was nothing of danger. Still, he hesitated.

Terrance put as much weight as he could on the words. "I need a minute alone here. We'll meet you upstairs."

When Loupe's man entered the elevator, Terrance turned back to Wally and hissed, "As a matter of fact, you haven't said or done a thing."

"You got a beef?"

"Of course not. What do I have to complain about? After all, you've contributed so very much to all that's happened since our arrival. Offering suggestions and advice and wisdom at every turn, that's our Wally."

She gave a cop's laugh, a quick huff of sound without humor. "You don't get it, do you?"

"Obviously not."

Wally shook her head. "You've lost it."

"On the contrary, I have everything under control."

Wally huffed another laugh, a verbal pistol with a silencer attached.

"I asked you a question."

She stepped over to where a pillar and a potted palm hid her from both the elevator and the reception desk. Having to follow Wally's lead made Terrance even hotter. Which, given the other frustrations of this rather fractious day, was not altogether a bad thing. At least he could let off some steam. "Would it be too much to ask for you to try and help me out here?"

"You're hopeless."

The words and their flat tone stung. "I am paying you good money—"

"You're paying me what I've already earned ten times over."

"Since our arrival you have done absolutely *nothing*."

Wally punched him in the chest with a finger of flesh-covered stone. "You think you're going to collar your guy, pay this Loupe his change, and just waltz off to never-never land. Is that it?"

"Not collar."

"Whatever."

"And you're the one paying Loupe, remember? It comes out of your share."

"You just don't get it."

"You've said that before."

Her every breath blasted him with heat and ashes. "Listen to me. The boss is not here because his guys goofed."

"That's what he said when—"

"Forget what he told you. This guy wouldn't know the truth if it arrived on the business end of a thirty-eight hollow point. He's here because he wants it *all*."

A snake of fear found the weak spot just north of his navel. "All what?"

"What do you think? *Everything*."

"He can't have it."

"Oh, is that so? And just who is going to stop him—you?"

"That's your job."

Her final huff carried very little force. "I may be good, Terry. But I'm just one gal."

Terrance stared around the lobby, as though searching

for a way out. A bellhop stared through the front window, watching the sky with a worried frown. "I told you not to call me that."

Wally closed in on Terrance with her lips drawn back from her teeth. A feral beast smelling of cigarettes and fear. "Listen to what I'm telling you. You want to have one single shred of anything left, you get out."

The snake just kept burrowing deeper, lodging itself with venomous ferocity, coiling around Terrance's spine. "You mean leave? I can't do that."

She bit off each word in even little gasps. "You have *got* to. *Now.*"

"You're running out on me, is that it?"

"Are you deaf? Do you not hear a word I'm saying?"

"All I hear is the woman who's here to protect me saying she's ready to run out on me."

"Not me, Terry. *Us.* We leave, we live to play with what you've got."

"But Val Haines is still out there!" The snake began dislodging oily drops of sweat that dribbled down his back. "One word from him and—"

She gripped his lapel and shook him. Punching his chest with the fist that held his jacket, while the snake fed on his guts. "Forget Val! You stay here and the man upstairs is going to take us down!"

"If I run now, Val will destroy us." Terrance was jabbering now. He knew it but couldn't stop. "Everything I've done to keep us safe will go up in flames."

"Safe? You call this safe?" Her eyes held a manic gaze. "I'm sitting up there just waiting for Loupe to tell one of his men to take us out back and smoke us."

"If they do that, they lose the money you promised to pay them."

"He's not after what we agreed on, Terry. This has gone way beyond that. We're talking *everything*. Including your *life*."

"Loupe doesn't know what I've got. Unless you told him."

"Do I sound like a rat? You think somebody working both sides would be telling you to run?"

"No." Terrance breathed. Or tried to. "No."

"Loupe will get what he wants out of you. It's only a question of how hard he's got to ask before you talk." Her gaze had gone blank on him. Just two empty glass voids, windows to nothing. "If Loupe starts asking, you tell him whatever it is he wants to know. Tell him fast."

"This can't be happening."

"Exactly. So we run. Now." Wally stood so close they might have been lovers. She whispered with the coarse burr of shared terror. "So Haines is still out there. So what? Last I heard, Barbados doesn't extradite."

"How can you be so sure about this? Loupe hasn't said a thing."

"I know these guys. Okay? Not Loupe. His kind. The boss. I'm into one of them for a lot of money. More than that. He *owns* me. This deal, it's my only hope of getting free. So it's in my own best interest to keep you alive and get you out while we still got legs to carry us."

"I have to contact Don. He's got to go along with this."

"Call him from thirty thousand feet. We run now, we just might live to . . ." She caught sight of something behind them and straightened. "Heads up."

"What now?"

"We got company." The hard mask was back in place. Wally stepped away. "You just be ready for my signal."

THEY CAME OUT OF THE PANTRY AND STARTED DOWN the hall. Val just managed to see above the pile of bathrobes and fresh towels in his arms. They came around a corner to find two dark-suited bruisers standing outside a suite entrance. Dillon tensed but played his part well. "Can I help you gentlemen?"

The pair eyed Dillon and Val like they would a free lunch.

"Right, sirs. Anything you need, just ring room service, I'll be up in a jiffy." Dillon guided Val to a halt at the neighboring doorway. "Six eighteen, this is where the lass said to do the drop." Dillon knocked, then asked the bruisers, "You know if anybody's around?"

"He's out."

"Makes our job tons easier, that." He knocked again just to be certain, then used his passkey. He let Val enter first, then said to the pair, "Trainee." And sniffed.

Dillon flipped on the light and called, "Housekeeping."

The room was empty. There was a closed door to Val's left, no doubt leading to the suite's parlor. Val could hear the soft murmur of voices.

Dillon shut the door and released a shaky breath. "Dump that lot in the bathroom."

When Val came back Dillon was doing a professional job on the bed, straightening the cover and plumping out the pillows. "Do what you got to do, mate. I can only keep this up for so long."

Val moved to the desk. The file opened on top was useless, all travel documents. The drawers were empty. He moved to the closet. Terrance's shoes were lined up like polished soldiers on parade. The two suits hanging overhead smelled slightly of their occupant.

The briefcase was set behind the shoes. Val slipped it onto the bed and knelt. The catches refused to give.

"Move aside, mate." Dillon flipped open a switchblade and jimmied the lock. "You didn't see me do that. And if you did, you won't tell Audrey."

The briefcase was new and almost empty. A series of files contained official documents related to the missing funds. Passport. More travel documents. Backup credit cards. Notepad. Silver Dupont pen. Val felt around the edges. "Is there a false bottom?"

"I'll have a go." But the switchblade did nothing save slit the threads connecting the leather base to the backing. "This isn't looking good, is it?"

In response, voices rose in the adjoining room. Both Val and Dillon looked up, frozen in the headlights of very real fear. A voice barked once, like a verbal gunshot. Beside him, Dillon jerked like he took the hit himself. "We can't stay here much longer."

The suite's door banged open and shut. They crouched and listened to footsteps thunder down the hallway outside their room. Then nothing.

Val shut the briefcase, stored it back in the closet, and cast frantically about the room. Then he found it.

The safe was tucked inside what formerly must have held a miniature fridge. "Can you open it?"

Dillon flipped open his wallet, pulled out a metallic blade like a shiny credit card. "Last time I did this, it earned me eleven months inside." He slid the card through a narrow slot running underneath the numeric keypad. Then he hit six numbers.

The safe pinged and the locks slid back. "I can't redo his code," Dillon warned. "Soon as he tries to enter, he's going to know."

"We'll worry about that later." Val flipped back the door. "Bingo."

Inside was a wafer-thin mini-laptop. As Val scooped it out, voices rose once more from inside the parlor. Someone shouted angrily.

Val slammed the safe door shut and punched in random numbers and hit the lock button. He handed Dillon the computer. The young man hid it under his jacket, catching it in place with this belt. He moved to the bath where he bunched up towels to make them look soiled and crammed them into Val's arms.

Dillon stepped to the outer door, opened it, and said loudly, "You got to speed things up, you want to keep this job."

They entered the hallway.

Dillon continued scolding as they hustled down the hall. "I'm telling you, mate, you got thirty rooms to turn down, you can't be crawling around like you're in some tortoise-and-hare race."

They were almost free. Two more steps and they would have turned the corner and been in front of the service lift. Punch the button and step inside and away.

"You two! Hold it right there!"

Val hissed, "Fire escape."

Dillon needed no second urging. He rammed open the stairwell door. Just as Val moved to follow, however, the elevator doors opened down at the hall's far end.

The day's discordant screech rose to a fever pitch. Val had no choice but to yell in reply.

———

Wally didn't like the way the pair hustled them toward the elevator. "Let go of my arm."

"The boss wants to see you."

Wally was not particularly large. But when she planted her heels in the lobby's carpet she put enough force into the act that the guy gripping her elbow jerked around. "I'm not asking you again."

"Look, the boss—"

"He's not the guy doing the grab here. You are. You want your fingers to stay intact, you let go of the merchandise."

The guy looked pained. His mate said softly, "There's people watching."

"That's right, boyo." Wally's face was stone, her eyes blank glass. "Listen to your pal. We don't want to make a scene, do we?"

The guy dropped his hand.

"Right. Now once more from the top. My friend and I are standing down here having a nice little chat, when you front us."

"The boss wants a word."

"So let's go." Wally gave him a meaningless smile. "See how easy things are when you play nice?"

Terrance tried to match Wally's easy tone and blank

wall of a face. But he was certain his thundering heart showed. He could feel the muscles beneath his right eye begin to pull down in tight little jerks. Like the strain of not screaming had to come out somewhere.

He walked alongside Wally to the elevators. One of Loupe's guys moved a half-step ahead, the other a half-step behind. In tight, but not touching. Close enough for Terrance to feel the heat and the threatening force. Whatever the boss wanted. No question. Those guys would do it and not blink.

The doors slid open. They stepped inside. The guy who had released Wally's arm hit the button. He glanced at the woman. "The boss didn't like knowing you two were down here alone." Almost apologetic now.

Wally shrugged. Like it was nothing. "Nice to know he's so concerned about our well-being."

The guy turned back and faced the doors. Overhead the elevator's speaker droned a tinny version of *The Girl from Ipanema*. Terrance glanced at Wally. Her warning had bruised his psyche. He wanted to convince himself that it was nothing. She had to be wrong. It was his money, his job, his work. They would finish this bit, take Val Haines out of the equation, and leave.

Then he saw it.

A tiny bead of sweat pressed out by her temple, penetrating Wally's stonelike mask. It trickled down the side of her face. Wally either did not notice or did not want to draw attention to it. Terrance could not take his eyes off the moisture until it disappeared into her collar. Wally glanced his way. Her eyes looked glazed with all the other sweat she was trying hard not to release.

Terrance turned to face the doors, as scared as he had ever been in his life.

The doors pinged open. Loupe's two men stepped out.

There was a shout from somewhere along the hall. Wally still had enough of the cop in her to want to be in open space if there was trouble. But the only person visible was a bellhop just this side of where the hall jinked around a corner.

Terrance was the last to exit the elevator. He had a sudden urge to take Wally at her word. Use this chance to slip away. Hit the lobby button and flee as fast as he could for the airport and the waiting plane and Jamaica.

But no. She was wrong. She had to be.

Terrance stepped out.

The doors pinged and began to close.

But before the doors could slide shut, a crazed bellhop raced forward. He tossed his pile of towels into Wally's face.

One of the bruisers started in with, "What the—"

The bellhop slammed into Terrance. And drove him through the closing elevator doors.

Then the fist smashed into Terrance's jaw. And suddenly he was fighting for his life.

VAL WAS SLIGHTLY OFF WITH HIS FIRST BLOW. HE KNEW before it connected that his aim was worse than his timing. He was still running when the rear wall of the elevator stopped Terrance up short and bounced him back into Val's incoming fist.

Even so, Terrance's eyes fluttered slightly as his brain went through the scramble brought on by taking one on the chin. Terrance flapped one arm up to protect his face. The other wrapped around Val's neck.

Val got one quick jab into Terrance's gut. The guy grunted, but again Val was off. Terrance gripped Val's neck harder and shortened the distance to nothing. Val tried to swing his fist around to the side, shoot off a kidney punch. But Terrance sensed it coming, or perhaps he was just thrown off balance. Whatever the reason, he caromed them over to the side wall. The elevator boomed from the impact of two bodies locked in strangle holds. A bell went off somewhere. The light flickered. The idiotic music faltered, then started back up with the elevator's downward motion.

Terrance clawed at Val's face with his fingernails for talons. The fingers felt like iron rods, jamming hard for Val's eyes. Val ducked down onto Terrance's shoulder, still going for the kidney shot. Terrance rammed him against the doors and the elevator bonged again. The alarm bell came on and stayed on.

"Where is Audrey?"

Terrance had no chance of answering. He flayed at Val with all limbs now. Their bodies were locked into a parody of dance, a vicious waltz to the music of rage. Val kneed Terrance hard enough to break the man's hold on his neck. He shoved Terrance against the side wall, bonging the cage so hard the brakes came on. The alarm bell was constant and shrill.

Val hooked Terrance on the ear. But his intent to slaughter his opponent left his own face open. The next thing he knew, an unseen hammer smashed into his wounded temple.

The sudden pain stunned him, and he fell forward into Terrance, who tried to shove him away. Val clenched harder, shaking his head. Terrance hissed in his ear, a shrill sound one note lower than a scream. Terrance pounded him in the ribs and got in two solid knees before Val's vision cleared. Partially, that is. Blood flowed anew from his wound, drenching his right eye. Val flipped it clear, spraying the wall and Terrance both.

The elevator started moving again. Terrance dislodged Val's grip enough to shove them slightly apart. But this time Val was ready. He jammed his arm between their bodies and got off two solid punches to Terrance's chin. The eyelids fluttered once more.

"What did you do with Audrey!"

In response, Terrance yelled with a fury to match his own and shoved.

Only the doors had opened, and there was nothing behind Val to halt his motion.

They careened out of the elevator and into a crowd of people drawn to the elevators by the alarm and their shouts and banging. Val's fall was softened by landing on a hotel manager and two bellhops. Terrance remained intent on locking his hands around Val's throat, his voice reduced to a constant beastly screech.

Val could feel his strength drain along with the blood flowing from his head wound. Thankfully, the blood kept Terrance from gaining a solid grip. Val got off one more hammer, putting everything he had into one solid right to Terrance's ear. When he felt his enemy's grip slacken, Val broke Terrance's hold and rolled away. He shoved his way free of the milling bodies scrambling with them on the lobby's carpet. He crawled to his feet and kicked hard at the hand gripping his ankle. Once free, Val lunged for the revolving glass doors.

Only then did he hear the tumult. The entire lobby was an arena of waving arms and shouting voices and running feet. Someone behind the desk was shouting for the police.

A hand gripped him from behind, one strong enough to wheel him about. Val half turned and faced one of the well-dressed killers.

Val clawed for something, anything. He caught hold of a brass ashtray standing by the nearest pillar. Val gripped the supporting rod with his free hand and whirled about.

The heavy was reaching for something under his jacket. Val reacted instinctively. He lowered his swing and batted the man's shoulder.

The man grunted in pain. His fingers flopped uselessly.

Val wrenched himself free and swung again, two-handed this time. He connected with the elbow that came up to protect the man's forehead, driving him back a step.

He was armed now, and his prey was still crawling out of the morass on the carpet. Val took a step toward Terrance and took aim.

But before he could unleash the blow, a woman slammed out of the stairwell beside the elevators. Her lips were drawn back from small animal teeth. She charged.

Val reaimed and caught her square on the shoulder, driving her to one side. She collided with another heavy, and they went down in a tangle of scrambling limbs.

People shouted and pointed and raced in every direction, just so long as it was away.

Two of the bruisers were rising to their feet, watching with deadly expressions. Val dropped the ashtray and sprinted with the others for the exit.

He shoved aside the bellhop who tried to halt him. He banged through the revolving doors. His head scarred the glass surface with red trails. Then he was through and lurching down the street.

His legs refused to obey his commands. They merely stumbled when he wanted to run.

Then Bert's van roared up alongside, climbing over the curb. Val could not make himself stop. He rammed into the side and stayed there as the door flew open and hands gathered him up and bundled him inside.

Dillon pulled Val into the seat beside him and stared aghast at Val's bloody face. Bert wrestled them off the curb and roared away. Only when they were three streets out from the center did Bert risk a glance and a grin in Val's direction. "My guess is you won't be offered a second chance at that job, mate."

Val remained silent. He bent over his legs, the aftershocks sending weak tremors through his frame. He was still being assaulted. Only now it was by memories.

Dillon stripped off his own bellhop jacket and handed it over. "Stick that on your face before you bleed to death."

Val pressed the jacket to his temple. The pressure did nothing to stem the flood. He remembered.

Bert demanded, "What's the matter, mate?"

Val straightened in stages. "Do either of you have friends servicing the rentals around here?"

"What, you mean cottages to let?" Dillon looked askance at Bert. "I might do. Why?"

When Val explained what he wanted, Bert laughed out loud. "I'm ruddy glad we didn't meet up back before I took the straight and narrow, mate. You're a right one with the planning, you are."

"You just watch the road," Dillon said.

Bert paid him no mind whatsoever. "Our Val is covered in it, and all he wants to know is, can we help him with what comes next."

Dillon asked, "What do we do now?"

"That's simple enough," Bert replied for him. "We're off to save the lady. Isn't that right, mate?"

Val only pressed harder at his temple. But the mental torrent would not abate.

He remembered everything.

THE STORM HAD NOT YET ARRIVED WHEN VAL LEFT
Gerald's study. He walked through the kitchen, easing his
shoulders and wincing at the bite of new bruises. Dillon
and Bert were busy at the stove making a late supper
nobody much wanted. They must have seen the frustration
in his face because they did not speak. The pressure of time
and unspoken terrors weighed heavily upon them all. A pot
of coffee had been sitting on the eye long enough to almost
congeal. Val poured himself a mug and stepped out back.

The greatest source of anxiety was that no one had
called. No threats had been made. No ultimatums.
Nothing.

The hillside was a dark silhouette cut from sunset and
the impending storm. The horizon was a solid wall of
black cloud. The air smelled of coming rain, heavy and
sweet. Thunder rumbled low and menacing. The chalk
veins glowed faintly, as if the heat Val felt fulminating
inside his heart lay exposed and gleaming.

He yearned for love. No incoming barrage of memories could change that. He yearned for the touch of a
good woman. A lady who cared enough to see in him
what only love could illuminate. What he had denied
himself for far too long.

Gerald let himself out the back door and came to stand beside Val. Gerald had dumped the contents of Terrance's laptop into his own computer, then he and Val had worked in tandem for three frantic hours. Now his voice carried the grainy tension of a quest unfulfilled. "Further north they refer to such hills as fells. It's a good Gaelic-sounding word, that. The fells. Brings to mind all sorts of dark and craggy depths. Places where evil might thrive unobserved."

Bert and Dillon let themselves out the kitchen door and padded over to stand beside them at the fence. Bert said, "You might as well go ahead and say it."

Gerald said, "All we have to show for our efforts is a long string of numbers belonging to a file named after this bloke here."

"That's something, right?" Bert searched both faces with frantic concern. "One of you tell me we're closer to getting the lady back."

When Gerald merely rubbed his tired eyes, Val explained, "It's something. But not as much as we hoped. My guess is, Terrance set up the accounts in my name so the U.S. authorities can track how the money flowed, maybe even get a figure on what's sitting over there. But that's it. Jersey banking laws make Switzerland's system look like fishnet."

"You guess," Gerald quietly scoffed.

But Val was seeing anew how the file with the numbers had been set up. It was marked simply as *Haines*. "Terrance can claim they found the account numbers in searching me out. That's why he can carry them like this, to show the authorities. But they'll have some pre-arranged electronic signal for moving the money on. That's what we didn't find. I should have figured Terrance would set up firewalls."

Bert complained, "You lost me back there around the first word."

"Maybe they set up a secure Web site somewhere. One way in, one out. He brought the computer because there's a signal embedded in here that opens the electronic door. We have no idea where to look on the Web. He could have this thing hidden anywhere. A server for the phone company in Tasmania, an insurance group in Shanghai, anywhere at all."

"Without the codes and the address, we're lost," Gerald said. "I say it's time we called in the police."

"Absolutely," Val said.

Dillon pointed out, "If we do, mate, they're bound to discover your role in all this."

"If you're hesitating on my account, forget it," Val said.

Gerald said, "So maybe we should arrange a trade. You for her. The one thief within reach for Audrey."

"I'm ready," Val said. Meaning it.

"No, mate," Bert decided, shaking his entire upper body. "We can't do that."

"Why not?" Gerald's voice was flat as a cop's.

"They'll murder the bloke. You know that same as me."

"So what do you think they're doing to Audrey?"

Bert sneered. "You're telling me it'd be right to feed the bloke to the lions?"

"If it saves Audrey, absolutely."

Val backed away from the three men. "I'm the one who brought this down on you people. I'm the reason the bad guys have Audrey. I've made a total mess of everything."

"What about your plan?" Bert said.

"Will you just listen to the man!" Gerald snapped. "We can't access the computer codes!"

"Your plan," Bert insisted to Val. "The one you were thinking of back before we hit the hotel."

"It could still work. Maybe. I'm not sure of anything anymore except that first you need to decide whether it'd be better just to offer me up for her."

A silhouette appeared in the kitchen doorway. Arthur d'Arcy held himself canted slightly to one side. He pushed futilely at the back door and then turned away. Val started back for the house.

Gerald shouted, "We're not finished here!"

Val kept going. A gale-force wind blasted out of nowhere. Thunder tore shreds from the feeble sunset. When Val let himself in through the door, Arthur d'Arcy was seated at the kitchen table. Arthur looked once in Val's direction, then planted his elbows on the table and placed his face in his hands. The motions of a defeated man.

Val understood perfectly how he felt.

The kitchen held a sulphurous odor. Far more than coffee had burned down to sullen residue. Val poured a second mug. The coffee was black as pitch and smelled charred. He doubted very much that Arthur would notice. Val set the mug down by the old man's elbow and took the chair on the table's opposite side.

Val tasted his own mug. "Apparently the fight with Terrance jostled my brain. Things are coming back to me now."

There was no sign from Arthur that he had heard at all.

"I remember everything. Well, not everything. But enough. I remember why I sent Audrey away. Right now, that's pretty much all that matters."

"I long to forget." Arthur did not raise his face from his hands. The words came out malformed, shards of trauma and regret. "My entire life has been quilted together from horrific errors. I should never have married Eleanor. But I was convinced my love was great enough for the two of us. I should have fought my father's decision. I should have . . ."

Val sipped his coffee and waited the man out. The voices out back had gone silent. The only sounds were the tick of the kitchen clock and distant thunder.

Arthur went on, "Everything Terrance accused me of was true."

"Partly," Val corrected.

Arthur lifted his head. He blinked slowly, having difficulty placing the man across from him.

"Partly true," Val repeated. "Finding his enemy's weakness and attacking hard are Terrance's trademarks."

"His enemy," Arthur croaked. "What a dreadful legacy I've created."

"What about Audrey?"

"They have her."

"That's not your fault. If you want someone to blame for that particular calamity, you're looking straight at him."

But Arthur was too lost in self-remorse to accuse anyone else. "I thought giving my family peace and harmony and stability was doing right by them. But that was what I wanted. Not them. They wanted . . ." He dropped his face back into his hands. He might have finished with the word "everything." But Val could not be certain.

The clock on the wall above the stove sounded like a pick working at the wound on Val's temple. Chipping away at his composure, exposing the bubbling fear that threatened to erupt at any time. They had Audrey. He had looked into the faces of four of them, Terrance and the woman and the two bruisers, and he knew them for killers. Val wanted to grab the clock and fling it onto the stone floor and stomp it to bits.

"Fourteen months after my wife left me for Terrance, I met Audrey," Val went on, his voice steady. "She showed me the same talent as her brother, only in reverse. Terrance hunts out weakness to attack. Audrey seeks only to help. She is the most giving person I've ever met. The most loving. I saw it even then. But I couldn't accept it. Back then I woke up every night drenched in rage. I couldn't see further than wanting to tear a man apart with my own bare hands."

Val looked down at his hands. He was amazed to find that they were not trembling. He could remember now what it was like, walking into the bathroom at one or two in the morning, knowing he would not return to sleep. Living on three or four hours of sleep a night because that was all he could have. All he would ever have. His bathroom was like the rest of the house, empty of life. Even when he was there. Two o'clock in the morning was a terrible time to face the fact that he had lost everything. All because of one man. His hands had trembled then. He would wash his face and clench his fists and press them to his forehead, trying to cram the rage and the hatred all back inside where it lay hidden during the day.

"Audrey arrived in Florida a week after I learned Terrance was stripping the pension funds. I had not slept in seven nights. I never knew a man could live without sleep. All I could think of was, how was I going to catch Terrance red-handed? If I blew the whistle too early, the fund would collapse and pull the company down with it. And Terrance would escape free and clear. And I wasn't going to let that happen. I was going to bring him down. I was going to crush him."

Val was lost in a morass of remembrances. The kitchen's sulfurous odor was identifiable now. It came from himself and the rage he had refused to let go. "Audrey caught me at my weakest. All she wanted was to give me hope in the future. I see that now. But at the time, I thought she was asking the impossible. She wanted me to forgive Terrance." The words were almost too large to fit inside his mouth. "She gave me an ultimatum. Give up the hatred, or her."

He could hear Audrey's voice so clearly she might as well have been seated there beside him. He felt anew her intense longing to reach him. To *turn* him. "She told me the only way forward was to release my desire for vengeance. Otherwise I would serve a life sentence, trapped in a prison of my own making."

Val saw her face again, the flame he had extinguished burning so strongly it illuminated his own heart. "But I wouldn't let go. I couldn't see beyond my hatred for Terrance. I knew it was consuming me, and I didn't care."

Val raised his gaze. Arthur had lifted his head free of his hands. Bert and Dillon were stationed by the rear door. The three men watched him with knowing eyes. Val swallowed against the hurt and the helplessness. "I'd made my choice. I wasn't going to be one of the good guys anymore. Audrey accused me of allowing Terrance to remake me into himself. She was right."

From behind him Gerald said, "So you sent her away."

Val nodded to the accusation in Gerald's tone. "Audrey never told me to stop going after him. But she wanted me to do it for the right reasons. To save the pension. To protect the company and the employees. But that wasn't enough for me. I wanted . . ."

"Vengeance," Arthur murmured.

"Everything," Val said, shamed by his confession. "I wanted it all."

"You wanted back what the man had stolen." This from Bert. "Audrey knew you couldn't have it. She offered you something else. You turned her down."

"Guilty," Val said.

Gerald came around to look Val in the eye. "Explain to me why you didn't go to the authorities as soon as you knew the money was missing."

"If I couldn't pin the loss on Terrance, from inside the company and knowing the books as I did, no outside examiner would find enough to put him away, much less recoup the losses. I couldn't blow the whistle until I had both hard evidence on Terrance and knowledge of where the funds had been hidden. But the more I looked, the more I realized . . ."

Gerald gave him a tight moment, then pressed, "What?"

"I realized the only way to track him was to put myself in his shoes."

"You mean steal funds yourself."

"That's right."

"Sounds very convenient to me."

"Gerald, mate, give it a rest."

"No, it's okay. He's right." Val stared at Gerald but saw only the past. "It wasn't Terrance that I first discovered at all. There was a woman in my department, Marjorie Copeland was her name. She had a severely disabled son and no life whatsoever. The last person you'd expect to be caught dipping. She revealed that she had found out someone else was taking huge sums. She was three years from retirement, and her son could not survive without her pension. I started looking and discovered she was not only right, but it was far worse than she had thought. Enough had been stolen to bring down the entire company. I knew it was Terrance. But I couldn't prove it."

Bert was growing impatient. "So you went after him by following his tracks. Sounds simple enough."

But Val kept his gaze on Gerald, his judge and jury. "It started off that way. But I knew the life Terrance had stolen from me was gone. Demolished. So I decided to take my own share of the pension, expose Terrance, and disappear."

Gerald repeated, more softly this time, "So you sent Audrey away."

"My life was over. I wanted to leave and never come back. I wanted to start over and do right all the things that had come out so wrong the first time."

He stopped then. And sat listening to his past and the ticking of the clock.

Gerald still challenged, but the heat was absent. "You said you have a plan."

Val took a breath, and stared into his dimly lit future. "That's right. I do."

TERRANCE D'ARCY PACED A DARKENED BEDROOM. THE room's only illumination came from a cheap bedside clock radio and light slipping beneath the closed door. He heard soft voices somewhere in the distance. His two suitcases lay open beside the bed with his clothes heaped on top. Such disorder would normally have sent him into a tailspin. Right now, however, he had more pressing issues on his mind.

When they had returned upstairs after the attack, Loupe had explained in his mildest voice that their struggle had attracted the wrong sort of attention. He asked if Terrance would temporarily relocate to their rented cottage. The silken voice had left no room for complaint. The police would be coming around, asking questions. Bound to happen, what with five of them involved in a dust-up in the hotel lobby and Terrance brawling in the lift.

His jaw throbbed where Val had struck. His body felt stiff with hints of pain yet to come. The bedside clock taunted him with red eyes that blinked out the minutes. He turned on the overhead light. Still the darkness would not go away. He was desperate for answers and had no one with whom he could talk. Wally had remained at the hotel. Don was still not answering his phone. But

Terrance's mind was such a muddle he needed someone to help him strategize.

Terrance stopped his pacing and stared at the side wall. To even consider such a move revealed just how frantic he had become.

Terrance stripped off the clothes trashed by his battle with Val. From the pile on the floor he selected a freshly starched shirt. A navy suit of finest gabardine with a slight hint of charcoal pinstripe. Baume et Mercier watch. Gold stud cufflinks. Donning the only armor he possessed.

He exited the room. Two of Loupe's men were seated at the kitchen table. They greeted his appearance with vacant gazes. "Everything all right, Mr. d'Arcy?"

"I just wanted to speak with my sister."

"Mr. Loupe didn't say nothing about that." The two men exchanged glances. "Think maybe we should call it in?"

"Look here. I was the one who ordered her brought in. She's my sister. If she is going to tell anyone where Haines is, it will be me."

The men looked doubtful but did not stop him as Terrance walked to the other bedroom and opened the door.

Audrey was handcuffed to a bedpost. She had risen to a seated position at the sound of his voice. She greeted him with, "I wouldn't dream of telling you anything."

Terrance gently shut the door. He picked up the room's one chair and carried it to her side of the bed. Audrey drew her legs up under her at his approach, as though fearful of contamination. "There is nothing I could possibly say of any help to you," she said.

Terrance opened the window wide. The mist floated in, and the room's air chilled. But it was his only hope of not being overheard. Audrey watched his movements but made no protest.

He lowered himself into the chair. He steepled his fingers. He spoke the words, "I am trapped."

Audrey remained motionless, her gaze guarded.

"I have only just realized how serious the situation has become. I don't know what to do."

"And you're asking me? For advice?"

"Help me strategize, and I will see that you are immediately freed." It was a lie, of course. But it was all he had. "I will set you and Father up in luxury and comfort for the rest of your days."

"You must be in far deeper than I thought." Audrey untangled her legs, and slid over. The handcuff rattled against the bedstead. "Brother, look at me." She waited through the long moment it took for Terrance to lift his gaze. "You have been trapped all your life."

"You don't understand."

"On the contrary. I understand all too well."

"Could we please dispense with the self-righteous claptrap for a moment? I am in very serious trouble here."

"Of that I have no doubt."

"You have remained persistently determined to misunderstand everything I am and do." Terrance felt the exasperation of centuries. "Why I came in here is utterly beyond me now."

"Because you're desperate. Because you have nowhere else to turn."

"You needn't sound so pleased."

"As a prisoner counselor, I deal with people in your situation day in and day out. The only difference is, they are wearing the cuffs. And their jailers are not normally in suits. But I have seen this situation more often than you can imagine. So I shall make things easy for you. You are completely trapped. You have nowhere to go. All your normal maneuverings have brought you nowhere but down into a pit of your own making."

He felt the old anger surge. "You and I are more alike than you ever imagined. You take precise aim for the jugular. Perhaps it's a family trait, one that passed over our dear father's generation."

"Don't you dare speak of him. Don't you dare." She stopped, pushed herself back. "Terrance, I have only one hope to offer you. One answer. One way out of the misery you have created for yourself and for everyone around you." She wiped a hand across her face. Plum-colored caverns had been excavated below her eyes. "Why did you come in here?"

A puff of wind blew night mist over them both. "You're right, of course. I shouldn't have bothered."

"No, no, that's not what I meant. You came in here looking for answers, isn't that so?"

"Clearly none of those you have to offer."

Terrance heard the phone ring in the distance. A moment later, one of the guards opened the door and announced, "The boss wants a word. In person."

"But it's four in the morning."

The guard shrugged. "The boss never was much for sleep."

Terrance rose and turned his face to the open window and the squall. The night was such a terrible foe. But he had triumphed over worse enemies. There had to be a way.

Audrey reached over and gripped his arm. "Listen to what I'm saying, will you please?"

Terrance looked down at her hand. He could not

remember the last time they had touched. "I was wrong to come here."

The guard warned, "Best not to keep the boss waiting."

"Terrance—"

He pulled his arm free. "Farewell, Audrey."

THE RAIN CAME WITH THE NIGHT. BY THE TIME DAWN spread a cold, grey blanket over the world, they had worked through Val's plan. Arthur held in there gamely, offering little besides his presence, refusing their repeated request for him to go upstairs and lie down. The five of them sat in grim determination, staring at the many problems for which they had no answers. Audrey's absence was a gaping wound Val saw in all their faces. Sharing this woe was a unifying force, the only answer he could find to whether he had the ability to pull this off.

Finally Gerald nodded once. A very small nod. "This is good."

Every tick of the clock was a hammer aimed at Val's temple, banging down on the need for speed. But he waited. There was nothing else he could do. To work this plan he needed them all. In truth, he needed an army. But these three men would have to do.

Arthur cleared his throat. "I would ask that you gentlemen do something for me."

"Anything." Bert's response was visceral. "Whatever you need, mate. Consider it done."

"When we got out of the joint," Dillon explained to Val, "Arthur here landed us both jobs."

"First honest wage I'd ever earned," Bert agreed. "You just name it, mate."

Arthur spoke for ten minutes. When he finished, the room remained locked in stunned silence.

Arthur slid his chair back and used both hands to push himself erect. "And now I fear I really must rest."

"We'll do it," Bert said, but weaker.

Dillon's voice was as strained as his features. "Are you certain—"

"Yes," Arthur replied. "I am. As certain as I've ever been in all my life."

"We can make this happen," Val admitted, though saying the words left him nauseous. "But we'll need your help."

"I thought as much."

Val followed Arthur down the hall and up the stairs, resisting the urge to help when the older man faltered. Only when Arthur entered the guestroom and sighed his way down onto the bed did Val say, "I'm not doing this for you, and I'm sure not doing it for Terrance. If I'd been the one holding the trigger and Terrance had been upstairs in that bank, I would not have hesitated one instant."

Arthur did not seem particularly surprised by his words. "And now?"

"I'm doing this for Audrey."

From the foot of the stairs, Bert called up, "Val, mate, it's time to roll."

Arthur's pale hands held out the keys to his battered old Rover. "I can only hope her love works on your magnificent stone of a heart."

Val accepted the keys. "I don't know if I'll ever be able to free myself like she wants—to let go of the hate and the pain. But I want to try. She deserves that much. Even if she won't give me another chance, still she deserves . . ."

Arthur watched him swallow against the tragedy of all he had lost, all he had done wrong, all he had failed to achieve. Arthur said at last, "This is the first good feeling I've had since the police stopped by."

Val set the portable phone on the bedside table and headed for the door. "I wish I could say the same."

———

Tension resided like an expanding bubble at the base of Val's ribcage. He swallowed twice as he descended the stairs, and three more times as he followed the trio out to Bert's van. The other men's grim silence only pushed more air into the bubble. The one sound in the van was the swish of the wipers. Val wondered if he showed the same lie in his own features. He had heard the way the breath caught in their throats whenever they mentioned Audrey's name. The only comfort Val found in that taut and colorless dawn was that they cared for her almost as much as he did.

They dropped Dillon off at the top of the road leading to Arthur d'Arcy's home. The young man solemnly shook hands with each of them before heading down the slope. They sat in tense silence until he unlocked Audrey's Rover and pulled away. There was no sign of unwanted interest. No sign of life along the wet and sleepy street. The remaining three men took a single unified breath of relief and headed out.

They skirted the industrial park and headed along the narrow high road toward Brighton. The early morning traffic was limited to trucks, delivery vans, and a few farm

vehicles. Wet sheep huddled against stone troughs and
sheltering groves. Cattle stared blankly at the passing
cars, unaware of the day's momentous hold.

The airfield was a pair of whitewashed hangars, a
stubby concrete tower, and one runway. The windsock
was pulled to nervous attention by the gusting wind.
They left the van and hustled into a steamy-windowed
café that formed the tower's base. Bert took a satisfied
breath of the grease-stained air and declared, "Believe I'll
have me a fry up."

Gerald grimaced in disgust. "You best be ready soon as
I say."

"Don't you fret, mate. You give us the word, and Bob's
your uncle." Bert watched Gerald depart with something
like fondness. "Just like Dillon, that one. Lad never did
have much of an appetite before a job. Mind you, after it
was over he could eat a horse and have room left over for
the saddle."

Val followed him over to the corner booth. There was
nothing to see outside but traces of rain patterned against
the steamed-over glass. "You and Dillon have been
together long?"

"Been years now. I claim to have raised him, just to
see him do his nut."

The day was such that Val could ask easily, "You were
both thieves?"

"We had our hands in a bit of this and that." Bert
smiled at the waitress. "Hello, love. I'll have the lot.
Beans, fried bread, four eggs, chips, rasher of bacon,
sausages, what have I forgotten? Oh my yes, and mush-
rooms. And tea. Oh, and toast. Got to have something to
wipe up the grease."

The waitress turned to Val. "What about you, love?"

"Just tea, thanks."

Bert smiled his thanks when the waitress returned with their teas. "What were we talking about?"

"You and Dillon."

Bert took a noisy sip. "Lad's the best second-story man I ever knew."

"And you?"

"Smash and grab, driving, fence, whatever paid, mate."

"Where did you meet Audrey?"

"Little place by the name of Wormwood Scrubs."

"A prison?"

"Worst there ever was." Bert watched the waitress deposit his plate, his good humor vanished. "Been there for donkey's years. Ghosts rattle around the place at night, ready to suck the breath straight out of your body." Bert used the scrunchy fried bread as a ladle for his eggs and talked around his food. "Audrey was counseling a mate of mine getting ready for parole. I went on account of any excuse being a fine one if it gave me visiting time with a lady. Took about six months before I realized she was drilling holes in this thick skull of mine. By then it was too late."

"Wish I'd had your sense."

Bert used his toast to sop up the grease. "Noticed you take something out and read it from time to time."

"Audrey wrote me a letter."

The knife and fork clattered down and he glanced at Val. A quick there-and-gone, nothing behind it. "Not my business to ask."

Val opened the letter. The creases had worn into soft patterns now. Val scanned the sheet, the biting affection known by heart. "She was just trying to reach me."

"Audrey has a way of talking," Bert agreed. "Brings to mind a sentiment I don't deserve."

Val refolded the pages. "Made me wish I was a better man."

"I remember once, she was talking to me on death. Death of hope, death of dreams. Watching life take the wrong turn that can't never be made right again." Bert turned and stared at the window, seeing something neither the rainswept day nor the misted glass could bar from vision. "What we do then is, we hide in our dark little cave and seal it up tight with a boulder of our own making. Before we can ever get out, we have to name the stone for what it is."

Rage, pain, hatred. Val found the words there waiting for him. All he said was, "I know exactly what you mean."

Bert said to his window, "Takes me back, that does. First time I heard her say the words, felt like she was tearing a hole in my chest."

The café's door opened. Gerald called through, "We're ready."

———

Val could not have come up with a better scenario to forget how bruised and bone-weary he was. He flew in the copilot's seat of a small single-engine plane. Below him was unmarked blackness. Above him was nothing at all. The windscreen was lashed by rain. The plane was buffeted by roller-coaster winds.

Val shouted above the roars, "Does it rain all the time here?"

"Don't be daft. It was lovely yesterday." Gerald pointed at the instrument panel with his chin. His complexion was green from the panel's illumination. At least, Val hoped it was the panel lights. "You just keep a sharp eye on the NAVS."

Bert filled both rear seats to overflow and groaned softly.

Val could not help but notice Gerald's death grip on the stick. "What's the matter with you?"

Gerald confessed, "I've never done this before."

"Done what, flown over water? Flown in a storm?"

"Take your pick."

Bert groaned louder. "Great time you picked to be letting us in on your little secret, mate."

"You can just ease up." Gerald never took his eye off the controls. "You heard him same as me. Val needed to get to Jersey without risking contact with the police. The authorities might be watching for him now that the news has broken."

"The important thing is getting there in one piece," Bert pointed out.

"Which I'm doing, if a certain somebody would tone it down with the distractions."

An hour later, Jersey appeared off to their right, a rainswept apparition rimmed by jagged white teeth. Gerald went through the landing protocol with an unseen tower. The voice coming back to them over the plane's loudspeaker spoke absolute gibberish as far as Val could tell. But Gerald altered his direction slightly and began a hard-fought descent. The wind struck them with invisible fists, jamming them about so hard the engine screamed to keep them on track.

They passed over a cliffside manor-hotel and a neighboring golf course. Two men working the first green halted their work, shielded their eyes against the tempest, and watched the plane's unsteady approach. The airfield appeared from the wet gloom. The landing strip looked about two inches wide.

Gerald took aim for the strip only to have a gust shove them brutally toward a neighboring grove of trees. He pulled back on the stick so hard his teeth were bared. The squall caught them full-force and sent them rocketing out and over the cliff. From where Val sat, it appeared they took aim straight for a grey and angry sea. Gerald continued hauling back and finally managed to straighten them out.

He regained altitude, dipped one wing, and circled back over the hotel. "Let's try that one again, shall we?"

"Just land the ruddy thing this time, all right, Gerald?"

Gerald straightened his shoulders, leaned in close to the windshield, and went for the strip. The wind mashed the surrounding grass into a shivering tabletop. The windsock by the tower looked ironed flat.

They hit hard. Bounced. The plane rose and almost touched one wing to the tarmac. They landed again. Gerald slapped the controls. The motor powered back. They stayed down.

When they stopped before the lone hangar, they crawled from the plane like cross-tied marionettes. Val glanced around the rain-swept vista. The workers by the first green had not budged.

TERRANCE SAT IN THE CORNER OF THE SUITE'S PARLOR.
He held a plastic hotel laundry bag full of ice to his jaw.
The swelling was coming in thick and purple. When the
skin stopped burning and turned numb, he switched the
bag to his eye.

A newspaper lay beside the silver coffee thermos. The
front page was folded back so that one word of the headline stood front and center. It shouted across the room at
him. *Insignia.*

Loupe sat at a room-service table set up by the empty
fireplace. The two heavies who had accompanied
Terrance in the elevator stood before him. The men
quaked in terror. Loupe did not raise his voice. Nor did he
threaten. "Explain it to me again. I'm trying hard to understand, you see. Describe how it was that two such great
hulking brutes could let the very man we've been tracking
for two days get by them."

"Boss, it's like this." The man swallowed loud enough for
the sound to carry across the room. "The bloke was wearing
a bellhop's uniform."

"A uniform."

"With a hat, boss. We didn't get a clean look at his
face, see."

Loupe turned his attention to his driver. The man stood sentry by the parlor's main doors. "What do you have to say for yourself?"

"I was right here. You called the house and ordered me back. I came."

Loupe pushed his breakfast plate aside and pulled out a cigar. He made a production of trimming the end and flicking open a heavy gold lighter. He sat back and puffed hard on the cigar, then inspected its glowing end. "A hat," the boss repeated. "This is the best excuse you can come up with? My so-called finest men?"

"All we saw was this hotel staff bloke carrying a wad of towels, coming down the hall. He wasn't nothing to us but the uniform."

Wally sat in the parlor's opposite corner, as far from Terrance as she could get. She watched Loupe with a cop's absence of emotion. Terrance wanted to shriek at her to give the signal. But Wally did not even glance his way.

Loupe asked, "What was it, the shiny brass buttons?"

"We just didn't recognize him, is all. Nobody knew who he was."

Terrance shifted the ice bag back to his eye. This was not supposed to be happening. He was the one in control. It was his forte. He *managed* things. He *manipulated*. All his problems came down to one man. Terrance whispered, "Val."

Loupe nodded vigorously in agreement. "Exactly. Val Haines is still out there. Who knows what mischief he might be cooking up?"

But a niggling concern had taken root in Terrance's mind. As though he needed another. He rose and headed for the parlor's side door, the one leading to what had formerly been his room.

Loupe tracked Terrance with his gaze but said nothing.

As Terrance entered the room, he heard the guard pleading openly now. "He came at us so fast, boss. Running down the hall, whacking our guy, then gone."

Terrance set the ice pack down on the tray holding the glasses and ice bucket. Val had been here. Terrance could sense the man's lingering presence.

Terrance crossed to the cabinet and opened the front. Dropping to his knees, he punched in the code to open the safe. Nothing. He repeated it, going more slowly this time, making sure the numbers were correct.

The safe's display replied that his numbers were invalid.

He walked back to the parlor entrance just as Loupe said thoughtfully, "Maybe I should show you both what a real whacking is."

"Boss—"

Loupe glanced over and noticed Terrance's expression. He waved the guards to silence. "What is it?"

"I know why Val was here."

"That's obvious enough. He came here looking for the girl. He failed. He went after you."

"That's not all. It probably wasn't even in the original plan." Terrance leaned against the doorjamb. "He's stolen my computer. I had it in my room safe. Now the safe won't open. Val broke the code, stole the computer, then shut the safe and recoded it to make it look like he hadn't been here."

There was a pounding at the door. Loupe motioned with his cigar. The sentry opened it.

Don Winslow burst inside.

Don was red-eyed and instantly raging. His gaze swiveled about the room like a sniper seeking prey. He fastened upon Terrance and shouted, "What are you *doing* here?"

Terrance could only shake his head. "You shouldn't have come."

"That's your idea of a news flash?" He sighted Wally and his scowl deepened. "So how come you're not out doing what we're paying you to do?"

Wally gave him an empty stare in reply.

Loupe demanded softly, "Who is this man?"

Don stalked over to where Terrance sat. "Do you have any idea the storm I left behind at headquarters? I've got SEC guys crawling all over the place with electron microscopes. So I fly over here, expecting to hear you're wrapping things up. What do I find?" Don flailed the air with his fist. "You guys sitting around having a tea party!"

"I asked you a question," Loupe said.

Don stared at the seated old man like he would a bug in the road. "I'm the top guy, is who I am. And the top guy is wondering why I'm talking to you at all."

Loupe paused long enough to puff on his cigar. He replied with the smoke, "I'm your new friend and partner."

Don laughed out loud. "In your dreams, pal."

The boss settled his cigar into the ashtray. "I fear that is the incorrect response."

"Like I care." Don wheeled back to Terrance. "Who danced on your face?"

"Val."

"Where is he?"

Terrance watched as Loupe set his cigar down in the ashtray. Terrance had never felt more helpless. Not even the day his father had betrayed him. Never. "We don't know."

Don's face reddened. "You're sitting here while the

man we need dead and disappeared is out strolling around the town?"

Loupe bent over and picked up one of the sofa pillows. "We were discussing strategy."

Don wheeled about. "I wasn't talking to you."

"Again, the wrong answer."

"What, you're making the rules now?"

Loupe slipped his hand beneath the jacket of his nearest man. He came out holding a pistol. Terrance was trapped in the amber of helpless foreknowledge.

Loupe brought up the pistol, cushioning the muzzle with the pillow.

And shot Don Winslow in the chest.

The bang was a sharp punch to the air, no louder than a single bass drumbeat. Everybody save Loupe jerked, knowing the next shot could just as easily be aimed at them.

Terrance watched his own life fall to the carpet with his former partner.

Loupe stood over Don and replied, "That is correct. I now make all the rules."

The boss nudged the body with the toe of his shoe. Then he handed back the gun, returned to the table, and reached for his cigar. He puffed long enough to get the cigar drawing fully, then said with the smoke, "Get rid of this filth."

The two men who had been awaiting judgment leapt to obey. Loupe watched them roll the body into a pair of blankets and toss it over one man's shoulder. "Don't either of you for a minute think I'm done yet."

A tremor went through both their frames. The driver opened the door, scouted the hallway, then pointed them toward the service elevator.

When the door shut behind them, the boss turned to Wally and said, "You know a gentleman by the name of Gennaro, I believe."

Wally might have nodded. But Terrance thought more than likely it was merely a shudder.

"Of course you do. He owns you, doesn't he?" Loupe tapped off the ash. "He and I had a little chat last night. I think it's time you went back and reported in, don't you?"

Wally struggled to her feet. She did not glance in Terrance's direction as she headed for the door.

As she opened it, Loupe added, "I don't need to say a thing to you, do I? About all that must remain between us and such as that."

Wally stared down at the hand holding the doorknob. She shook her head and murmured, "No. You don't."

"The first time I set eyes on you, I knew you for a smart lady. Be sure and give Gennaro my best, now, will you?"

Loupe waited until the door shut behind her to say, "I do so hope these new arrangements meet with your approval."

Terrance did not respond. Of course, he was not expected to.

Loupe dragged a chair over to Terrance's corner and seated himself. He patted Terrance on the knee with the hand holding the cigar. The smoke clogged Terrance's every pore.

The boss said in his mild tone, "Now perhaps you'll be so good as to tell your new partner just exactly what the stakes are in this little game."

AS FAR AS JOCKO WAS CONCERNED, THE ISLAND OF Jersey was a wee tight place. Especially for two men who'd shared a berth in Wormwood Scrubs, as cramped a set of quarters as ever there were. The walls here might be liquid, the food a ruddy sight better than inside the grey-bar hotel. But the sentence Jocko served out was the same. Forever and a day.

They were set up in a hotel across the street from the bank's only entrance. The room Jocko shared with Matt was almost as small as their cell. The hotel was a glorified boarding house, not even deserving its single star. But it was the only one they could find with a clear view of the place. When Matt had complained, Loupe had offered to fit them out with something smaller. A barrel, perhaps.

So there they sat, day in and day out, one or the other of them staring at the ruddy entrance until their eyes were ready to fall out of their heads. They even did it all night long, which was the stupidest thing going, according to Matt. The bank had these great steel doors that wheeled out at five every afternoon, locking the place up like a streetside vault. They made no sense, as orders went. Jocko's mate, the brains of the pair, was given to complaining more with every passing hour. Jocko, though, he found the alternative a ruddy sight less appealing. He had been around long enough to hear the tales of what Loupe did to those who disappointed him. Jocko had no interest in finding out if the tales were true. No, mate. Not him. He'd sit by the ruddy window until he fused with the chair, he would.

Which had almost happened. Jocko had been at it for five poxy hours. Sitting by the window, watching the grey light strengthen and the rain fall and smoking his head off. The noisy bedside clock taunted him all night with how slowly time moved. Finally he couldn't take it anymore.

Jocko walked over and kicked the bed. Again. A third time, and finally his mate was up and complaining again. The rain, the day, the stink from Jocko's cigarettes even with the window wide open. Matt's voice was persistent as a drill. But at least Jocko heard some other noise now besides the drip-drip-drip of this rain.

Soon as Matt was dressed and moaning by the window about another day lost to nothing, Jocko left. The hotel manager was already at his desk. The old geezer didn't think much of two men sharing one of his cramped front rooms. Jocko left the hotel and walked through the cold rain and wondered why anybody would ever want to live in such a place. Stone the crows, but this was a miserable excuse for a town. Cramped rooms and tiny streets and small-minded people, surrounded by miles and miles of empty water and rain. Jocko stopped by the newsagents' and bought a *Sun*. He rounded the corner and entered the steamy café. He took his regular place in the booth by the window and ordered his regular breakfast. He opened his paper and almost moaned over that first sip of tea. Breakfast was the one thing this place had not managed to ruin.

Jocko was about midway through the morning feast when something caught his eye.

At first he wasn't sure what it was he'd seen, what with the window so misted over and the rain falling in sheets. Jocko rubbed the pane clean. Yes. Stepping away from a shop connected to a church. Walking there on the main road. Headed for the bank. A man who looked a lot like . . .

Jocko sprang from the booth and barged out the door. He raced around the corner in time to watch the bloke walk up the front steps and enter the bank. It might have been their man. Only Jocko was looking at this bloke from the rear. And it had been a while. And the wind was rising and blowing this pelting rain straight into his eyes. Jocko swiped angrily at his face and started forward.

Then he stopped. Because there were two men stationed at the front of the bank. One of them was a bloke big as himself. Definitely someone who knew how to handle himself.

Jocko took another step. This one took him over by the corner of the hotel. He squinted against the driving rain.

He'd seen that man before.

Jocko turned up his collar and sauntered along the lane. He took the hotel stairs easy as you please. Once through the hotel entrance, though, Jocko hurtled across the lobby and thundered up the stairs.

Jocko flung open the door to their room, only to discover his mate seated by the window, his head in his arms, dead asleep.

Jocko kicked the chair out from under him.

Matt fell to the floor, picked himself up, and cuffed Jocko. The blow was about as potent as a fleabite. Cross and sour, Matt picked up the chair, slammed it back down, and started complaining about how Jocko didn't even bother to bring him a cup of tea and something hot—

"He's here."

Matt paled. "The boss? Here?"

"No. Our target."

Matt almost fell out the window in his panic. "Where?"

"The bank. Maybe."

"What's that supposed to mean, maybe? Either he's in the bank or he's not."

"Only saw the bloke from behind, didn't I. And look there. See the muscle? They showed up with him."

His mate was seriously alarmed. "Are they ours?"

"Have a look at the bloke on the right. I've seen him before."

"With Loupe?"

"No. Inside. He was in another section. Somebody pointed him out. Savage. Yeah, that's the bloke's name. Bert Savage."

"The boss didn't say anything about heavies."

Jocko squinted out the window, wanting to tighten down his gaze and pierce the stone wall. "Maybe it wasn't him."

"But what if it is?"

"Think we should call it in?"

"Have you gone totally round the bend? What if you're wrong? You want to give Loupe another reason to bring us in for a little chat?"

Jocko did not need to answer that one. "What do we do, then?"

"I'm going over."

"Wait, the boss, he said we weren't supposed to show our faces."

"We've got to know, right? You heard the boss same as me. The second that bloke shows up, we're to phone it in. Not thirty seconds later. Not even two." Matt grabbed his jacket. "Wait here."

VAL, BERT, AND GERALD SHARED A TAXI INTO ST. HELIER, the capital of both Jersey and the Channel Islands. The town was fairy-tale clean and laced with sea salt and safe mysteries. Not even the pelting rain could wash away the island's romantic feel. Early morning tourists clambered about the cobblestone lanes, so enchanted they accepted the windswept chill as part of the magic. The wealth on display was very discreet, like a lady's subtle hint of silk.

The taxi let them off by a church tea shop down the block from the Syntec Bank of Jersey. By the time they'd settled at a table with their tea and scones, a numbness had invaded Val's bones. He felt enveloped within an altered state somewhere between exhaustion and an electric high. Val was no longer angry. The day held no space for such mundane elements as personal feelings. The three of them shared a rapidly cooling pot of tea and waited for the clock to crawl once around the dial.

At nine sharp they watched through the tea shop's front window as two uniformed guards rolled back the curved steel gates sealing the bank's entrance. Silently, Val and the others left by the shop's side exit.

When they arrived at the bank, Bert took up station under the front awning. "You get yourself in there and save the day, lad. We'll camp out here and wait your word."

"You both know what to do?"

"We've been over it a dozen times, mate. More."

Gerald almost smiled. Not quite, but almost. "I don't suppose it would help to say the fate of the world rests in your arms."

"No. It wouldn't." Val entered the bank alone.

Syntec bank's public chamber was a long, narrow hall with brass-caged teller's windows down the right-hand wall. Brass footrails ringed the oval marble writing stand. Brass chandeliers hung from the high ceiling. The floor was marble, the front windows high and arched. The back of the room was given over to executive stalls with waist-level mahogany partitions. The woodwork gleamed. The entire chamber smelled of centuries of money and polish and the subtle terrors Val carried in with him.

Val took off the raincoat and shook it. His clothes were borrowed from Gerald. They consisted of a grey flannel suit, Oxford shirt, and a silk tie printed with the emblem from Gerald's college. He felt only marginally better dressed than when he wore the bellhop's uniform. Then again, it probably was not the clothes that constricted his gut and made it hard to draw a decent breath.

A guard approached. "Can I help you?"

"I'm here to see Mr. Francis Richards."

"Is *Sir* Francis expecting you?" The guard gave gentle emphasis to the title.

"I called earlier this morning and left a message on the bank's answering machine."

"Certainly, sir. May I have your name?"

"Jeffrey Adams."

"Very good, sir. If you'll just come this way." The sentry guided Val to the rear of the chamber, where a receptionist was already on her feet. "A Mr. Jeffrey Adams to see Sir Francis."

"Do you have an appointment, Mr. Adams?"

"My visit came up at the last moment. I called before you were open and asked for this meeting."

"Are you a client of Sir Francis?"

"In a manner of speaking. But we've never met."

"Might I trouble you for some form of ID?" When Val handed over his fake passport, she said, "If you'll just wait here a moment, I will see if Sir Francis is available."

When the receptionist cupped the phone to her ear and turned slightly away, Val asked the guard, "What is Sir Francis's position?"

"Senior account executive, sir."

The receptionist swiftly returned. "If you'll just come this way, sir."

Val was ushered upstairs and into an antechamber of rosewood paneling. Cigar smoke hung vaguely in the air, like a lingering fragrance of the previous day's millions. Val found the odor faintly nauseous and breathed through his mouth. His heart sounded loud as gunfire.

A slender man approached with outstretched hand. "Mr. Adams?"

"That's right."

"Francis Richards. What a delight. Received your message first thing this morning. Shame about the weather, don't you agree? Tragic spring we're having. Lashes of rain and cold and no end in sight. Won't you come this way?"

Richards wore a double-breasted navy jacket with gold-embossed buttons. A scarf matching his overloud tie dangled slightly from his breast pocket. An ornate family crest was woven into this same pocket. His hair was long and foppishly styled. His teeth were huge as he smiled Val into his office. "I believe you'll find that chair quite comfortable."

The office was rather cramped and narrow. But a royal crest matching the one on Richards's jacket hung from the wall behind his desk. Val took the seat before the desk as directed and looked carefully about. The room's only window overlooked the rainwashed street. A photograph of a grand estate hung from the right-hand wall. The manor looked enormous. But the photograph was in black and white, and the man standing upon the front steps was dressed in a bygone style.

Richards crossed behind his desk. "I checked our records after hearing your message, Mr. Adams. I failed to find any record of your being a client of our bank. Not that you're not welcome, of course. It's just we do rather like to keep tabs of whose money we're holding."

Val would normally have disliked the man and his upper-crust bray on sight. Today, however, he considered him ideal. No man, dressed like a titled duke and bearing his overarched accent, would be doing duty as a bank staffer unless he possessed more title than cash. He pointed to the photograph. "That's some spread."

"Ah. Yes. It is rather nice. Or was, I suppose I should say. Lost in the Depression, along with far too much else. I really should dispose of the wretched photo."

Val nodded slowly. He could well understand why Terrance had chosen to do business with this man.

Richards steepled his fingers. "Is there something I might do for you today, Mr. Adams? We are rather pressed for time, you see, and—"

"My name is not Adams."

Richards froze. "Pardon me?"

"It is Valentine Haines."

"Haines, Haines. Now that is a name I do recognize." He slid his chair over and tapped into his computer terminal. "Of course. Mr. Haines." Then a light dawned. "Did I not hear something of your recent demise?"

"All false, I'm afraid."

"And how frightfully glad I am to hear it. I don't suppose you happen to have any form of identification on you."

"No. But you have my photograph in your records." Stored in advance, to ensure personal security and access to their funds. "Along with my fingerprints."

"Indeed we do." Richards turned to his credenza and came up with an electronic pad. "If I might ask you to be so kind?"

Val pressed his hand onto the glass screen. And waited.

It did not take long. "Verified and confirmed." Richards was now all smooth professional. "What might we do for you today, Mr. Haines? Or should we remain with Adams?"

"I'm here to make a withdrawal."

"Certainly, sir. How much would you be after?"

"Two million, two hundred and eighteen thousand dollars."

The banker tabbed the keyboard. "But that's—"

"All of it," Val confirmed. "Plus any interest I've earned. And I want it in cash."

———

Matt did the innocent's walk across the street to the bank entrance. Ambling along, collar up against the wet, not looking at anything really. Just minding his own business and headed inside. Going up the stairs, he slowed enough to give both the blokes a careful look. Up close the muscle to his left didn't look any more familiar than from the window. Which didn't mean Jocko was wrong. The two men gave Matt an inspection of their own, using the cold eye of blokes who know their way around a tight corner.

For a moment Matt hesitated. He did the pocket-pat, like he belonged there at the bank if only he could find his papers. Thinking maybe he should go back for Jocko. But if they were there guarding the man Matt was after, leaving and coming back would only alert them. And what good would it do? Matt's orders were to call in soon as they spotted the bloke. Nothing more. Having a dust-up on a dank street in the middle of this poxy town was not on the list.

No, best just play the hand and act like he owned the place.

Which might've worked, only one of the heavies decided to follow Matt into the bank.

Inside, the bloke just stood there by the entrance. Hovering. Ready.

Matt gave the place a quick look-round. The bank was almost empty. Three customers up front, all women. One old geezer in the back, talking soft like he'd spent years learning how to handle coin. Definitely not their man. Which meant either their bloke was upstairs some-where, or Jocko was wrong.

What to do?

Matt sighted the guard sauntering over. Taking it slow. Not wanting a fuss.

Matt turned and left. The muscle followed him out.

Matt scampered down the stairs and across the street and into the hotel and up the stairs and into the room.

Jocko was all over him in a flash. "What'd you see?"

Matt collapsed into the chair. "Go bring me a tea and two fried-egg sandwiches."

"Was it our guy?"

"He wasn't there, was he?"

"So he's upstairs somewhere?"

"If it was him."

"What do we do?"

"We wait." Matt snapped his fingers. "Large tea. Extra milk. Hot mustard and white toast, and the eggs better be fried up hard enough I can nail them to the wall."

"What if it's him?"

"We call it in. Say he's just arriving." Matt didn't take his eyes off the bank's only entrance. "Now hop to it. I need you back here and ready."

THE BANKER PUT UP A RATHER HIGHBROWED PROTEST at Val's demand for over two million dollars in cash. But obviously Val was not the first person to come in seeking that sort of withdrawal. The papers were eventually filled out and passed over for Val's signature.

The conversation drifted over inconsequential matters as the money was gathered. Suddenly Val spied a face in a window across the narrow street. He leaned forward, searching his memory. But he couldn't be certain. Then he spotted a second man, a larger one whom Val had seen much closer and for far longer than the narrow-faced man. Suddenly he was back on the ferry.

Val stood and turned his chair around. When he reseated himself, he realized the banker was observing him with mild alarm.

"The light," Val said. "It bothers me."

The banker stared out his window. "But it's raining cats and dogs."

"Exactly," Val said.

The banker's secretary returned with a polished rosewood tray. On it resided a very substantial block of cash. Richards could not completely hide his avarice as he surveyed the money. "Perhaps you might like to count it," he suggested brightly. "Then you can be on your—"

"We're not done yet," Val said. He turned to the secretary and asked, "Would you mind leaving us alone?"

Richards gave her a befuddled nod. "Give us another moment, would you, Fiona?"

"Certainly, sir."

When the door closed again, Val reached into his jacket pocket and brought out several sheets of paper. He handed over the first page, which held the six strings of numbers they had found on Terrance's computer. "Have a look at these, please."

The banker's eyes rounded as he read the data. He swung his chair around and tapped into his computer. His eyebrows crawled up into his hairline.

It was the response Val had been seeking. The one they desperately needed for this to work. Val interpreted for him. "Your bank holds deposits totaling four hundred and eighteen million dollars. These accounts are in the names of Val Haines and Marjorie Copeland. As you have heard, Mrs. Copeland died in the explosion that destroyed your New York offices. This leaves me the sole holder of these funds."

Richards continued to study his screen. It was all the confirmation Val needed. "I am countermanding whatever standing orders you have controlling access to these accounts."

Richards read off the computer screen, "I require detailed codes to unlock them."

"They were destroyed in the explosion." Val handed over a second sheet. "I want all these funds transferred to this account."

Richards worked his mouth a few times before managing, "But this is . . ."

"That's right," Val agreed. "It is."

The banker looked from the page to Val and back again. "Without the codes, I fear—"

"But wait, there's more. In a couple of minutes, your phone is going to ring." Val offered the banker a third sheet. "This man will be calling you. He is going to ask if the funds are still in the account here in this bank. Tell him yes. He will then probably give you transfer instructions. He will have the codes. Tell him you'll do as he orders, but only once you have confirmation that this person is released. Confirmation must come from the father, Arthur d'Arcy. Who must come on the phone and speak with you."

Richards sputtered, "I couldn't possibly even consider—"

"Do these two things," Val said, "and all the money piled here on the desk is yours."

The banker went pale.

Val carefully repeated the instructions. "There will never be anything in writing about this conversation. No record whatsoever of this ever having happened." Val pushed the tray slightly closer. "One transfer. One phone call. And it's yours."

———

The instant Val slipped through the front entrance, Bert gripped his arm and spun him about. "Face the wall, that's a good lad."

Gerald explained, "Bert thinks we've got some unwanted attention from the hotel across the way."

"I spotted them from the banker's office," Val said.

Bert shielded him from the street with his bulk. The bank had a circular awning of colored stone, from which the rain dripped in a steady translucent curtain. Gerald asked, "What's the word?"

"He went for it."

The two men sighed in unison. Gerald announced quietly, "Dillon rang. His contact came through."

"We have to be certain."

"You can count on the lad." Bert looked from one face to the other. "Then we're good to go, are we?"

Val forced himself to say, "Let's make the call."

Bert took his phone from one pocket and a slip of paper from the other. He dialed the hotel's number, listened, and handed Val the phone. "Good luck, mate."

The phone spoke to him. "Good morning, Hastings Palace Hotel. How may I help you?"

"Suite eight-eighteen, please."

"One moment."

The phone rang twice before a male voice answered with, "We're still waiting on a fresh pot of coffee up here."

Val swallowed hard. "I'd like to speak with Terrance d'Arcy."

"Who's this?"

"Just tell him there's four hundred and eighteen million good reasons for him to get on the phone."

TERRANCE LAY IN THE SUITE'S SECOND BEDROOM AND watched daylight stain the walls. It had stopped raining during the previous hour. A steady drip-drip pattered upon the windowsill beside his head. Every now and then one of the sentries glanced through the parlor's open door. Terrance lay in his clothes except his jacket, which was cast over the back of a nearby chair. His tie was down a notch. He rubbed his chin. He needed to shave. He could not recall the last time he had been so bedraggled. Or a time when it had mattered less than now. He stared up at the ceiling where the window drapes formed a guillotine's shadow.

One of the sentries stepped into the doorway. "The boss wants a word."

Terrance knew there was nothing to be gained by arguing. Besides which, he had no interest in lying there any longer. He donned his jacket, tightened his tie, slicked back his hair, going through the motions as though they mattered.

"Pour our guest a cup of coffee," Loupe ordered.

Terrance did not want any, but he accepted it and held it. Loupe slurped happily from his own cup. "We were discussing the safety measures you kept in your machine. What did you call them?"

"Firewalls. We've gone through this before."

"Indulge me. Firewalls. Yes. A fascinating concept. Are these firewalls secure?"

Old cigar smoke clogged the parlor. "Anything can be broken into, given enough time and expertise."

"So nothing has changed. We enter a new electronic age, and yet the old rules still apply." Loupe seemed to find a bizarre satisfaction in that pronouncement. "And there is no way for you to access your accounts except with your machine?"

"My laptop, my home computer, Don Winslow's computer. But only with them." The codes had to be entered in a precise fashion. All electronic banking was done in this manner, but Terrance had introduced new restrictions such that the bank's computer would only communicate with another computer that reconfirmed as it worked, an ingenious means of ensuring that no outsider could access their accounts. It required both the codes and a knowledge of which bank they accessed.

Which Val Haines possessed.

"Which means we must not grant our opponents sufficient time to move." Loupe toyed with his cup. "Remind me once again the sum we are discussing here."

"Four hundred and eighteen million."

"Dollars."

Terrance wanted to raise his fists and scream. "Dollars. Yes. Dollars."

Loupe finished his coffee and sighed contentedly. He asked the sentry, "Still nothing at the old man's house?"

"Not a peep, boss."

He asked Terrance, "You are certain there is no other number where we might . . ."

His words were cut off by a pinging from the hotel phone. The nearest muscle answered and said they were still waiting for the coffee. Then he held the phone out to Loupe.

———

The man on the other end did not bother to cover the phone as he spoke to someone else. "There's a bloke on the phone asking for d'Arcy. Sounds like a Yank. He knows about the money."

A longish pause, then a slightly accented voice asked, "Who am I addressing, please?"

"Val Haines."

"Mr. Haines. How wonderful. I have been so looking forward to having a little chat."

"Who is this?"

"Let's be frank, Mr. Haines. There's only one name that matters here, wouldn't you agree? And it's certainly not mine."

The two men supported Val with their steady gazes. "Audrey."

"It's so good to deal with someone who can move directly to the matter at hand, don't you agree?"

"I asked to speak with Terrance."

A faint steel edge crept into the voice. "You're dealing with me now."

Val fought hard to keep his quivering stomach muscles from affecting his voice. "Long as I get what I want."

"My thoughts exactly, Mr. Haines. You have something of ours, I believe."

"That's right."

"So how would you wish to play this out?"

"A straight swap. The hotel lobby."

"I would prefer somewhere a bit less public."

"I know you would. But this is how it's going to be. I want Terrance and Audrey in exchange for the computer."

"I do not care for your tone, Mr. Haines. Perhaps I should have one of my men help your dear young lady to sing for you."

"I'll be there in three hours. The two of them for the computer. Your call." Val punched off the phone. Clenched it to his chest with one hand and reached for the metal pillar supporting the veranda's roof. Pumped his lungs hard. "I'm going to be sick."

Gerald looked as nauseous as Val felt. But Bert replied, "No time for that, lad. You said it yourself. Timing's everything now. Straighten up, big easy breaths, that's the ticket."

"Time for the second call," Val said weakly, and handed Bert the phone.

"No, mate." Bert coded in another number and handed it back. "You're the captain of this ship."

The phone rang once, then Arthur d'Arcy said, "Yes?"

"We're on."

"Bless you, son." The old man sounded positively joyful. "A thousand times over. Bless you."

"You be careful."

"Don't worry about me." Arthur almost sang the words. "God is on our side."

Val cut the connection and handed back the phone. "You won't believe what he just told me."

Bert pointed over his shoulder at the hotel across the way. "I might've recognized one of the blokes. From inside."

The sick feeling started to press up into his chest again. Val damped it down as best he could. "Nothing we can do about that now."

"No, suppose not," Bert said, and followed Val back inside.

———

"Is it him?"

"For the tenth time, I can't say." Matt pounded the windowsill and hissed across the street, "Turn around!"

"I'll go over there and sort this out proper."

"Stay where you are."

"But—"

"The boss didn't say anything about getting ourselves made, did he?" Matt clawed the sill. "What're they doing standing around in this weather, that's what I'd like to know."

"We can't sit here doing nothing."

"Hang on. He's going back inside." Matt groaned. "And the muscle is going with him. Of all the ruddy luck."

"What do we do?"

Matt slumped back into the chair. "What we been doing since we started this life sentence. We wait."

WHEN THEY ARRIVED UPSTAIRS, THE BANKER'S SECRE-
tary was waiting to show Val back into the banker's office.
Her eyes widened at the sight of Bert. Most likely she did
not often see bruisers with arms larger than her waist
come waltzing in, wanting to talk about two million dollars in cash. Val said simply, "He's with me."

"Of course, sir." She scurried to stay well ahead of
them. "Right this way."

When they arrived back in Richards's office, the cash
was still there on the desk. Richards's gaze rounded at
their entry. But less so than the secretary's. He was too
busy with his mental games, playing out what he could
do with over two million dollars.

Val said, "This is my associate. I have to leave. He will
remain here through the telephone conversation, then
depart. He knows what you need to say."

Richards rocked back in his seat. "And if I don't?"

Bert warned, "A deal's a deal, mate."

Whatever Richards saw in Bert's face was enough to
drain his own features of blood.

"No, none of that," Val said sharply. "You agreed. But
if you decide to change your mind, we'll just take the
cash and leave."

"A little late for that." Bert punched the air between them, causing the banker to flinch. "We've already set things in motion because of him."

"Bert." Val waited until the big man stopped glaring at the banker and turned around to say, "Audrey wouldn't go for that."

Bert's shoulders slumped. "What a thing to be telling me now."

Richards cleared his throat. "Audrey?"

Val kept his eyes on Bert. "We do this right, or we don't do it at all."

"The right thing for the wrong reason is just adding to the problem," Bert mumbled to his feet.

"Is that from Audrey?"

"Sure didn't come from me, mate." Bert nodded once. "Okay, then."

"You're sure?"

"Yeah, I'm right as rain."

Val turned to the banker, who was watching with wide-eyed confusion. "It would help us to know now what you're going to do. A woman's life may hang in the balance."

Bert covered his eyes.

Richards's gaze went from one man to the other. "Something's happened?"

"The man who is about to call you is holding her against her will. We don't think he will hold to his side of the bargain and let her go. You're part of our insurance policy."

"I-I'm not quite sure I understand."

"You don't need to," Val replied, and waited.

Richards touched the knot of his tie, rubbed his jaw, patted his foppish hair. "Well, naturally, if we're intending to help a damsel in distress, who am I to refuse?"

"Then you'll do it?"

"Certainly. For a good cause, and all that."

"And two million two in cash, free and clear."

"Well, yes." His gaze swiveled back to the money. "There most certainly is that."

Val pulled the final sheet of paper from his pocket, inspected it carefully, and said, "There's just one small thing more."

Richards blanched. "I beg your pardon?"

"Nothing complicated. Just a straight transfer, for which I do have clearance." Val handed over the page. "Can you handle that while you're waiting for the call?"

Richards had difficulty bringing his computer records into focus. "Oh. Yes. Of course. I see no problem here."

"Great." Val rose from his chair. "Is there a back door? If I can, I'd like to slip out unobserved."

"There's the employees' entrance at the rear." Richards saw nothing beyond the cash on his desk. "I'll have my assistant show you the way."

"Ask her to bring my associate in from your front porch before she does. His name is Gerald." Val patted Bert on the shoulder. "We'll call as soon as we've got something to report."

Bert did not look up. "You just make ruddy sure things go to plan, mate."

"I'll try."

"And when you see her, tell the lass Bert says hello."

———

Matt leapt from the chair. "I don't believe this!"

"What is it now?"

"They've all disappeared!"

Jocko pressed in beside him. "They can't have."

"They did, I'm telling you. One comes out, two go in, now a lady shows up and the third does like smoke."

"You think they made us?"

"How am I supposed to know that?"

Jocko leaned out the window and was drenched by the rain. "It's like they never were there."

"The boss hears about this and we're good as dead." Matt pounded the windowsill. "What do we do now?"

Jocko ducked inside and wiped his face. "You want me to go have a look?"

Matt let his hand drop to his side. "What good would that do?"

"You're asking me?"

"Wait, let me think." Matt's face glistened with the same fear churning through Jocko's gut. "Okay. Here's the deal. You go have a quiet look around the outside. I'll keep watch. First sign it's really our man, we call like we just spotted him, right?"

Jocko swiped his own face clear of the fear-sweat. "But what if they don't show, Matt? What if we sit here all ruddy day and the bank closes and we still don't get another look? The guy's scarpered, we've let him go, what then?"

Matt's features were green. "Then *we* scarper."

"What?"

"Morocco. Or the Philippines, maybe. Someplace far away."

"Leave England?"

"We've already left England, you dolt."

"This is different."

"Too right it is. This time we're never coming back."

GERALD PHONED THE AIRFIELD FROM THE TAXI AND promised a huge tip if the plane was fueled and ready to go. When they arrived, the mechanic was there to unhook the wings.

The mechanic slipped Gerald's cash into his coveralls and asked, "Where are you headed in such a rush?"

"England."

"In this?" Rain dripped off the hood of his jacket, causing him to squint. "Better you than me, mate."

Gerald powered up the engines before Val had his seatbelt fastened. The wind mocked them with its force, rocking the plane before they were even moving. Now that he was once more behind the controls, Gerald's features adopted the same grim cast as before.

He taxied them out to the runway, rogered his take-off to the tower, then glanced at Val. "You ready?"

"Just remember," Val replied. "If we crash and burn, this whole thing goes to pot."

The roller coaster started as soon as their wheels left the ground. The plane yawed furiously, swept up by a sudden gust, tilted sharply, and the engine howled in protest. Val took white-knuckle grips on the edge of his seat and the roof. The cliffs swept by beneath them, to be replaced by raging whitecaps stretching out to where everything became lost in the rain and wind.

An hour and a bit into the flight, however, everything changed. One moment they were flying through grey skyborne froth, surrounded by a dismal noonday twilight. The next, they entered a vastly different realm.

The storm peeled away as though ripped from the earth. The wind calmed.

They entered a placid universe, so different Val doubted his own senses. Even the motor was comforted into a softer purr.

Val looked at Gerald. "What is this, the Twilight Zone?"

Gerald released his death's grip on the stick. "Just your basic schizophrenic English spring."

The sky stretched blue-black ahead of them, washed sparkling clear. Below and to Val's right, two freighters carved white streamers from a jewellike English Channel. Up ahead he could just glimpse the white coastal teeth and the emerald fields beyond.

Gerald asked, "Do you think we might take this as a sign?"

Val refused to answer.

The phone chimed just as Gerald began his initial approach to the Brighton airfield. "Get that, will you? Right jacket pocket."

Val pulled it out. "Haines."

It was Dillon. "Can you believe this ruddy weather?"

"I understand why you talk about it all the time. It never ceases to amaze."

"Where's Gerald?"

"Landing us."

"I'm sitting at the entrance to Alders Way. Ask him does he know where that is."

Gerald replied, "Tell him yes."

"You lads get over here right sharp. I found the house they're using."

"You're sure?"

"Pretty much."

"We can't be wrong on this."

"Just don't hang about. We'll see what we see when you get here."

———

Fifty-five minutes later, Val and Gerald pulled into the entrance of a cul-de-sac jammed hard against the base of a steep hill. The mound grew out of nowhere, punching up into the impossibly blue sky like a grass-covered block. A pair of trails crawled up the side, probably where kids climbed and played over the flat top. The houses ringing the base were nondescript clones, ten in all. White stone bases rose to red mock-Victorian fronts, three linked together, then a tight space, then three more. Only the middle house stood alone. Opposite the cul-de-sac's entrance, the sea sparkled between rooftops and Hastings's narrow lanes. A few sailboats were already leaving port and putting tentatively to sea. The morning's storm was merely a fading memory.

Dillon rose from Audrey's grey Rover at their approach. He had his phone plastered to his ear. He wore an open-neck shirt and jeans wrinkled below the knees by the rain. He waved them around the corner. Gerald halted his van behind a house, blocking them from view.

Dillon walked over and nodded a tight welcome. "Everything go right in Jersey?"

"Far as we know. Where's Audrey?"

"Hang on a sec." He tapped one hand nervously on the van's roof. "The house is in the middle, the only one standing all by itself. Inside that little wall there, see it? Number eight. Three toughs came tearing out of there and jammed into a car. Black beemer."

"When was that?"

"An hour back."

Which meant they were gathering forces before Arthur's arrival at the hotel.

"I ducked down as they came roaring past, but not before I got a good look," Dillon went on. "Audrey wasn't with them. So I phoned for some backup. Here she comes now."

The woman could have been forty or sixty. She turned the corner and approached the van with a balanced limp, as though both feet hurt her equally. She wore a buttoned cardigan and a flowered dress and reading glasses draped around her neck. She carried a rolled umbrella in one hand and a metal clipboard in the other. She bussed Dillon on the cheek. "All right, love?"

"Yeah, not bad." Dillon slid open the van's rear door. "Lads, this is Doris. Doris, these are the mates I told you about."

"Help me in, that's a dear." Her features held the dignified sternness of someone who bore much in silence. Her hair was a chemically induced shade of copper. When Dillon slipped in beside her and shut the door, she asked, "Staying out of trouble, love?"

"Up to this morning." Dillon explained to the others, "Doris is mum to a young lady I'm seeing."

"Only so long as you keep your nose clean."

"I'm trying, aren't I?"

"Trying isn't good enough."

"Yeah, so you keep going on about." Dillon said to the men up front, "Doris runs the largest holiday rental agency in Hastings. Yesterday one of her cleaners was telling her about a cottage where all the men wear suits. And we're not talking about your basic business geeks, are we, Doris?"

"I manage eighty-three cottages. The things you see don't bear thinking about." She shook her head in disgust. "Do I want to know what's happening here?"

"Probably not, love. No."

Val turned fully around in his seat. "Dillon is not going to get involved in anything, ma'am."

Doris inspected him carefully. "You're going to see to that, are you?"

"Yes ma'am. I am."

She studied him a bit longer, then nodded her head. Satisfied. "I've had a word with Susie, like you asked."

"Susie being the cleaning lady," Dillon explained. To Doris, "You trust her, do you?"

"She's a good lass in her own simple way. We're not after rocket scientists here. We're after honest, hardworking folk who won't pocket what's not theirs."

"She saw something, your Susie."

"Four men, just like you said. All in dark suits. Expensive cut. Drive ever so nice a motor. Foreign, she thought. Dark like the suits."

"Not your normal sort of tourists."

"What's normal in this day and age, I ask you? So when you phoned back I decided to go have a look for myself. Delivering fresh towels, carrying my clipboard, just going about for a normal inspection. The bloke in there tried to give me some lip."

"Just one man?" Val asked.

"That's all I saw."

"You gave him some lip right back, didn't you, love?" Dillon said.

"They rent from us, we've got certain rights and obligations, I tell him. It's our way of keeping up with the houses in our care. So he lets me in, but he doesn't half keep an eye out. Stalking me, he was. And he wouldn't let me near the back bedroom. Claimed there's a mate of his in there, not feeling well. I can't complain about that, long as he lets me into the lounge and the kitchen and the loo. Which he does."

Val asked, "Tell me what you thought of the guy."

"Big hulking brute," she said crossly. "A thug in a suit is still just a thug. Made my skin crawl, just being inside with the likes of him."

"Thanks, Doris." Dillon slid open the door. "You've been ever so helpful."

"We run a proper service here for proper people." She started for the door, then paused. "Straight up, now. You're not back on the game, are you, son?"

"Not me, love. No. Not ever."

"That's right, he's not," Val confirmed. "We're just trying to help a friend."

"I'll be off, then." She stepped from the van. "You lads play nice."

WERE IT NOT FOR THE PIPED-IN MUSIC, THE ELEVATOR might as well have been a coffin fitted for six. They rode downstairs in silence. Terrance was hemmed in on all sides. Loupe had hardly spoken to him since getting off the phone with Val. Something about the conversation had unsettled the man. It was not a pleasant sight, the boss being unnerved. All his men were brought to the edge of barely contained violence, just waiting for Loupe to tell them which way to explode.

They entered the hotel lobby in a phalanx of muscle and gabardine and crossed to the opposite end from the front desk. Men were stationed at either side of the empty corner, their expressions telling anyone who approached that this entire area was off-limits. Terrance spotted more of Loupe's men around the lobby and still others outside on the street. The old man sighed his way into the sofa, and pointed Terrance into a chair by his left.

Dust motes danced in the air. A stringed quartet played Debussy over the ceiling speakers. Elegant people passed wearing springtime pastels. The lobby held an atmosphere of moneyed calm. To Terrance's left, sunlight splashed upon high rain-speckled windows.

The sight of his father limping into the hotel struck
Terrance with such pain he actually gripped his chest.

Loupe observed Terrance carefully. "Who is that?"

"My father." Terrance carted his stricken gaze back
and forth between the two men as his father approached.
"What is he doing here?"

But Loupe had dismissed Terrance now. The boss rose
to his feet and demanded, "Where is Haines?"

Arthur d'Arcy glanced once at Josef Loupe, then
returned his gaze to Terrance. "How are you, son?"

"Your boy is fine," Loupe said. Their highly public
surroundings kept his snarl very soft. "For the moment."

Arthur's gaze remained gentle upon his boy. "You look
tired."

Terrance was kept mute by the rising dread of this day.
Just when he'd been certain it could grow no worse,
another blow arrived. A constant rain of hellish force. His
father, of all people, here to witness his failure.

Loupe was not accustomed to being ignored. He
snapped, "I was addressing you, sir."

Arthur d'Arcy displayed a remarkable strength of will
for so frail a figure. "You do not control this moment. You
only think you do."

"Where is Haines?"

"Where is my daughter?"

"So." Loupe drew out the word until it stretched his
features with a tight smile. "It appears we must deal with
the emissary at hand. Sir, I believe you have something I
want."

"I asked you a question."

Loupe gave a dignified smile and resumed his seat. "I
do so hope we shall be able to avoid any unpleasantness."

"Where is my daughter?"

"She is safe." Loupe snapped his fingers. Instantly an aide brought out his phone, keyed the pad, and handed it over. Loupe said, "Put her on."

Very real pain coursed through Arthur's features as he took the phone and murmured, "Hello, darling. Are you all right?"

A boulder was lodged where Terrance's heart should have resided. Every word his father spoke caused the stone to tremble. The motions bruised his chest. He reached up and massaged the spot over his ribs. The agony was fearsome.

"Enough." Loupe gestured with one finger. Instantly the aide reached forward and slipped the phone from Arthur's hand.

Arthur said, "You promised Val my daughter would be here."

"It appears we have both been somewhat inconvenienced."

"You don't want Val. He means nothing to you."

"True." Loupe extracted a cigar from a leather case, then pulled a tiny gold guillotine from his inner pocket. As he trimmed the cigar's tip, he went on. "Your daughter will rejoin you soon enough."

Arthur glanced around the room, taking in the men stationed like soldiers in Cerutti uniforms. "I must call Val."

"By all means." Loupe lit his cigar and nodded to the aide. "Allow me to explain to him how things stand."

THEY SAT IN THE VAN AND WAITED. THERE WAS NOTHING
more to be said. Every now and then one of them walked
to the end of the block and back, just checking on the
cul-de-sac and the middle house. In and out of sight in a
matter of seconds. Everything was placid, calm, just
another lovely day by the seaside.

The call came right on time. Arthur sounded faintly
breathless, but steady. "It's me."

"And?"

"Audrey isn't here. He says he won't release her until
the money is in his hands."

"Put him on."

The afternoon's glory was tainted by the voice on the
other end. "I was so very sorry not to have the pleasure of
meeting you, Mr. Haines. You're not living up to your
part of the bargain."

"That's something, coming from you. Maybe I should
tell Arthur to walk away."

"Very dangerous, that. People who get in my way tend
to regret it as long as they live. Which is not as long as
they might like. Do I make myself clear?"

"Yes."

"So I advise you to instruct d'Arcy senior here to

hand over what is mine." There was a protest from the other end, to which the man said, "Do be quiet, that's a good lad."

"Was that Terrance?"

"What d'Arcy junior wants or does not want at this point is immaterial."

"Call the Jersey bank. The man in charge is a Mr. Richards." Val's words were punctured by his thundering heart. Short verbal bursts proved easier to hold steady. "Terrance will access the codes for you. Richards will only release the funds when Arthur confirms that he, Terrance, and Audrey are safe."

"I can well understand your desire for personal vengeance on young d'Arcy here." The words were softly spoken. Merely a quick breath of smoke. But the dragon's flames licked the side of Val's face. "But do you think you are any more capable of wreaking havoc than I?"

Val pressed a fist tight against his gut. "That's the deal."

"I fear you do not hold all the cards, Mr. Haines. Do I need to send you a taped message from the young lady to prove my point?"

The cramp wracked his gut so tight that Val doubled over, drenching his knees with the sweat from his face. "No."

"Now here is how things are going to play out. You will tell d'Arcy senior to hand over the computer which you stole. I will walk through the transfer process with d'Arcy junior. The two gentlemen will depart. When I am satisfied that everything has gone smoothly, and no pesky authority figures come around asking difficult questions, I shall release your young lady." He might have been smoking a cigar. Or perhaps it was merely that the flames had finally escaped and were eating away at the phone. "Do we have a bargain?"

"Put Arthur on the line."

"A wise choice."

There was a moment's pause, then, "Yes?"

Val swallowed hard against the gorge. "You heard?"

"I did."

"We have no choice."

"No."

"Good luck."

"Ah. That is not required."

Val shut off the phone. The effort of dragging in another breath left him unable to lift his head. He felt a heavy hand pat his back. He heard Dillon ask, "All right there, mate?"

"No."

"Ease up, now. That's it. Can't go to pieces on us now."

Gerald asked, the dismay and nausea there in his voice, "What did he say?"

Val let his hands guide him upright. There was a dark stain of dread on his knees where his face had rested. "They're not going to let her go."

Dillon's voice carried the pained ease of one used to life's impossibles. "We knew that going in, mate."

But now was different. Now it was no longer a plan spoken in the safety of a night-draped kitchen. Val heard anew the anguish in the old man's voice and swallowed hard. The two men waited him out.

Finally he managed to unclench his grip and hand Gerald the phone. "It's time."

LOUPE REFUSED TO EVEN GLANCE TERRANCE'S WAY AS Arthur rose from his seat. Terrance watched his father cross the lobby in that odd tilted gait of his. Loupe sat and smoked his cigar, examining the glowing tip between puffs, until Arthur limped back inside the hotel. Terrance's computer was at his side. He reseated himself and placed the laptop in Terrance's hands.

When Terrance did not move, Arthur said gently, "Son, this man intends to kill you."

"Nonsense." Loupe spoke the words to his cigar tip. "What an absurd concept. Young d'Arcy is a valued ally."

Arthur ignored him entirely. "His kind does not share. You know this far better than I."

"My kind." Loupe seemed mildly amused by the exchange. "My kind."

Arthur reached over and opened the laptop. "Give the man what he wants."

Terrance watched his own hands betray him. They turned on the laptop, coded in the ID, made the wireless online connection, and entered the secret Web site. He swiveled the computer around, pointed to a line of numbers across the top of the screen, and fell back into his seat. "That's it? That's the lot?" Loupe snapped his fingers. The driver handed him a cell phone. Loupe asked directory assistance for the Syntec Bank's main number in Jersey. Terrance listened as Loupe asked for Mr. Richards. But all Terrance truly heard was the shards of ambition and of his plans falling about his feet.

Loupe read off the numbers, then demanded, "What is the total in those accounts?"

Terrance watched as the boss flushed at what he heard on the phone. Dust. All was dust and ashes.

Beads of sweat appeared on Loupe's forehead. "I want you to transfer the entire amount to my account in Luxembourg." He gave the bank details from memory.

The banker replied with something that caused Loupe's eyes to shift from father to son and back again.

Loupe said, "I was given to understand that these computer codes granted me full access without any such conditions." He waited a fraction. "I see. Very well. You will please remain on the line."

The hand holding the phone out to Arthur trembled slightly.

Arthur replied, "Not until my son and I are seated in a taxi."

Loupe was already rising to his feet. "Mark my words. Any hint of mischief and your daughter—"

Arthur raised his voice for the first time. "Threaten me or my family in any way, and I will call for the authorities."

"Just so long as we understand one another."

In response, Arthur pushed himself from the sofa, then motioned for Terrance to rise. When he did not move fast enough, Terrance felt himself lifted by one of Loupe's men. Arthur gripped his son's arm and turned him toward the door. "Not long now."

Loupe said into the phone, "Are you still there? Excellent. We will only be a moment longer."

As they exited the hotel and entered the blinding sunlight, Arthur said, "Do you know, this is the first time in six months I am not in pain."

Had he been able to speak, Terrance would have replied that he felt sufficient agony for them both.

VAL FORCED HIMSELF TO STEADY UP. "GO AHEAD."

Gerald darted nervous glances first at Val and then Dillon. The younger man agreed, "Do it."

Gerald asked, "What was this neighbor's name again?"

"Smathers. Lives at number nine Alders Way. For the twentieth time."

Gerald puffed like he was finishing a marathon, and gave it a high-pitched breathless note. "Yes, good morning. It's Smathers here, down Alders Way. I've been hearing the most horrid noise from next door. Yes, Smathers. What kind of noise? Oh, a horrible racket. Just the worst possible sort of din. Like a woman screeching. Yes, that's right. Like she was being hurt something fierce. Oh, oh, there it goes again. Can you hear it?"

Gerald listened a moment. "Number nine, Alders Way. Down at the bottom. What is the number . . . Oh, you mean next door. That would be number eight, wouldn't it? There's some strange lot renting over there, I saw them move in yesterday. Six or seven men, great hulking brutes and all wearing dark suits. What sort of holiday rental is that, I ask you? Carrying on at all hours of the day and night."

Dillon stuck a fist to his mouth and turned to look out the side window.

Gerald went on, "I've been after those agents before, you know. Here we sit, down here for a bit of peace and quiet. Oh, there they go again. That poor woman, I know they must be up to something beastly in there. It's the agency, you mark my words. They'll rent to anybody with ten quid in their pocket, never mind us who have to live with this horror. We're left waiting for blood to run down the front steps. Yes. All right. Good-bye."

Dillon took a moment to turn back around. "That was inspired, that was."

"Long as we're in time." Gerald looked at Val. "Perhaps I should stay."

"Can't neither of us pilot the plane, mate," Dillon replied.

"Go collect Arthur and Terrance." Val opened his door. "Take them to the plane. Be ready to move the instant we arrive."

———

"If I'd been planning a job, one look at this place would've earned it an instant pass," Dillon told him. "One way in, one out. A recipe for disaster, that is. And ruddy little to show for the effort besides. Basic two-up, two-down fifties council house, not worth a second glance save for the location. That's what people who don't know better pay for. Take a nothing sort of place like this, give it a garden the size of a throw rug, set it in tight like sardines on toast, throw in a bit of the sea, and people think they're somewhere exotic."

They were seated in the Rover. Val was behind the

wheel. The old car smelled of dust and oil and age, with a vague sense of Audrey's perfume thrown in for good measure. Dillon had grown talkative with the wait. Val did not mind the noise. The quiet was unnerving. Nothing moved on the cul-de-sac.

"Before you two showed up this morning, I was busy recollecting my first talk with Audrey. Not my first meeting, mind. That came four months before the other and doesn't bear thinking about. When I got out I tried a couple of times to apologize for the things I said back then. But Audrey always claimed not to remember. It being Audrey and all, I almost believed her."

Val nodded slowly. "I know just what you mean."

At the sound of a car, Dillon turned and then slid below the dash. "Crouch down, mate. It's the old bill."

"The police?"

"What I just said." Dillon eased himself up a fraction as the police car passed them. "Quite a difference from the early days, me being glad to see the likes of them show up. Back then, one glance of the men in blue was good for heart failure."

Val glanced up, but lowered himself at a hiss from Dillon. Dillon kept popping up for the occasional glimmer. "Leave the looking to an expert at not being seen, why don't you."

"Tell me what's happening."

"Two blue bottles are approaching the house. A third is hanging well back, hand on his radio. It's taking a while for somebody to answer their ring. Hang on, here he comes. Hello, what's this?"

Val risked a look. The man who answered the door looked straight out of a tourist brochure. Pleated shorts and polo shirt and a watch that glittered down the length of the lane. No socks. Deck shoes. Legs springtime pale but well muscled.

"Took time to lose the suit, didn't he? Smart move, that. Look at the smile he gives the johnnies, will you. A real charmer. Chatting up the coppers like he's paid for the duty. Which he is, in a manner of speaking."

Val watched his hopes fade. The cops wanted to go inside, but the guy wasn't having any of it. Why should he, since they had no warrant and him standing there with a valid rental contract. "This is bad."

"He's got the coppers off-balance, no question." Dillon chewed his lip. "They're turning this way; get down."

Val slid back below the level of the console. Dillon waited a moment, then risked another look. "That tears it."

"What's happening?"

"The copper who was hanging back, he's headed round to the house next door. Going to question this Smathers bloke who called it in."

"Who won't be there."

"Too right. We got us a sweet old dear in fuzzy slippers answering the door. Waving a hello to her neighbor." Dillon slapped the dashboard. "The coppers are apologizing to the bloke and calling in their report. Bang and done and on their way. What do we do now?"

"Get out of the car. Stay low." Val fiddled with the gearshift and controls, trying to orient himself to everything being on the wrong side. "If something goes down, I'm going to use a false ID that claims my name is Jeffrey Adams."

Dillon must have seen something in Val's expression. "Not on your life. I've never run out on a mate, and I'm not starting now."

"You're not running. You're being sent." When Dillon

looked ready to argue, Val added, "You just heard me promise Doris."

Reluctantly Dillon opened his door. "What are you going to do?"

"Whatever it takes." Val started the car. "You just hang back and be ready."

Val rammed the car into first as the cops slipped back into their car. The Rover's gears meshed improperly, as though the old car was well aware of the fate in store.

Dillon stepped away. He might have said something more, but the roaring engine cut him off. Val had a little trouble on takeoff, as he'd never driven a car with steering on the right. Pity his first lesson would be so brief.

"In for a penny," Val said. It was another of Audrey's sayings. He recalled how she had carried a photo of Arthur standing beside this old car in her billfold. Two hundred and seventy-seven thousand miles on the clock, and it still managed a full-throated roar as Val jammed the accelerator right down on the floor.

Arthur had bought the car soon after the sky had fallen. Disinherited, divorced, and a son who refused to even speak his name. Arthur could not afford anything else at the time. After a while he wanted nothing more. A contented man, was how Audrey had described him, touching the photograph where the old man stood beside the car. Audrey claimed to have kept the car as a symbol of all the good that could come from bad. If only one learned the secret formula to a happy life. Another of her wise little sayings.

Val smiled as he took aim down the empty road. Memories were such a grand thing.

The old car was a bit sluggish on takeoff. But by midway down the lane it had built up a full head of steam.

Val slid into second, liking the way the motor bellowed up through the revs.

The cops caught sight of him about then. Which Val decided was not all bad. After all, if he was about to do an Evel Knievel of his own, it would be nice to have an appreciative audience.

His last thought before striking the curb was that it'd be just his luck to discover Audrey had been shipped off to Yalta.

The curb had a bit of lip to it, enough to lift the car like a launcher and send him straight for the bowed front windows. Val thought he might have glimpsed an astonished face staring out at him. But it might have been just wishful thinking.

Val took out all three windows and a fair-sized portion of restraining wall before coming to rest in a hail of plaster, brick, and shattered glass. The curtains lay over the fractured front windshield like a shroud to all the miseries of his now-distant past.

The floating dust had the cops coughing so hard they couldn't place him under arrest as they dragged him from the wreckage. Val, too, found it hard to form the words, and at first nobody paid any attention to what he had to say. But as they dragged him back into the brilliant sunlit afternoon, he managed to form a very hoarse shout, "My fiancée's chained up in there!"

This, following Gerald's phone call, got the police's attention. "Say again?"

"They kidnapped my fiancée! She's being held in the back room!"

"Get him out of here." The senior cop pointed at the policeman not holding Val. "You. Come with me."

The thug in the pleated shorts decided not to hang

about. He burst out the back door, leapt the side fence, and started for the hill.

"We've got a runner!"

"You there! Police! Halt!"

Val's view of the proceedings was cut off by the third cop hustling him back to the car. He was planted on the side, legs spread, hands in plain view. All the neighbors were outside by now, gaping at the proceedings. Dillon arrived then, his head turned to the sunlight and smiling broadly. Val grinned in reply. It felt as though his face was trying to recall something from the very distant past.

"Something funny, sir?"

"Just glad you're here, officer."

"We'll see about that."

Then there was a shout from the house, echoed on the policeman's radio. The cop thumbed his radio and barked, "Say again?"

Val caught enough of the repeated words to know they had found someone. He set his forehead down on the roof and shut his eyes tight. Just giving thanks. Just getting ready. Because here she came, clearly the worse for wear but walking out on her own two legs. Dillon and the officer helped her clamber through the opening, like Val had carved the way just for her. Which, in a sense, he had.

"Oh, Val." She rushed up to him and gave him a fierce embrace. "What on earth have you done?"

"Remain as you are, sir."

Val kept his hands in plain view as she hugged him. "Are you all right?"

"I am now."

"Madam, I must ask you to step away."

"Adams," Val told her softly as the policeman pried

her arms from his neck. "The ID in my pocket says I am Jeffrey Adams."

"Please, madam, you are only making matters worse."

Val could not stop grinning. Not even as the policeman wheeled him about and ringed his wrists with cold steel.

"Stop that! What on earth do you think you're doing?"

"We have to follow procedure, madam."

"But this man just saved my life!" When the policeman continued undeterred, she demanded, "Where are you taking him?"

"Eastbourne, ma'am. He'll be booked and processed there."

As Val was guided into the police car's backseat, he heard other sirens whooping in the background. Val told her, "Dillon's going to stay with you—"

The door was slammed in his face. Audrey shouted her protest and tried to reopen the door. But the policeman remained adamant and gently but firmly moved her away.

Val smiled out at Audrey. As the car pulled away, he cast a final glance at his handiwork.

Shame about the car.

AS FAR AS ELLEN LAINEY WAS CONCERNED, THESE DAYS Insignia's head office held all the warmth and congeniality of an open coffin.

The only reason she stuck around at all was, she had inherited Val Haines's position. The suits upstairs called it a promotion. But Ellen had made it this far by staring facts and figures straight in the eye and calling them as they stood. Her predecessor had been toasted in a bomb blast that had the investigators crawling around the office like roaches in Gucci. The office to her left was home now to a half-dozen pinheads with badges and bad attitudes. The future looked decidedly grim.

Rumors continued to fly. New ones popped up every morning. This morning the coffee cluster had it on best authority that Don Winslow was missing. Which meant nothing, really. At seven the previous evening she had heard the same group talking about alien abduction.

A young accountant knocked on Ellen's open door. The guy had been on the job for six weeks. Ellen knew what he thought of her. A hard-timer, just punching her ticket and working the corporate treadmill, hiking her way toward an Ocala retirement community with a pink poodle for company. He assumed her flat-panned expression was the product of a thousand fifty-five-hour weeks. What he did not know, what Ellen was keeping all to herself, was how the SEC goons had locked up the pension funds tight as a Wall Street safe. All her fund-related systems were shut down. She could not access anything. Her questions had been answered with blowtorch glares and silence. Ellen was not asleep at the wheel. She knew something was seriously wrong. She also knew her job description included an unwritten order not to fuel the rumor fire. She could play the poker-faced lady and keep what she suspected locked up tight. For the moment.

The new accountant was named Jerry. He was both very smart and very shy. He also had a tendency to stutter slightly when he was nervous. Which he almost always was when he was in the presence of his boss. Any conversation with him could stretch over eons.

Ellen greeted him with, "I do *not* have time for you today."

Normally this would have been enough to send Jerry scurrying for his cubicle. But not this morning.

He stepped further inside her office. "We have to talk."

Ellen started to scream at him. She had not slept at all the previous three nights. When she lay down, she tended to watch the corporate figures dance across her darkened ceiling. What they added up to made for a waking nightmare she could not banish with thoughts of her new title.

But were Ellen to vent the worry-steam in Jerry's direction, the guy would probably do an implosion right there in her doorway. Which would mean getting buried by more paperwork. Ellen sighed, went back to her file shuffling, and said, "So talk already."

"I've been doing my weekly check of all the office petty cash accounts, like you ordered."

Unbelievable. Here she was, imagining a corporate meltdown the papers would call Florida's very own Enron, and the guy wants to point the finger at somebody overspending on stamps. Ellen did a solid drumbeat on her desk with the stack of folders. "Jerry, this can definitely wait."

Jerry slipped fully inside her office. And shut the door. This was enough to halt her next outburst.

Jerry flitted up close to her desk. "I've found it."

"Found *what*?"

"The money. All of it."

Something inside the guy's expression had her heart pounding. Which of course made no sense at all. "*What* money?"

"At least, I think it's all. I never saw any figures. Did you?"

Ellen worked at making words. But nothing actually fit the moment. So she shut her face and waited.

"All I'm going on are the rumors." He cleared his throat. "But I think it's all there. It's got to be. As much as it is, it's the only thing I can figure out."

She was not aware that she had risen to her feet. "Just how much are we talking about here?"

Jerry revealed a true accountant's heart in how he reverentially said the numbers. "Four hundred and eighteen million dollars."

"You're telling me you found four hundred million dollars *in our petty cash account*?"

"I called the bank. They confirmed that the transfer came in last night." His eyes had gone round from the revelation. "It's just sitting there. Waiting for us."

THE ISLAND OFFERED THEM A GLORIOUS WELCOME THE day they laid Arthur d'Arcy to rest. Val stood by the entrance to the stone church on the outskirts of St. Helier and hoped his remaining strength did not let him down. He was drawn as finely as he had ever been, stretched by days and nights of planning and work and worry. Audrey had done little since their arrival save sit the death watch with her father. Bert and Dillon and Gerald had done what they could. But most of the critical issues not related to Arthur's passage had rested on Val's shoulders alone.

A comforting breeze drifted down the little lane, flavored by wildflowers and the sea. The village was lost beyond two sharp bends and a hillside blanketed in spring finery. Overhead the sun played games with scuttling clouds. Undulating meadows shivered and sheened with the paintings of light and shadow. In the distance the waves wrote their own frothy script of farewell.

Val heard voices before the crowd rounded the corner and came into view. Bert and Dillon had volunteered to go down and meet those arriving with the afternoon ferry. Val pushed off the ancient stone and went to greet them. There were perhaps four dozen mourners, a motley assortment of polished gentry and rough trade, united now in grey cloth and grief.

Dillon pulled him to one side and said, "Gerald says you're needed back at the cottage."

"Terrance?"

"The bloke's just sitting and staring at all the yesterdays he's wasted. Needs a swift kick, if you ask me."

"Not today."

"No, suppose not. How is it you're the only one who knows how to wind his motor?"

Val started down the lane without replying.

A copse of trees separated the hamlet from the parish church. Val arrived at the cottage's front walk just as Gerald came out with Audrey, and resented the sight of another man standing where he wished to be.

Audrey made even grief look alluring. "Terrance says he won't come."

"He'll be there."

"He wouldn't even look at me. I begged and he wouldn't even meet my gaze."

"Leave your brother to me. You've got enough to worry about already today."

"He's right, you know," Gerald said. A truce had settled between Val and Gerald. Whatever else, they had been through enough to know the other's measure. Their unspoken agreement was loud and clear. Audrey would have to decide between them. "If Terrance will mind anybody, it's the lad here."

Audrey's hair caught the sunlight in a brilliant weave. "Perhaps I should just let him be."

Val started for the door. "We'll meet you at the church."

The stone cottage was so old that the lichen decorating

the slate roof grew in layers. They had rented the place because it was within walking distance of the St. Helier hospice. The three downstairs rooms were more charm than comfort. The four upstairs bedrooms were closets with windows. Val found Terrance just as Dillon had said, seated on his bed and staring at an empty side wall. Val had accepted Audrey's request to try and reform her brother, rather than send him to jail. Val had even suggested the method. And he did his best to do away with his burden of hate. Even when Terrance had confessed to doctoring the lab reports and stealing the child Val had always known was his. Even then.

During Arthur's steady decline, Val had done what he could to ensure their future safety and Terrance's ongoing obedience. Nights already turned sleepless by tending to Arthur had been extended even further. He had carefully quizzed Terrance and then prepared a script. In the backroom of a local photographic studio, Terrance had sat beside Val and read the script in the buzzing drone of a crypt dweller.

They had express mailed a copy of the DVD to an attorney in London, who had hand-delivered the package to the address the same attorney had located for Loupe. They had included no message. No warning. Nothing.

The fact that they were all still alive was the only evidence Val needed that the message had been received, loud and clear.

Arthur had held to his considerate nature right to the end, slipping away quietly six days after their arrival. Audrey was asleep by her father's bed at the time, awakening to a glorious spring dawn and birdsong and a man who looked so very pleased to journey home.

———

Terrance gave no indication that he was even aware of Val's presence. Terrance had not shaved since performing for the camera. Nor did it appear that he had slept. His eyes had retreated back into plum-shaded caves. Nowadays Val addressed Terrance in a prison warden's manner, unemotional direct commands.

Val told him, "We leave for the church in ten minutes."

Slowly Terrance's head lifted. "What did you do with the money?"

"We've been through this a dozen times."

"Tell me the truth."

"I already have. I wired it back to Insignia's accounts."

"You couldn't have."

"Terrance . . ." Val had a sudden sense of staring into a mystic mirror, one that revealed how close he had come to living solely for vengeance.

"What?"

"Do this thing for Audrey," Val said, still captured by the image of his journey to the brink. "I won't make you come with me when I visit Stefanie."

Terrance's head sank back to his hands.

Val retreated from the room. "You've got ten minutes to shave and dress."

———

The church's interior was unpainted stone. The slate floor was washed by the tide of centuries. The windows were tall and narrow and set deep in slanted recesses. The priest's robes were from another era, as was his chant as he lit candles at the coffin's head and feet. Audrey sat between Val and Gerald. Terrance sat further along the same pew, sandwiched between Bert and Dillon. Incense wafted from two burners set to either side of the altar. The painted medieval frieze behind the priest's lectern came alive in the smoke. In Val's exhausted state, the ceremony's measured cadence carried him back through time, joining him with centuries of worshippers long gone, yet with them still. Then he felt Audrey's hand reach over and take his own. He wrapped her hand in both of his, and wondered if perhaps she recalled another time, when she had brought him to such a place and sought to give him only the best of what she had. And what she had, he needed as strongly as breath.

The priest invited those who wished to come forward and say a few words. Audrey rose and walked over to stand above the coffin. Val tried hard to hear what she said. But his heart spoke too loudly just then. Strange how such a time and place could generate such an overwhelming sense of gratitude.

As she returned to her seat, she glanced at Terrance. But he gave no sign he saw her. Dillon nudged the man. Still Terrance did not respond. Audrey sighed and shook her head, a single tight gesture.

Val rose to his feet, slipped from the pew, and stood at the coffin's head. He said, "Arthur's daughter told me recently that everything good in her came from this man. I can only say that he must have been a very fine man indeed. One I wish I had known better."

He looked at her then. And said, "One whose example I can only hope to follow."

VAL ARRANGED THE MEETING FOR SIX FORTY-FIVE IN THE morning, precisely the time he had been scheduled to be blown up. The sense of living irony helped steady his nerves as he stepped out of the elevator and walked through the penthouse foyer. The Insignia chairman's office was empty, but he heard sounds emanating from the adjoining boardroom.

Jack Budrow was tucked into a sumptuous breakfast and surrounded by a lovely spring sunrise as Val stepped into view. The chairman's expression was almost comical, his fork frozen in midair as he searched for an appropriate response. All he could think to say, however, was, "I can have security up here in thirty seconds."

"Don't bother."

"You're that man. What's his name."

"Val Haines."

"I . . . I don't understand. The call came from . . ."

"Terrance. He decided to remain downstairs."

The mental tumblers flipped and spun. But nothing of worth came to mind. Jack Budrow pushed his plate aside. "I can't tell you how glad I am to see—"

"Save it." Val walked to the front of the room and slid

aside the shoji screen hiding the television, then slipped the DVD into the slot. "I want you to see this."

It took him a moment to work out the remote's unfamiliar controls. By the time the television and sound came to life, Terrance was already into his spiel. He heard Jack Budrow choke on the sight of Terrance seated there beside Val.

"—Arranged with my two partners, Jack Budrow and Don Winslow, to defraud Insignia Corporation's pension funds of four hundred and eighteen million dollars. We arranged to pin the theft on Marjorie Copeland and Valentine Haines."

Terrance looked like a talking corpse as he read from the prepared script. His hands trembled slightly in time to his voice's tremor. "Using the services of Suzanne Walters, we arranged to blow up the New York offices of Syntec Bank, destroying both the people we were framing, the banker through whom we had worked, and all records not held in-house and doctored by myself."

"Turn that off!" Budrow sputtered. "I didn't know anything about this!"

"But Val Haines did not die as expected in the New York blast," Terrance droned. "With full support from Winslow and Budrow—"

"That is a lie!"

"—I flew to England with Suzanne Walters. We accepted the services of a local mobster, Josef Loupe." In a cryptlike monotone, Terrance detailed their work, Loupe's scheme to steal all the money for himself, and finally, "I personally witnessed Josef Loupe murdering Don Winslow with one shot from an automatic pistol to his chest."

Jack Budrow stumbled around the boardroom table.

He pawed the other chairs out of his way, leaving wreckage in his wake. He grabbed the remote from Val and hammered it with tight bursts of breath, as though throwing punches. When the television finally cut off, he threw the remote to the ground. "I knew nothing about any of that. Winslow and d'Arcy were acting completely without my knowledge—"

"Here's how it's going to play out," Val said. He slipped the DVD from the machine, placed it back inside the jewel box, and slid it down the table. It sparkled in the growing sunlight as it spun and slid and finally came to rest beside Jack Budrow's unfinished breakfast. "Today you are going to resign all your positions with Insignia."

"You can't possibly think I would even consider—"

"You will relinquish all retirement benefits. You will refuse any consulting position. You will turn over your stock options and all your shares in the company to the Insignia pension fund. It is a benevolent final gesture to repair the damages made to the hopes and futures of all your loyal employees."

Jack Budrow's face had drained of blood. One hand gripped his chest. The other used the doorjamb for support. "You're insane."

"If that announcement is not made public by tomorrow, copies of this DVD will be delivered to the chairman of the SEC. Others will go to the *Wall Street Journal*, the local papers, the television, and everywhere else I can think of."

Budrow whimpered a protest that died before it was fully formed.

"One day," Val repeated. "And one day more to make good on the promises. Otherwise I go public."

Val slipped past the chairman and started for the exit. He turned back and repeated, "One day."

———

When Val arrived back at the car, Terrance gave no sign that he was aware Val had departed, much less returned. His gaze carried the bleak emptiness of a man staring a life sentence in the face. Which, in a sense, he was.

From the rear seat, Audrey observed Val with cautious reserve. "How did it go?"

"Fine." He started the car. At least she had decided to accompany them to America. Nor had she bothered to claim it was to keep an eye on her brother. Val started the car and said, "Everything is just fine."

Forty minutes later, they pulled up in front of a mammoth steel-and-glass building, headquarters of the long-distance and cell-phone company that ran its international operations from this campus north of Winter Park. Outside, brilliant Florida sunlight splashed against the stream of corporate employees racing the morning clock. In the rearview mirror, Val saw that Audrey was still watching him. He hoped his sense that something was melting inside her was not just his imagination. Until he was certain, however, he was determined to wait it out. He wanted to give her whatever space she needed. This time he wanted to get it right.

Terrance touched the knot of his tie and murmured, "I suppose I should be reporting for work."

Audrey leaned forward and said to her brother, "You're doing the right thing, Brother."

Terrance opened his door, grabbed his briefcase, and walked into the sunlight.

Audrey sighed and leaned back. Shook her head. Closed her eyes.

Val turned around in his seat. "Give it time."

"He's had a lifetime. That isn't long enough?"

"You've reached hard cases before," he replied.

She opened her eyes. "Have I?"

"Absolutely."

After a long moment, Audrey opened the rear door, rose from the car, and slipped into the seat vacated by Terrance. She asked, "When do you leave?"

He started to say, when he could be sure she would be there when he got back. But that sort of statement was too far a reach into a tomorrow she had not yet offered him. "A few days. As soon as Terrance delivers the first batch of goods, and I can be certain he'll be okay on his own for a while."

She spoke the words with slow caution, as if needing to assess the texture of each individually. "Do you want me to do anything while you're gone?"

"Does this mean you're going to stay?" He swallowed, then added the words, "With me?"

"Let's just take this one step at a time, all right?"

In reply, Val put the car into gear. Wondering if perhaps the faint stirrings he felt at heart level meant there really might be a future he could call his own.

VAL HAD THE CAB WAIT FOR HIM OUTSIDE THE HOTEL
Everest. Vince watched him push through the doors. "If
it isn't Mr. Smith. How we doing today?"

"So far so good."

"Glad to hear it." Vince gave him a careful once-over.
"I don't see any open wounds. You meet any trouble?"

"Some."

"There ain't no partial when it comes to trouble.
Either you did or you didn't."

"Yes."

"And you came out on top?"

"Sort of."

Vince gave that flicker of a smile, like he tasted something alien. "You come walking in here without a limp, I
say you did okay."

"So would I."

"Way to go." He glanced at the wall clock. "You got
my money?"

Val took out the zippered pouch supplied by the bank
and set it on the counter between them.

The final transfer request Val had given to the Jersey
banker had been in regard to Marjorie Copeland's funds.
It had been her idea for Val to have signatory rights over

her account as well. Just in case, Marjorie had said, asking only that Val make sure her child was taken care of. Just in case. The majority of the funds, after this sum for Vince and their expenses on Jersey, was now safely resting in a trust established in her son's name.

Vince opened the pouch, peered inside, zipped it closed, and made it disappear. "What do you know. Looks like I was right to trust you, Mr. Smith."

"The name is Val. Valentine Haines."

"This trouble you were in. It's officially over?"

"Getting there."

"Which means you won't need to be staying uptown again. You're moving back to the other side of the park, right?"

"I'd still like to drop in from time to time, if that's all right."

Vince gave a fractional head-shake. "You don't want to hang with me. I'm street. It might rub off."

"Not a bad thing. Especially where I'm headed."

"Yeah? Where's that?"

"Looking for trouble."

Vince liked that enough to offer his hand. "Feel free. You hear what I'm saying?"

The man's touch was surprisingly light, as though Vince did not want to connect too heavily even through a handshake. "Thanks. For everything."

"You're not a bad guy, for a sucker. You need something, you say the word."

———

Val sat in the outer office, surrounded by New York bustle. He might as well have been invisible. Which he did not mind. A moment to rest in the eye of the storm was fine by him. He leaned his head against the wall and closed his eyes. The image was there again, the same one he had carried since traveling to New York by way of a certain Miami waterfront condo.

Val had stood by the living room window and stared out at the waterfront palaces and the floating wealth as Stefanie had cried her way through Terrance's on-camera performance. Val had remained mute and motionless while she regained control. There were a number of things that would have to be said. A multitude of legal matters to be rewritten, a myriad of issues to be resolved anew. But not this time. Val did not want to mar this moment with anything other than the reason for his coming. Which was not revenge. Nor to tell her that he had been right all along. None of that mattered. He could see just enough of his reflection in the sliding-glass door to know that this was not merely fatigue or momentary ruminations. He stared into eyes that seemed full of the day's sunlight, a translucent image so powerful he could almost blank out the sound of his ex-wife sobbing behind him.

When he was certain the tears were over and her composure restored, Val turned around.

He said, "I'd like to see my daughter now."

The aide ushered Val into the office. The SEC's chief investigator eyed him with open curiosity. "You're Haines?"

"Yes."

"Valentine Joseph Haines?"

"That's right."

"You got some ID?"

Val handed over his recently recovered passport. The man inspected it carefully. "You want coffee?"

"No. I'm good."

He tossed Val's passport onto his desk. "Now this is real interesting. First off, funds you supposedly stole suddenly wind up in Insignia's petty cash account. Then, if that's not good enough, a guy who's supposed to be fully dead calls me up and says he wants to stop by, talk to me about a job."

"That's right."

"With me."

"Right again."

The chief slung one arm over the back of his swivel chair. "So talk."

Val opened his leather portfolio and extracted a set of documents. "You're concerned about possible financial improprieties at a major Florida-based telephone company. But you don't have the required evidence to go in with a full investigation."

The chief unslung his arm. "Who says?"

Val offered the papers. "These might help you move forward."

The chief studied them intently. From behind the man's desk, a silver-plated clock ticked precise New York minutes. That and the flipping of pages, a ringing phone, and the sounds of Wall Street traffic rising from far below were the only sounds.

"Where did you get these?"

"I've got eleven in the business," Val replied. "I know all the tricks. I can help you."

The chief picked up his phone and punched in a

number. He said, "Get in here. I don't care. Come here *now*."

A harried young woman entered without knocking. "You of course realize we are due in the mayor's office in three hours, and I am two weeks from ready."

The chief handed over Val's documents. "Tell me if we're looking at the real deal here."

The woman went through them with rising delight. "Where did you get this?"

"Is it real?"

"Looks that way to me."

"Is it enough?"

"It's a ton more than what we've got now, I can tell you that much. The rest will have to wait."

"Call the mayor's office and cancel. Have the team in here and ready. One hour."

"You know the mayor. He won't like this."

"Move."

The chief waited until they were alone again to say, "You've got an inside source."

"One that will move from project to project," Val agrees. "One that answers only to me."

Val and the chief talked through the entire hour. Only when the woman returned to get the chief for the meeting did the man say, "When can you start?"

"It looks like I already have."

The chief nodded acceptance. He shook Val's hand, ushered him from the office, and finally said, "One thing I don't get. What's the motive here?"

Val did not turn back to reply, "Penance."